Other Novels by Mike Gilmore

<u>The Randy Fisher Series</u>
Levels of Power: The Senator
Levels of Power: The Legislator

"The Toilet Salesman"

LEVELS

★ ★ ★ OF ★ ★ ★

POWER

THE DIPLOMAT

Mike Gilmore

authorHOUSE®

AuthorHouse™ LLC
1663 Liberty Drive
Bloomington, IN 47403
www.authorhouse.com
Phone: 1-800-839-8640

This is a work of fiction. All of the characters, names, incidents,
organizations, and dialogue in this novel are either the products
of the author's imagination or are used fictitiously.

Published by AuthorHouse   04/15/2014

ISBN: 978-1-4918-6661-0 (sc)
ISBN: 978-1-4918-6660-3 (hc)
ISBN: 978-1-4918-6658-0 (e)

Library of Congress Control Number: 2014903330

Any people depicted in stock imagery provided by Thinkstock are models,
and such images are being used for illustrative purposes only.
Certain stock imagery © Thinkstock.

This book is printed on acid-free paper.

The Characters

The Americans

Harold Miller	President of the United States	
Randy Fisher	United States Senator—South Carolina	
Tom Evans	United States Senator—California	
Warren Fletcher	White House Chief of Staff	
Leslie Overman	Assistant White House Chief of Staff	
Ralph Peters	Representative from Texas	
Jasper Lawrence	United States Senator—Wyoming	
Jimmy Diamond	Vice President of the United States	

The Chinese

Huang Zhao	Vice Chairman—CNOOC
Lian Wu	Chairman—CNOOC
Chang Chen	Minister of Land and Resources
Fang Li	Senior Admiral—Southern Command
Deshi Yang	Southern Command Operations Officer
Jin Wang	Commodore—*Liaoning* Aircraft Carrier
Dong Zhang	Vice Premier
Ji Liu	*Liaoning* Flight Operations Officer

The Vietnamese

Tran Van Huong	President of Vietnam
An Nguyen	Ambassador to the United States & ASEAN
Binh Huy Pham	Admiral—Chief of Naval Operations
Trieu Thank Le	Rear Admiral—Chief of Staff—Vietnamese Navy
Dc Thuc Ho	Rear Admiral—Vietnamese Navy Commissar
Sub. Lt. Huynh Tan Phat	Commander—*Ly Nam De* Torpedo Boat
Captain Cam De Ho	Captain Lada Submarine—*Da Nang*
Captain Cam Le	Captain Lada Submarine—*Ha Noi*

The Filipinos

Bayani Limbaco	President of the Philippines
Isko Bello	Ambassador to the United States & ASEAN
Crisanto Olan	Philippine Chief of Naval Operations

Chapter 1

The federal government was only two days away from shutting down for the 2014 calendar year. Actually, the government never completely shuts down. No agency involved with national security ever takes a day off. The armed forces never take a day off. Small interior renovations, planned and completed, inside federal buildings occurred during the two weeks that Congress was not in session. Newly elected members of Congress were arriving to get their offices set up even as outgoing members were packing up their personal effects and cleaning out their offices. Of course, the federal employees at the government agencies still worked their weekly nine-to-five jobs.

In the months leading up to the midterm elections, the newspapers and national broadcast news networks filled their pages and airwaves with pre-election coverage, but the elections had been rather dull as was common. There had been less than a dozen changes in the makeup of both the House and Senate officeholders—certainly not enough to change which political party controlled the legislative branch of the United States government.

The lull in political news ended immediately after the elections on November 4. The press had a new and very big story to discuss with the American people until the new Congress returned in January. On November 5, Jerrod Wyman, vice president of the United States, tendered his resignation to Republican president Harold Miller effective December 31, 2014.

1

The newspapers changed their normal font for their front pages to large bold letters as they informed the country. The talking heads filled the airwaves with their beliefs about the reasons behind the vice president's decision to resign. The most favored rumor among the political commentators was the prediction that Jerrod Wyman would run against his own party's incumbent in the 2016 presidential elections. There had been plenty of stories leaking from the executive branch regarding President Harold Miller and his vice president, not only that they disagreed on many policy decisions, but that their relationship had deteriorated to the point they only nodded at each other when they met in the hallways of the White House West Wing.

Washington insiders predicted Jerrod Wyman would go back to his home state of Texas where he had been a popular governor for two terms to prepare his campaign for the 2016 elections. With a net worth of nearly four billion dollars from the sale of his oil and gas refinery business years before, money for a national campaign would not be a problem.

Following the news surrounding Wyman's resignation, the most important piece of information everybody wanted to know was whom President Miller would select as his new vice president. It would be logical to assume that there would be many willing applicants for the prestigious and certainly important position, but there again, the talk circling around Capitol Hill from the more extreme liberals was that maybe the list of potential candidates was a little on the short side.

President Harold Miller was currently experiencing the lowest favorability ratings of his political career. Elected president in November of 2012, Miller had been the senior senator from the state of New York. He had won the election by a narrow majority over the incumbent Democrat. Early in his presidency, his polls were in the mid-fifties, but 2013 had started as a rough first year for the new president. His polling numbers were below 50 percent and little had happened to turn the favorability ratings back to their previous higher numbers.

The relationship between the Miller White House and the legislative branch of the government neared a breaking point in 2014. Two major pieces of legislation authored by Senators Tom Evans of

California and Randy Fisher of South Carolina passed through the Congress with over a two-thirds majority vote.

The president had initially opposed the first bill, the Sierra Vista Border Security Plan. Congressional approval of the bill, along with the president's signature, would authorize the US Customs and Border Protection Agency to increase the number of border guards by five thousand additional agents as well as by two hundred fifty more customs officers. Additional electronic surveillance equipment, including four new drones to improve border coverage, was also in the package.

The president kept telling the American public the country's current security procedures were adequate, but the killing of five border agents during a bold daylight incursion of the Juarez drug cartel forced the president to reverse his earlier position on the legislation. The bill passed by a large margin in both houses of Congress.

The second bill, The Fisher / Evans Pathway to Citizenship, was another bitter pill for the president to swallow. He had fought it all the way to Capitol Hill, claiming the ten-thousand-dollar fee for each applicant was allowing illegal immigrants to buy their way into citizenship. He even went so far as to accuse Senators Evans and Fisher of being willing to take a "bribe" by allowing illegal immigrants to become citizens of the United States in return for their support for the Democratic Party.

The bill might not have received its narrow two-thirds majority for passage were it not for an amazing incident that occurred in a small city in Ohio called Coshocton. Captured on video, four illegal Mexicans, working on a nearby construction site, participated in the rescue of over 120 students and faculty members from a massive fire in a junior high school building with no resulting loss of life. The state governor, the two US Senators from Ohio, and the member of Congress representing the district where the school was located all successfully campaigned for the illegal Mexicans to receive their green cards, which would allow them to remain legally within the country. The heroic efforts of the four Mexican construction workers helped convince the country and Congress to approve the new citizenship bill against the wishes of the president.

The president's administration during its first year in office came under fire because of several high-profile political scandals.

Immediately after termination by the president for stealing money from the department's special research funds, his energy secretary committed suicide in his own cabinet office. The first incident had barely been off the front pages and airways of the broadcast media when his education secretary, along with his pregnant private secretary, were involved in a minor traffic accident in downtown Washington DC. Early into the investigation of the accident, the secretary revealed that he was the father of the baby, resulting in his forced resignation. Scandals in 2013 followed by two major legislative losses for the president in 2014 capped the end of his second year in office.

The political scandals and major legislative losses by a Congress asserting its authority over the president made it appear to the American public the office of the president was not as powerful as it had once been. Combined, these events were keeping qualified people from having their names added to the president's short list for his selection of VP candidates. Who wanted to hook his or her political future to a president facing a very tough reelection—maybe even against his former vice president?

Randal Edward Fisher, Democratic US Senator from South Carolina, was forty years old and had recently celebrated his election for a new six-year term. He was in his office in the Russell Senate Office Building, using a few quiet hours to catch up on some reading. The Senate had adjourned for the day, and he was free until 8:15 that night when he had to attend yet another Christmas party.

The office was empty, his staffers having left for the day. Even his workaholic chief of staff, Tim Smith, had needed to leave right at 5:00. Randy was reviewing a stack of newspapers and their bold headlines about new possible candidates for the VP spot. Some were also running stories about possible presidential candidates for the 2016 election. Jerrod Wyman's name was on the short list as a possible Republican contender, along with that of Randy's friend and mentor, Democratic Senator Tom Evans. These two senior members of their respective political parties topped the list as major rivals to the president for the job. Eight other politicians for the Democratic nomination followed Tom Evans's name. Randy was glad that he would not be faced with a presidential campaign. Running for his own first election had been enough of a learning experience for him.

Randy looked at the calendar printed on his desk blotter and ran the figures in his head. Seven hundred ninety-one . . . two years and one month since he had walked into Loading Dock Six at the grandstand within the state fairgrounds in Columbia, South Carolina, and found himself faced with a terrorist setting up a nuclear device rigged to explode during the presidential debate between incumbent Jonathon Blakely and then-Senator Harold Miller.

Randy had been the southeastern regional sales manager for a large manufacturer of industrial electrical control equipment and had been on a typical sales call. Before he could think of any type of response, the customer he was with had been fatally shot, and Randy had taken a bullet to his right shoulder.

Despite the bullet wound, Randy had been very lucky that fateful day. The terrorist assumed he was dead and turned his back on both men. Randy was able to get up and attack the terrorist. He disarmed him of the handgun. The terrorist then pulled a knife from a leather sheath and came at Randy again. During their fight, Randy had tripped the terrorist using a leg trip or takedown technique he'd learned from his army service as a military MP, and the terrorist fell and impaled himself on his own knife.

Barely conscious, Randy had been able to telephone authorities to warn them of the bomb and prevent a terrible nuclear incident that would have affected the entire country. Two months later, after his recuperation, South Carolina governor, Jessica Brooks, appointed Randy to complete the final two years of a six-year elected term of retiring US Senator Robert Moore.

With the latest elections behind him, he had won the office on his own merits. He promised the people of the Palmetto State he would work to bring jobs to South Carolina and to help make their lives a little better. The Emerson Electrical plant in Greenville, South Carolina, had been a new addition to the industrial base and was located in the upstate region. Randy and his staff had had a lot to do with the one hundred fifty new jobs. Emerson had two more plants due to open next year in his state.

Randy did not even hire a campaign manager until after the passage of the immigration and border security bills in June of this year. He had about $400,000 set aside from speaking fees he had earned in the previous eighteen months and had been willing to use about $250,000 from his personal assets provided by royalty income from a patent for an electronic air-conditioning control switch his late father had designed and sold to the Trane Company. To his surprise, the Democratic National Committee came through with a check for $250,000 and a commitment for another $500,000 if needed.

Starting in the middle of July with a new campaign manager and a staff of mostly volunteer workers, Randy began a blitz of weekend events throughout his state. As soon as the Senate would recess for the week, he would leave Washington and fly to one of the airports in South Carolina to begin traveling from one event to another. From mid-July through October, Randy was in his home state every weekend attending events scheduled by his campaign manager.

It was a major help when the Republican Party decided not to run anybody against him, but Randy would not take the voters for granted. He wanted to let them know he still needed their votes even though he was unopposed.

By election night, Randy was able to bring in a huge win without using the extra half million dollars offered by the DNC and without dipping into his personal funds. He and Annie, along with hundreds of campaign volunteers, celebrated at the Hilton Garden Inn Hotel near the South Carolina Convention Center in Columbia.

Chapter 2

Washington DC
Wednesday—December 17, 2014
6:00 p.m. (EST)

Randy Fisher glanced at his Timex watch. The South Carolina junior senator still had another two hours before he needed to leave for tonight's Christmas party. He leaned back into his office chair and stretched his six-foot, 185-pound frame as he reflected on the holiday season thus far.

Every evening last week, he and Annie had attended a foreign embassy Christmas event. The first on Monday of last week had been at the British Embassy. The following nights of the week, he attended holiday events at the German, Canadian, and Spanish Embassies, ending at the French Embassy on Saturday. Randy was relieved to be able to stay home on Sunday night. It was typical for a US senator to receive special event invitations, and Randy sat on several high-profile committees in the Senate. The Armed Services and the Select Committee on Intelligence were important assignments, and he wanted the invitations to use these events to meet with many of the foreign ambassadors and their senior staffs.

On Monday evening of this week, Randy and Annie had attended the Mexican Embassy's holiday event. With the passage of his two pieces of legislation this year, he could not turn this event down. Annie had begged off from last night's holiday event held at the OAS (Organization of American States) Building. Randy attended because he would meet with dignitaries from all the member nations. He told Annie it was like attending thirty-five parties in one night.

Annie was forgoing tonight's event as well. She needed to finish a portion of an electrical design for a hospital renovation before they left Washington for their own Christmas break. She had been an employee at the Department of Energy when she and Randy first met. After the Raymond Cleveland suicide event and the attempt on her life by Thomas Dean at the DOE, Annie decided to look for work outside the government. She had accepted an electrical engineering and design position with the Global Architectural Firm. GAF was an architectural company specializing in the designs of schools and hospitals for third-world countries. With the use of computers and the Internet, Annie was able to work at home most of the time. She would have to drive into the Global Architectural DC office one day each week for meetings with other members of the firm to help coordinate the design and accompanying work schedules.

Randy cleared away the newspapers he had been browsing and picked up the top folder from his "must read" file. There was never an end to the reports or internal papers members of his staff felt were important for him to read. Tim would review the summary page and decide if the paper deserved Randy's attention.

He opened the folder, finding several articles from newspapers or magazines dealing with the political tensions building up in the South China Sea between the People's Republic of China (PRC) and the member nations of ASEAN. In 1967, five Southeast Asian countries first established the Association of Southeast Asian Nations. The Philippines, Malaysia, Thailand, Singapore, and Indonesia were the original chartered members, with the Philippines, Thailand, and Malaysia having all been part of the former ASA or Association of Southeast Asia. Today, in addition to the original chartered members, ASEAN included Brunei, Myanmar, Cambodia, Laos, and Vietnam.

Randy scanned the papers quickly to see what the focus of the articles was. In a few minutes, it was easy to understand why Tim had placed these in his important file folder. China needed more energy, and the South China Sea was their answer. China had proven oil reserves of only 1.1 percent of the world total; however, China consumed 10.4 percent of total world production and 20.1 percent of all the energy used on the planet.

The US Energy Information Administration quoted several reputable authorities that estimates of oil reserves in the South China

Sea exceeded 213 billion barrels—ten times the proven reserves of the United States. The same US agency estimated the natural gas reserves in the area to be 900 trillion cubic feet.

Most of the exploration would be in the Spratly Islands, Scarborough Reef, and Paracel Islands, all within the South China Sea. Most, if not all, of the member nations of ASEAN claimed ownership of these islands and contested the same claim from the PRC.

Another disputed point was the right of passage through these international waters. China was using its ever-growing naval power to expand its influence throughout that part of the world, and even India was threatening to send its navy into the region to keep the international waters open to every country.

Randy slowed his reading when he came to several papers describing clashes between fishing fleets from Vietnam and small Chinese Navy patrol crafts. It was easy to understand the ASEAN member nations' complaints against their colossal neighbor to the north. China and the Philippines each claimed ownership of the Scarborough Reef. The Philippines' Subic Bay lay only 130 miles from the oil-rich rocks and small island group, while China's coastline was five hundred miles northwest of the same location, which they called Huangyan Island.

Other nations claiming partial or full ownership of the Spratly Islands were the Philippines, Vietnam, and Malaysia, the ROC (Republic of China or Taiwan), and Brunei—all disputed by China.

Randy laid the papers down on his desk and turned his swivel desk chair. He looked out the windows of his Senate office at the dark and cold Washington night. There were over six hundred million people in the member nations of ASEAN and another 1.35 billion Chinese, all claiming rights to the rich oil and gas reserves beneath the South China Sea.

Chapter 3

Washington DC
Wednesday—December 17, 2014
8:15 p.m. (EST)

Randy Fisher shut the engine off for his new 2015 Ford Explorer and removed the keys. He was still young enough to be excited about owning a new car. It had been a surprise present from Annie, who knew he needed to replace his 2006 model.

After the campaign blitz and working seven days per week for three and a half months, culminating with a late victory party, Randy Fisher went to bed in the early morning hours and slept until almost noon on Wednesday, November 5, after the election.

Their first wedding anniversary had been on November 1, and they had taken time for a quick and—Randy was thankful—*quiet* dinner. He still had another campaign event the same evening. They had decided to do something special after the election.

Annie decided to act on her own. She had gone on the Internet and obtained several quotes from local Columbia dealerships and had purchased the new car with instructions that it would be delivered to their home in Arcadia Lakes the morning after the election.

He had awakened from his long and restful sleep, grabbed a shower, and walked into the kitchen. Annie was waiting very impatiently with the big surprise. She told him someone must not have been happy with his reelection because his car had been "egged" during the night. They probably should have parked it inside the garage, she said.

Randy had immediately gone to the front door of their home to see what mess he would need to clean up, discovering the new car instead. A large poster was lying under the windshield wipers with the words "Mr. Fisher goes back to Washington." He could not miss the reference to the old Jimmy Stewart movie directed by Frank Capra.

Annie claimed it was Randy's anniversary present and his birthday present for the next two years. Randy could not have been happier with the gift. He insisted on taking her out for lunch at a local restaurant.

He opened the car door and stepped out into the cold night air. He ran his hand through his thick brown hair to repair the damage from the cold wind blowing through Washington that evening. To help ward off the evening's dropping temperature, he pulled the collar up on his London Fog overcoat and pulled on soft leather gloves after tucking the car keys into his coat pocket. The walk to the Philippine embassy was only about two blocks. He made it without any problems, carefully avoiding patches of snow and ice on the concrete sidewalks. As he approached the intersection across from the embassy, he stopped for a few moments to admire the beauty of the structure.

The dark night hid the outside beauty of the three-story stone and glass building, but the internal lighting from the very high and narrow multi paned windows glowed brightly. Every interior light, turned on for the evening's event, helped to enhance the beauty of the building.

The front windows and doors received their own festive decorations with miniature white twinkling lights and seasonal green wreaths with red satin bows.

The Philippine national flag, hanging from a pole near the front entrance and illuminated by a ground-mounted spotlight, moved freely in the cold evening breeze. Even from across the street, he could hear the snap rings clicking against the flag's aluminum pole.

Randy stopped to look both directions along Massachusetts Avenue. Fifty-six national embassies were located along Embassy Row, a stretch of Washington real estate that included Thomas Circle and Ward Circle as well as Scott Circle. Other embassies were located on Wisconsin Avenue, but this was the high-rent foreign political section in DC.

He crossed the street and approached the entrance to 1600 Massachusetts Avenue. An embassy employee opened the door immediately, greeting Randy with a smile and, "Good evening, sir." He stepped inside, presenting his invitation to a young Filipino woman with thick black shoulder-length hair, who was holding a clipboard. The warmth of the foyer was a welcome change from the outside cold air.

She took a quick look at the invitation. Her eyes widened, and her smile seemed to brighten just a little more. "Merry Christmas, Senator Fisher, and welcome to the Philippine Embassy."

Randy accepted the greeting and offered his own in return. At her gesture, he moved off to the side and removed his coat, stuffing his gloves in the side pocket. He handed the coat to another young woman behind a counter and received a numbered plastic ring to use later in retrieving his coat. He then walked through a temporary metal detector and entered the main lobby of the embassy.

Taking notice of the extra security, he guessed that it probably consisted of off-duty Capitol Hill police moonlighting for some extra holiday pay. Once he had collected his watch and car keys, he proceeded into the lobby interior.

There were people all around the inner lobby area. A few recognized the famous senator and stopped him with their greetings and well wishes for a Happy New Year.

The Philippine nation had a long history going back many thousands of years, but its current history started in 1521 when Ferdinand Magellan claimed the Philippines for Spain. In July of 1898, the Philippine people revolted against the oppression of their Spanish rulers and tried to force the Spanish out of their country. They would have failed in their quest had not the United States Navy, under the command of Admiral George Dewey, come to their aid. In December of the same year, Spain ceded the island nation to the United States to avoid a defeat of their forces. The United States continued to manage the affairs of the country, and by 1935, it was a self-governing commonwealth. Their planned independence, interrupted by the invasion of the Japanese at the start of World War II, would have to wait. They received their independence on July 4, 1946.

The relationship with the United States had always been good but became strained by the United States' continued support of the brutal regime of Ferdinand Marcos from 1965 to 1986. After his removal from office, relations resumed near-normal conditions, except for the removal of most of the US military assets, which had been stationed in the Philippines since 1898.

The Philippine ambassador was not the official host for this evening's event. This was the official Christmas party of ASEAN, and the current ambassador to the United States from the association was the ambassador from Vietnam.

Vietnam had two embassy locations in Washington. They were commercial office suites for official business and improving trade between the United States and their country and were not large enough for tonight's event. The Philippine ambassador was gracious enough to offer his official home to the ambassador from Vietnam for the festivities.

This was an ASEAN event, and Randy's goal was to meet with each of the official representatives from the member nations. With ten nations and less than two hours, he had a busy night ahead of him.

He entered a large open room to his left, which was filled with the guests, and made his way to the closest bar in the right corner off the entrance. There was a long line in front of him. Several bartenders were working quickly to fill drink orders. Randy requested a 7-Up, leaving the straw from his glass on the bar top. Nobody would know he was drinking a soft drink, and he wanted to keep a clear head for the evening.

Moving away from the bar and into the room's interior area, he almost bumped into the Philippine ambassador. Isko Bello was nearing seventy years of age and a seasoned politician. Next year, 2015, would be his last year as ambassador to the United States. Randy had met with him several times in the past two years and both liked and respected the man.

The two men greeted each other warmly and wished each other a happy holiday season. To Randy's delight, Bello decided to escort him around the room to meet with the representatives from some of the other member nations.

The representatives from Laos, Thailand, and Cambodia were together and were the first stop for Randy and Isko Bello. To Randy's surprise, they were speaking the official working language of the association—English.

Randy's working knowledge of foreign languages was, to say the least, terrible. Even after three years in Germany during his military service, he could speak only a few words of German. He knew just enough to order a sandwich or beer and could ask directions to the men's toilet. He found it embarrassing and frustrating but finally had to accept the fact that foreign languages were simply beyond his capability. He was grateful not to have received an appointment to some foreign posting. Communications in Washington DC were difficult enough.

The discussion among the three member nations centered on Laos and its need to improve exportation procedures. The country was landlocked, and trade routes were by roads to Cambodia and Thailand. The major obstacle was the time required to cross the borders. Lengthy delays caused by custom inspectors were costing the Laos merchants too much money and time in their efforts to get their goods to market. Some of the shipments were taking as long as five to seven days to be processed.

The ambassador from Cambodia asked Randy for his thoughts. Randy was not sure if the politician really wanted his ideas or was just being polite. He probably waited several seconds too long to respond, judging first by his facial expressions. However, he finally came out with his answer.

"We had the same problem with our trading partners in Mexico and Canada. Sometimes large semitrailers would be required to off-load their cargo for inspection at the border, adding several days' delay to their deliveries. We created the NAFTA agreement, which allowed certain products and goods to transfer quickly over the borders. We started slowly by designating certain groups of products and gradually increased the items until the system was refined. It took several years for the entire program to obtain full implementation, but it works very well now. We have the largest free trading zone in the world with Mexico and Canada."

The three men quickly began peppering Randy with questions about the program. When he was finally able to answer, he suggested that he could arrange for them to meet with the US International Trade Committee responsible for overseeing NAFTA. This seemed to make the men very happy. Randy removed his Blackberry to record a notation, a reminder to himself to reach out to the USITC and request its assistance. He promised to get back to each representative after the first of the year. They traded handshakes all around, and Ambassador Bello gently took Randy by the elbow to move to the next group.

As they were walking, Randy recognized an American woman nearby talking to the foreign cultural attaché for the Philippines. Margaret Anderson was the chairperson for the Senate Foreign Relations Committee. Randy did not sit on her committee but knew her well and always listened to her ideas and advice.

Anderson noticed Randy and raised the glass in her hand, bobbing her head just slightly to let him know she had seen him. She followed up with a quick smile and then focused her attention back on the political officer at her side.

Randy and Ambassador Bello had almost reached another small group of men when a loud commotion behind them caused everyone in the room to look for the disturbance.

Randy and his escort turned with everyone in the room to look at three men off to the left of the entrance. They were talking loudly, and from their postures, Randy could tell it was not a pleasant conversation.

The room was growing silent as other conversations stopped. Randy recognized the Chinese ambassador from the one meeting he had attended at the Chinese embassy. There was a large Chinese naval officer standing behind and to the left of the ambassador. The third man, he did not recognize. He started to pivot to Ambassador Bello to ask his identity. Bello anticipated Randy's request. Bello moved a step closer to Randy and whispered that the smallest of the three men was the Vietnamese ambassador and their actual host for the evening's event.

Randy had never met An Nguyen before nor even seen his picture in any intelligence reports. The diminutive man appeared to be in his middle sixties and stood nearly toe to toe with the Chinese ambassador. His country was a lot smaller than China, but you could not tell that from his body language. He was standing firm against the two Chinese officials. Randy was disappointed that he could not interpret the rank insignia of the Chinese officer, who had yet to speak.

Luckily, Isko Bello came to his aid once again. "That's Admiral Fang Li of the PLAN."

Randy knew the officer was a member of the naval branch of the People's Liberation Army and Navy but was surprised when informed that he was looking at the current commanding officer of the Chinese Southern fleet based in Zhanjiang, China.

The two men were not speaking in English, and Admiral Fang Li continued to remain quiet but moved a step closer to his ambassador as though to protect him if the Vietnamese ambassador took any provocative actions toward the Chinese political representative.

Another young man approached Ambassador Bello on his side away from Randy and started whispering in his ear. Randy suspected that he was an interpreter for the ambassador. Randy decided to concentrate on the body language and facial expressions of the two men. Bello could fill in the details of the verbal exchange later.

Throughout the heated exchange, the Vietnamese ambassador was not giving any ground to the towering Chinese politician. He continued to point his left index finger at the Chinese ambassador with each comment he made. Randy stole a quick glance over to where Margaret Anderson was watching the exchange between the two men. She simply raised one eyebrow to show her concern.

It was almost two full minutes before the men seemed to realize the entire room was witnessing their heated exchange. The Chinese ambassador took a half step closer to Nguyen, leaving only a few inches between their bodies. He made one last statement, turned on his heel, and walked from the room.

Admiral Fang Li simply stood for another few seconds staring down at the smaller man. Suddenly, he pressed a smile on his face, leaned toward the Vietnamese ambassador, and spoke his only words since arriving at the embassy. When he was finished, he stepped back and looked at the rest of the room. His smile became a little wider as he gave the room a slow, shallow bow from the waist. He turned and exited the room.

Ambassador An Nguyen was completely silent, and the people in the room followed his example. Finally, he turned around to face his other guests. Putting on his best face amid an embarrassing situation, he addressed the group. "My friends, please excuse my unforgivably bad manners. This was not a proper occasion to discuss political issues between neighboring countries. I trust I have not ruined your evening." He moved his arms up and spread them slightly to include every person in the room. "Please continue with your conversations and enjoy the evening. Please accept my apologies once again to each and every one of you."

Randy, along with most of the other guests, was confused. He turned to Ambassador Bello. "Can you tell me what the confrontation was all about?"

Bello looked at the young man who had joined them and then back to Randy. "This is Rodel Quiamnao. He is one of my aides and is the best interpreter in our embassy." He turned his head to the aide. "Rodel, please explain to the senator the exchange between the two ambassadors."

The young Philippine assistant was perhaps twenty-five or so years old with thick black hair. "The Chinese admiral was not on the invitation list. This was to be a political-dignitary-only event. His presence here got the conversation off to a bad start. Nguyen then mentioned a recent skirmish between a Vietnamese fishing fleet and a Chinese Navy corvette near the Paracel Islands. Apparently, one of the fishing ships sustained heavy damage, and three crewmembers were seriously hurt. The Chinese ship left the scene and failed to offer either assistance to the fishermen or an apology."

Bello looked at Randy Fisher. "The Chinese continue to bring more combat ships into the South China Sea. With no one willing to stand up to them, they continue to act as if they are the sole owner of the international waters. I'm afraid every ambassador here tonight will be making a report of this incident to his home office before he retires for the evening."

Randy looked back to the interpreter. "What did Admiral Li say to the ambassador before he left the room?"

"He said the fishing fleet was operating in Chinese territorial waters. Vietnam needed to learn its place. Next time, they might not be so lucky."

Chapter 4

Randy Fisher entered the Senate dining room and looked around for his lunch companion among the filled tables. He spotted Margaret Anderson over by a window table and moved to join the foreign affairs committee chairperson. Margret Anderson would be starting her fourth term in office next year. She was the highest-ranking female in the Senate by years. She had been married for thirty years to the same man, and all of her four children were grown. She kept her hair blond with the help of an artificial coloring agent and dressed conservatively to match her age of fifty-five.

"Hello, Mags," he said. Her friends called Margaret Anderson "Mags," and Randy felt honored to be among the group with that privilege. "I'm glad you were able to meet me for lunch. I was very concerned after the rowdy display between the two ambassadors and Admiral Fang Li last night."

Mags Anderson emptied an envelope of sweetener into her cup of hot tea. "Well, if you hadn't called me, I was going to call you. I have been to many political and social events in my eighteen years in Washington, but last night takes the cake. I assume you got an interpretation from Bello?"

"Yes," Randy answered. "Admiral Fang Li warned the Vietnamese ambassador that the next time his fleet comes across a Vietnamese fishing fleet in the South China Sea, there will be another confrontation. It seems their two countries are both trying to occupy the same waters over there. You would think the South China Sea is large enough for everybody, but I guess that is wishful thinking."

Mags Anderson had finished mixing the sweetener into her tea and laid the spoon beside her cup on the saucer. "I'm afraid the situation over there is not going to get better by itself. Someone is going to have to step in and try to bring these differing sides to the table for discussions."

Randy agreed. "The combined military forces of the ten ASEAN members are not enough to take on the Chinese. Only if the Indians were to move their fleet into the South China Seas would the opposing sides be closer in size. We would have two nuclear powers facing each other. I don't like the prospect of any increase in naval presence happening over there."

Mags nodded her head in agreement. "I think I must have read the same report as you. I need to check the current status and strength of the Indian navy."

Randy offered some of his own information on the Indian navy. "They've got two aircraft carrier groups that they like to parade around to flex their political muscle. It will not be a happy event if they tangle with the Chinese. Both have a lot of firepower to throw at each other."

Randy asked the other question that had been on his mind since he left the party last night: "What is Admiral Fang Li doing in Washington?"

Mags picked up her menu booklet to browse the restaurant's selection of salads or soups, sandwiches, and entrees but looked over the top at Randy before she spoke. "I was surprised myself to see the admiral in Washington. I would not have recognized him. It was my first time to actually see him."

"I'm in the same boat with you, Mags. We need to send this up the ladder to the intelligence people for their information, though I hope they already knew before last night. I am having a quiet dinner tonight with Marion Bellwood. I can let the DDO/CIA know about this latest incident."

"Good," she said. "I've got a call in to William McGowan to ensure his staff is up to speed on our Chinese friend."

Randy's dinner companion later that evening would be the

deputy director of operations of the Central Intelligence Agency. Mags Anderson was trying to reach out to the secretary of state for President Harold Miller.

"Now," she said, "is there anything on this menu besides salad that won't add to my waistline?"

Chapter 5

Washington DC
Thursday—December 18, 2014
7:00 p.m. (EST)

Marion and Marci Bellwood lived in a small city about twenty miles northeast of Washington called Greenbelt, Maryland. Randy and Annie left their apartment in Alexandria for the drive, accessing the 495 east Outer Belt and circumventing the capital city until they reached the Baltimore/Washington Highway. They drove north on the BW about fifteen miles, bypassing the exit to the National Security Agency at Fort Mead. The exit to Greenbelt was only about four or five miles further north.

From the exit, they only had to travel a few more miles to the subdivision where the DDO/CIA lived with his wife and three kids. The kids were now young adults who were more interested in after-school activities with their friends than in their father's government occupation.

Marci had told Annie when she called with the invitation that it would be a quiet and informal dinner for just the four of them. Annie and Randy were looking forward to a relaxing evening now that all the public parties were over. Annie would drive from her own office tomorrow after the Global Architectural Firm's office party. She would continue to the Russell Senate Building for the smaller party with Randy's staff. This year, his gift was a large can of mixed nuts and chocolates to all of his staff members in DC and South Carolina. The staff members were sure to enjoy the cans with a festive painted Christmas scene on the lid. They would probably appreciate their

Christmas bonus of a week's salary a lot more than candy and nuts though. The bonus money came from Randy's own pocket. The federal government did not authorize a bonus to its federal Senate staffers.

After tomorrow, the two would travel to South Carolina and visit the four offices Randy had in the state. They would then drive north via I-95 to Richmond and Annie's parents' home in Glen Allen, Virginia. There, they would spend the Christmas holidays until the twenty-seventh. Afterward, they would fly to Los Angeles and spend a week with Randy's aunt, Frances Ward, at her beach home. Randy was looking forward to the sunny weather and the warm breeze blowing in off the Pacific Ocean.

Randy pulled into the driveway of the two-story brick colonial home of the number-two spy in America. Randy, Marion, and Marci all met in Germany. Marion was a CIA case officer, and Marci was a lieutenant in the Army G-2 section for intelligence. Their mutual background in intelligence served as a bridge for Marion and Marci to develop a strong relationship with each other. They became engaged while in Europe. They were planning their wedding once they were both back stateside.

While on patrol one evening checking the security of a classroom building, Randy, an MP, discovered an open door. Inside a classroom, Marci's body lay backward across the classroom desk, stunned and helpless by the assault from a crazed Special Forces operator. Randy immediately moved to the woman's assistant but was nowhere near the skill level of the rapist. He found himself in a deadly situation fighting off the attack now turned against him. The killer, moments away from plunging a knife into the MP, was hovering over Randy with his K-Bar knife held high above his head. He had just begun a downward motion with the knife when Marion Bellwood arrived to pick up Marci. Taking less than a split second to make a decision, the CIA officer drew his Glock 9MM automatic handgun and fired two rounds into the SF operator, saving Randy's and Marci's lives.

Marci shortly afterward rotated back stateside after the incident and resigned her commission when her enlistment period was completed. Randy and Marion spent many off-duty hours together in Germany until Randy's tour of duty concluded and he returned home. They had not talked often until Randy received his Senate appointment and moved to Washington. Now the two couples would get together at one or the other's place almost every other week for dinner, or as their busy schedules allowed.

The Bellwood's front door opened before the Fishers reached the entrance, and the fifty-year-old Marion Bellwood welcomed them inside the foyer. Annie received a warm hug and Randy the usual handshake from the man who had saved his life. For his part, Randy was instrumental in Marion's being appointed to his current position, so to a small extent, Randy had returned the favor. Marci Bellwood, two years younger than her husband, hurried in from the kitchen to join her Marion in welcoming two of their closest friends.

The four had long ago stopped using the formal dining room for their get-togethers. Both the Bellwood's home and the Fishers' apartment had a prep area in their kitchens large enough to seat four, and they favored the more casual setting. Marion was the first to suggest the eating arrangement. He admitted, since he couldn't tell anyone what he did for a living, it was a real treat for him and Randy to be able get together with their wives and not have to worry about someone trying to probe too deeply about his work. Still, they had a strict ground rule. The conversation could cover politics, religion, family, and a host of other topics; the subject of national security was off the table.

The dinner was perfect, and Randy enjoyed the easy openness between his friends and not worrying about their conversation being the headlines in tomorrow's newspapers. Conversation about politics, never completely forgotten, always seemed to drift into their discussion, but Randy would try to steer the talk toward Annie's work with GAF. Marci was particularly interested in whether the Fishers would purchase another home in the DC area now that Randy had a guaranteed seat in the Senate for six years.

The younger couple had mixed feelings about the subject. They both loved the apartment in Alexandria but wanted to start a family. The apartment was the perfect size for two but would not work well with another family member. They had decided to keep the apartment for the time being. They planned to begin the search for a new home in earnest once Annie became pregnant. Nine months for the baby to come full term would give them plenty of time for house hunting.

Marci had a skeptical look on her face as she pointed her finger at both Fishers. "Listen, friends. You do not want to be in an advanced stage of pregnancy before you make a buying decision. No mother wants to be in the final trimester and packing and moving to a new home at the same time. Even if you hire a moving firm, don't underestimate the stress of the moving process."

Randy gave a little chuckle. "I'm sure my wonderful mother-in-law will be certain to see that Annie will not be overburdened by any move we make. Once she knows that her status of mother is going to change to grandmother, we will be given all the advice we need." He caught the look on Annie's face and decided to add to his last statement, "and we will be most happy to hear everything she has to say."

Marion picked up his partially filled wineglass and held it up to his friend. "Nice save, friend."

Annie leaned over to kiss her husband on the cheek. "A perfect choice of words, dear. Now we all know why you're the politician."

The group laughed. Randy knew his wife was not upset with him. Millicent Willis was a wonderful woman, but she would never stop being a strong mother to her daughter.

Annie and Marci removed the dishes and started to load them into the Bellwood's dishwasher. Randy asked if he could speak with Marion in the older man's study. After the two left the kitchen, Marci and Annie looked at each other. Marci gave a little shrug of her shoulders. "After fifteen years, I still don't ask what is going on in his life. I'm just glad he's not overseas running agents anymore. At least his domestic schedule allows a little more time for me and the kids."

The two men entered Marion's carpeted study, which was lined on two walls with floor-to-ceiling bookshelves. Marion took his seat behind the highly polished wood desk, and Randy flopped down on the leather sofa. Randy looked at the only wall in the room with windows. The closed curtains would prevent prying eyes. He looked toward his friend. "You still have that neat little scrambler device with you here in the house?"

Without a word, Marion reached into the pencil drawer of his desk and removed a small rectangular black box about the size of an iPod and placed it near the edge of the desk closest to Randy. He pressed a button on the side to activate the device. It put out a signal capable of scrambling any conversation should someone be listening with any type of electronic device. It would cover a space of about ten square feet in diameter, and no listening device was capable of hearing their conversation through the jamming. Marion might not risk his life on the jamming device, but it would be good enough for their conversation unless Randy went into something so sensitive that he would have to stop the Senator.

Assured of their privacy, Randy told the spy about the incident at the Philippine embassy. "Did you know Admiral Fang Li is in the country?" Randy asked after he had finished his recap of last night's events.

Marion nodded his answer. "We knew he was here as soon as he stepped off the Chinese jet at Reagan National, but we don't know the reason for the visit. With his current command position in the Chinese PLAN, our Far East division suspects he is briefing the Chinese ambassador on their next moves in the South China Sea."

"What do you people think the next move will be?"

Marion looked at the jamming device to see if it was still working. The illuminated green diode glowed brightly. "We think they're going to put a massive effort into more oil drilling platforms around the Spratly Island area and some of the other oil-rich island groups in the South China Seas. The area is ripe for an eruption of new military conflicts among the other countries claiming drilling rights to the same area."

Randy wanted to ask another question. "I assume you've told our friends over in the White House. What is their thinking on this?"

"They want to get the hell out of Afghanistan and bring the balance of our people home. They have little interest in the South China Sea. I've kept the president's national security advisor fully briefed, but the only questions I get back from the White House deal with Afghanistan."

Randy sat back deeper into the sofa. He did not have to be a member of the Senate Select Committee on Intelligence to know the president's policy for Afghanistan. The goal was to reduce the US level of commitment to around ten thousand troops from the high of nearly 140,000 and to use the remaining troops for training and as a rapid response force for putting out any fires that might flare up from the Taliban or al-Qaeda. It was what the people wanted, and even Tom Evans had publicly supported the program. Randy had other thoughts and worried the terrorist groups would just wait for new opportunities once the US commitment levels got too low to be effective in the mountainous country. He had not yet broken rank with Tom Evans on the policy and would not until he had a private discussion with the Senate majority leader. What was popular was not always the correct action.

Randy looked at his friend. "What's your advice for keeping events from flaring up over there in the South China Seas?"

Marion shut off the jamming device as he rose from his chair. "Talking is better than shooting any day."

Chapter 6

**Washington DC
Thursday—December 22, 2014
10:30 a.m. (EST)**

Warren Fletcher took a sip of his Earl Gray tea. He carefully set the china cup back down on the matching saucer with the White House emblem baked into the glaze. He swiveled his chair around to look out the window of his corner West Wing office. Warren was the chief of staff to the president of the United States and only a few years younger than the sixty-five-year-old president. His office was located down the hall from the Oval Office.

The West Wing in the White House is roughly square by design, with offices for senior staffers located along the outer perimeter. The cornerstone of the West Wing was, of course, the Oval Office itself. Next to the Oval Office were the president's private study and his personal dining room. The deputy chief of staff had her office after the president's private dining room. Next along the outer wall was the office for the secretary to the COS to the president. Fletcher's own office was located in the corner of the outside wall. Warren could step from his office into the main hallway and take a right turn. A dozen long strides and he would reach an angled turn in the hallway and the Oval Office. If he instead turned left in the corridor from his office, he would only walk the width of his own office to the end of the hallway. From there, he would make a right turn to reach the office to the vice president's secretary's or take a few more steps and reach the official office of the vice president. Further on was national

27

security advisor's office at the end of the hallway and directly "catty-cornered" from the Oval Office.

A person could leave the Oval Office and enter the connecting hallway system or the president's secretary's private office. Past her location was the large cabinet room, and around the corner was the press secretary's office.

Inside the wide hallway, connecting all of these rooms, was the Roosevelt Room and the entrance lobby for the West Wing, which all visitors had to pass through to gain access to the president and his senior staff members.

The West Wing was a little quieter today than normal. The president and the first lady were not currently in the White House, and a number of the staffers had left for their own Christmas break. POTUS and FLOTUS (president of the United States and first lady of the United States) were spending the early part of their Christmas vacation at Camp David, where they would remain until December 27, and then would travel to Florida near Naples where they owned a second home.

Fletcher and his wife had been discussing vacation ideas since before the midterm elections, mostly to spend their Christmas vacation with their son and his family in Southern California. From the day they had made the decision, she had been mapping out the details for him. Most of them involved spending as much quiet time as possible. She had requested a list of books he wanted to read and movies they might want to watch together. She had informed their daughter-in-law of Warren's desire to spend time with them and their three grandchildren, but her primary goal was for her husband to just relax and recuperate from the last fifteen months working for the most demanding person she had ever met. She liked the president, but Warren was an emotional person who brought the job home from work every night. It was taking a toll on her husband's health, and she could not stop worrying about the long-term consequences.

The decision by Jerrod Wyman to resign from his position as vice president completely disrupted the well-laid plans for the Fletchers. The president had tasked Fletcher with the job of compiling a list of potential successors and screening them for any problems or skeletons in their closets. Now, instead of leaving last Friday for the West Coast, he was still working in the West Wing, trying to have the list completed by the time Harold Miller returned from his Christmas vacation on January 6.

There was no question if he was qualified to make up the short list of candidates for the president. Warren Fletcher had been the Republican governor of Virginia for two terms and then the chairman of the Republican National Committee prior to accepting the position of chief of staff to the president. He knew everyone in the Republican Party who might be close to being qualified and most of their strengths and weaknesses. What he did not know was the one or two things in their private lives that might disqualify them from the position. The president had given a final warning before leaving for vacation. He could not afford another Raymond Cleveland or Robert Hodges. It was a warning Warren Fletcher certainly did not need to hear. From his old position as the former chairman of the RNC, he had been a firsthand witness to the scandals that racked the new Miller administration, and he knew their party could not afford any more loose cannons like Cleveland, Hodges, or Thomas Dean.

He picked up the china cup and took another sip of his tea, but it had gone cold and he did not really like the taste of the beverage anyway. He had tried to reduce his intake of coffee, but the long hours in the West Wing made him reach for more of that caffeinated beverage.

Fletcher had assembled a team of several White House staffers, including his deputy chief of staff, Leslie Overman, and three people from the RNC he completely trusted to keep their mouths shut during the vetting process. Leslie had been the working leader of the group and reported to him. Their efforts from almost six weeks of work were now on his desk, and he would spend the rest of December and his Christmas vacation either in his office or in his private study in his Georgetown home carefully reviewing the committee's selection.

He had not indicated any potential favorite to Leslie so as not to force her to look at any one person but simply to come up with six finalists from their first round of candidates. They would then complete the first stage of vetting and turn the six names and personal information over to him. He would select two names from their list, and another round of vetting would begin. That was another instruction the president had left with him. Vet the candidates once and then really dig into their personal and public records. No mistakes this time around.

Fletcher rose from his desk and passed through the connecting door to his secretary's office. It was empty since he had allowed her to take her time off, but she kept a coffeemaker on a credenza next to the common wall of their offices. He picked up the empty glass pot and walked out of her office to the water cooler in the hallway and started to fill the pot.

The West Wing was not empty. Even through the holiday season, the work of the executive branch continued. People were going about their work, but the activity was less hectic than normal. There was always a difference when the president and first lady were out of the White House, and the office of the vice president was now empty, even though Jerrod Wyman would still be the vice president for another nine days. He would finish his term from Texas unless a national crisis demanded that he return to Washington.

Warren returned to the coffeemaker in his secretary's office and started the brewing process. As he waited for the coffeemaker to complete its magic, he returned to his desk and picked up the brown expanding folder holding the files of the potential finalists. An elastic band held the folder's cover in place. He removed the band and lifted the flap of the folder. Inside were six files, one for each of the contenders, and he removed the thick packets containing everything Leslie and her team had put together for his review.

He laid them down on the desk and decided to look just at the names of the candidates—no details yet. He just read the names and formed a first impression. Leslie had taped a typed list of their names to the top folder.

Tom Postman—current governor of Virginia whose second term would end in December

Harper Collins—current secretary of the Department of Energy

Larry Frye—speaker of the House

Ester Chives—secretary of the interior

James Diamond—former governor of Florida

Carl DuPont—governor of New York

Warren left his desk and went back to the coffeemaker. The machine had completed the brewing process, and he poured a full cup. He would compromise with his wife and just drink the coffee black, without his usual three sugar packets.

Back at his desk, he stared down at the list of names as he took his first sip and then another of the hot coffee. He could not stop his brain from processing a quick review of the candidates.

Tom Postman was his own replacement for his former position as the governor of Virginia. He had campaigned for Postman because he had the best chance to defeat the Democratic rival, but Warren never really liked the man. Tom was too quick to smile, and he always seems to have a smug look on his face. The man talked a little too loud, and Warren felt Postman was not as smart as Postman thought he was.

Harper Collins—Really, there was no problem with the man, but they did not want to do anything to focus the American press back on the Department of Energy. That would only lead to more stories about Raymond Cleveland.

Larry Frye—Fletcher felt he was the best candidate on the list, but they needed him in his position as speaker of the House. In addition, the president had a mental black mark against Frye for failing to follow his orders to bury the bills for border security and immigration in the House.

Ester Chives—This was Leslie's hope for a female VP. She was probably qualified for the position, but she would not be a good match for Harold Miller.

James Diamond—He was a good possible selection. To Warren's knowledge, Diamond had a solid political record in Florida.

Carl DuPont was qualified, but they would need him to bring New York in during the 2016 reelection. Another problem, he was another big-money man who got his start on Wall Street. Too many people might question his selection.

Warren set the list down and drained the coffee cup. He was going to take today and the remaining time between now and Christmas Eve to make his selection for the two finalists. After a shortened Christmas vacation, his team would start the second round of vetting and have their choice to present to the president when he returned to the White House on January 6.

Warren looked at the thick folder on Tom Postman. He decided a second cup of coffee was in order before he started the review process. He returned to the coffeemaker for his refill. With his mind concentrating on his workload, Warren did not realize he put the normal three paper packets of sugar into the refilled cup.

31

Chapter 7

Beijing, China
Monday—January 5, 2015
10:30 a.m. (CST) (China Standard Time)

The American architectural firm of Kahn Peterson Fox described the global corporate headquarters of the Chinese National Offshore Oil Corporation as shaped like the bow of a ship and suspended on piloti columns to resemble an offshore oil derrick.

The architectural firm designed the massive 940,000-square-foot structure of glass, concrete, and reinforced steel to hold the more than 5,300 employees and provide ample space for future expansion of the CNOOC Organization. The piloti columns were made from a combination of iron, steel, and reinforced concrete and supported the building above an open ground level. Internally, the structure was hollow all the way to its roof and allowed offices with windows on both the interior and exterior walls.

The CNOOC company logo was round, with a three-layer blue background designed to resemble the blue waves of the ocean and a large red letter C superimposed on top. Inside the "C" was a slightly smaller, red "N" with the first up-leg or line of the "N" and the second down-leg made to resemble the "A" shape of an oil-drilling platform. The other red letters, OOC, were smaller and continued after the shorter final up-leg completing the "N."

The senior-level offices overlooked the Second Ring Road at Chaoyangmen in Beijing's eastern Dongcheng District. The building provided balance to the huge Ministry of Foreign Affairs building located on the opposing corner.

A twelve-member board of directors controlled CNOOC. They had a chairperson, vice chairman, two executive directors, four nonexecutive directors, and four independent directors. These twelve men issued the orders and controlled the worldwide company, which generated over 241 billion RMB (Renminbi being the official currency for China) or almost forty billion US dollars per year. CNOOC, listed on all the stock exchanges, had earned a net profit exceeding twelve billion US dollars per year. The company's past year's annual growth had exceeded 12 percent and would normally be a figure any corporation would brag about on their annual report to stockholders.

The board members, seated around the large glass and steel conference table, were unusually quiet today. The rectangular table, reflecting the minimalist look of the modern skyscraper, was large enough to seat fourteen people comfortably. The first meeting of the New Year found all the table spaces filled with the board members and their two guests. The senior finance officer, Kun Zhou, was just concluding his preliminary revenue figures for the 2014 fiscal year. The 12 percent increase from the 2013 revenue figures was an impressive performance, and he would have normally been proud to make this presentation. However, the prevailing winds from the National People's Congress and, more specifically, the Chinese Ministry of Land and Resources responsible for all oil production for the country were not happy with the year just closed.

Listed on the corporation charter as the governing body for CNOOC, the chairman, the vice chairman, and the other ten members of the board, in turn, reported to the senior chairman heading up the Ministry of Land and Resource and the thirteenth man sitting at the table.

Land and Resource Minister Chang Chen was in attendance today to listen to the 2014 fiscal report and hear about the production goals for 2015. Perhaps it would be more accurate to say he was there to tell the board members how much oil and gas production they would be responsible for in 2015.

The group was silent as Kun Zhou, the finance officer, took his seat. Normally, at this time, he would hear praise from his fellow board members on the report just delivered, but they all sat quietly waiting for a response from Minister Chang Chen.

The minister was writing some figures in his tablet. The secretarial staff had placed one tablet and one pen, both imprinted with the company's logo, in front of each place at the table before the meeting. He looked up and located the finance minister. "Please put back up the slide indicating the revenue for each of the corporate operational divisions."

Kun Zhou took the position again back next to the projection screen and activated the remote control for the projector. He pressed several buttons, reversing the direction of his presentation until he came to the screen showing the total gross revenue and the breakdown of the production figures for each division that made up CNOOC.

The slide showed the breakdown in millions of barrels of oil and millions of cubic feet for gas.

Division	OIL	GAS
Bohai	38.0	10.2
Western South China Sea	6.6	35.7
Eastern South China Sea	11.5	14.5
East China Sea	0.1	3.0
Overseas	12.9	41.4

It was easy to see Bohai Bay in China's northeastern region was the most productive internal field for the oil drilling company. The lucrative field had an estimated 146 billion barrels of crude oil beneath its surface. It was also easy to see their overseas operations were producing almost as much as the productions platforms in the South China Seas. With transportation costs and shipping time delays, the overseas operations were less cost effective than production from the Bohai and South China Sea platforms.

Not receiving any more questions from Minister Chang Chen, the finance officer left the projector operating and the division figures on the screen and returned to his chair.

Minister Chang Chen finished scribbling on his notepad and looked around the room at the board members. The forty-five-year-old slender minister with thinning hair put his ink pen back inside his suit coat pocket and picked up the tablet. "We have located thirty-eight more fields for the harvesting of gas and oil in the South China

Sea. We want production from all of those fields by the end of 2018. We want you to start twelve new platforms per year through 2018. The Central Committee will want your plans for years 2019 through 2025 for doubling the current production and the extra production from the thirty-eight new platforms that will be erected and started through 2018."

Finance officer Kun Zhou looked down at his own paper tablet and was making quick notes to meet the new demands from the minister. He was very glad this answer was not his to provide.

The CNOOC board members were all quiet for nearly thirty seconds. CNOOC Chairman Lian Wu was sitting at the end of the conference table with his back to the windows to be better able to view his board members. The sixty-five-year-old chairman was trying to grapple with these huge new demands. He looked to his vice chairman, Huang Zhao, who was responsible for production. "What are our current capabilities to erect twelve new platforms this year and build up for years 2016 through 2018?"

Huang Zhao was almost twenty-five years younger than the CNOOC chairman and easily the youngest man in the boardroom. He had worked years to reach this position of importance. Initially, it was working in the oil fields and studying all the textbooks on his profession. When he showed great promise in his specialty, the guiding authorities sent him to special schools for more training and more time in the fields. He even spent several years studying in the United States and earned a degree in geology. A special visa allowed him to travel to other parts of the world, such as Venezuela, Iraq, and Iran, to study their production techniques and to bring valuable information back to China. Of all the members of the board, he was the only one called by the Western term "wildcatter" oil driller, because he had worked on actual producing rigs to learn his trade.

Now he was looking at production requirements completely unrealistic for their current production equipment. If he failed to provide the expected positive answer to the minister, his career would be over.

He addressed the answer to the group and the minister. "We have four new oil derricks scheduled to go into service during the first quarter of 2015. They were to be located in Bohai, but we can easily change their destination to the new fields in the South China Sea.

We have issued contracts to our construction builders for delivery of four more by the end of this year. I can talk with them, see if they can improve their delivery dates, and see if they can improve the number from four to eight. If not, we can try to locate other rigs from alternative manufactures."

He suddenly felt anger rising within his body. "But having the drilling rigs available doesn't mean we will have trained men available to properly operate them. Where do we look for the skilled oilrig platform operators? We cannot just pull some autoworkers from their assembly line and put them on an oilrig platform. It takes years to properly train a man to work efficiently and safely on these rigs."

Lian Wu stared hard at the man he had promoted over others for the position of corporate production manager. He fully supported Huang Zhao's upward movement in the oil production industry and had taken a risk to put him in this position. Nobody in his right mind would talk to a minister in such a manner and certainly would not question the goals of the National People's Congress.

The fourteenth man sitting at the conference table was Admiral Fang Li, commanding officer of the Southern Command of the PLAN Navy. The admiral was sitting next to Minister Chang Chen and was smiling to himself. The young production expert reminded Fang Li of himself many years ago. He possessed the same hot temper and determination at that age, which helped to get him to his current senior position in the People's PLAN and People's Liberation Army Navy and as commander of all naval forces for the southern region. Huang Zhao would be capable of the job if he could learn the proper time to use his temper.

Minister Chang Chen was not thinking the same about the production manager as Admiral Fang Li. "Your job is to supply the equipment and meet the new production goals assigned by my ministry. If you do not feel capable of fulfilling the requirements of your position, then I'm sure your chairman can find a suitable replacement."

Chen looked over toward Chairman Wu. "I'm sure if you do not have confidence in your young production manager, I can find a suitable replacement."

Chairman Lian Wu wanted to change the topic from production to security. "Minister, I know Huang Zhao will exceed your requirements. My concern lies with security for our new operations in the South China Sea. We are well aware of many of the locations for the new production fields, and they lie in contested waters. Who is handling the negotiation with the member nations of ASEAN?"

Minister Chang Chen smiled back toward the CNOOC chairman. "You have no worries about security. That is precisely why I brought Admiral Fang Li here with me today. Admiral, please explain your negotiation program to the board members."

Admiral Fang Li had been sitting in a relaxed position during all the presentations and discussions during the board meeting. None of them up to now concerned him. However, security was his responsibility. He shifted his body to a full upright position in the chair. "My superior naval fleet will be used as my negotiation tool for our expansion into the South China Seas. For the last several years, we have increased our naval presence and pushed every other naval craft back closer to its respective country. We will bring our newest ship, the aircraft carrier *Liaoning* and the pride of the Chinese Navy, into the area. With the *Liaoning's* jets and helicopters and our other support ships, I will control the South China Sea. We will no longer tolerate the members of ASEAN and their unsupported claims of ownership on the PRC's rightful territory."

Chapter 8

Beijing, China
Monday—January 5, 2015
1:30 p.m. (CST) (China Standard Time)

Huang Zhao kept his barely controlled anger within himself through the balance of the board meeting and the luncheon for the board members and their two distinguished guests. The board members were now gone from the building, and the minister and Admiral Li had been whisked away in a private limousine with their personal security escort. He was free for the moment from their presence. He marched into Lian Wu's office waving outstretched arms, finally venting his pent-up anger.

"How can we possibly meet those demands? They are completely impossible to achieve with our current production capacity, even with all the equipment we have ordered. I do not have to check with our suppliers to see if they can improve their delivery schedules on our new platforms. I'm already threatening them with performance penalties if they don't improve their delivery schedules."

Liam Wu made no comment. He simply watched with a hard, stoic face as the younger man walked to the windows behind his desk and laid his left hand against the steel frame.

For a few seconds, Huang Zhao tried to enjoy the view his position offered, but he could not force himself to remain calm. His anger once again rose to the surface, and he slammed his hand against the window frame hard enough to rattle the glass panel.

Liam Wu's body jumped in his seat. He quickly turned his chair and stepped up to the window next to his protégé. He laid his left hand on Zhao's right shoulder. "You need to get yourself under control or Chang Chen will have you replaced or perhaps something worse. Do you want your family forced to follow you to some remote part of the country as you try to scratch out some sort of living? We have received our instructions, and I need your mind clear of confusion and anger about something we can't change."

Both men stared down at the street many floors below. At this time of day, the Chinese workers filled the streets and sidewalks, returning from their lunch period.

Lian Wu sat back down in his chair but remained facing the window. "I'm well aware, my friend, of the production capabilities of our oil derrick suppliers. Talk to them anyway. Determine if they have contracts with other oil-drilling firms. Perhaps they might be able delay delivery to other companies and divert equipment to us."

He waited a few moments and then issued his next order, knowing the response he would receive from his "wildcatter." "Contact all the salvage yards. See what you can find from those companies."

To his credit, Huang Zhao kept his temper under control with his old friend. He slowly turned from the window to look down at the chairman of the Chinese oil production company. "You know what they have to sell. Worn-out equipment no sane oil driller would agree to work on. We would be taking a terrible risk for equipment failure and risking the lives of our workers. With that older equipment, the possibility of an environmental disaster increases. The International Greenpeace community and every other environmental organization will raise a terrible noise if we bring worn-out equipment into the South China Sea.

Lian Wu sat back in his chair and raised his hands in a gesture of hopelessness. "We have our instructions, and we must perform. Have the salvage yards paint every piece to look new. If it will float, then buy the damn equipment."

He started to swivel his chair back to his desk but stopped and reversed the motion. "And don't worry about the international environmental community's concerns about our equipment. They'll have plenty enough to complain about with Admiral Fang Li and his precious Southern Fleet to worry about us."

Chapter 9

Washington DC
Tuesday—January 6, 2015
7:30 p.m. (EST)

Governor James Diamond avoided the two small lounges and overstuffed chairs in the White House West Wing lobby. He preferred to walk slowly about the room, looking at the paintings and sculptures that were part of the decorations while awaiting his appointment with President Harold Miller. The two-term Florida Republican governor had been retired for two years since the end of his last term and was still having doubts if he had made the correct decision to take this meeting with the president and his chief of staff.

Did he want to be the next vice president of the United States? *It certainly would look good on a résumé,* he thought, with a private chuckle.

Jimmy Diamond was seventy years old and a straight-voting Republican since he cast his first vote almost fifty-two years ago. In 1972, at the age of twenty-eight, after graduating from Florida State University's College of Law, he had started his political career as a city council member in Fort Myers, Florida, and held that position until he was thirty-six.

He was next successful in his bid for a statewide office as commissioner of agriculture and was reelected to a second four-year term. In Florida, the commissioner of agriculture is a high-ranking position, considering the value of the Florida agriculture industry. After agriculture, he cast his eyes toward the position of attorney general to maybe put his expensive law degree to some good use.

Another campaign win and he kept the office for the legal limit of two terms. At fifty-two years of age, the political fire was starting to wean in his soul, and he decided to retire from politics and return to Fort Myers to open a small law practice.

For eight years, he worked his legal trade, preparing wills and contracts and making a few court appearances. However, it seemed Florida politics would not leave Jimmy Diamond alone. In 2004, members of the Florida Republican Party approached Jimmy, now sixty, and asked him to consider a run for governor in an attempt to unseat a popular Democrat.

Jimmy Diamond had been a happy and satisfied person living in Fort Myers. He was still married to his high-school sweetheart and had four grown children with successful marriages of their own, producing a litter of grandchildren. What more could a man ask for?

Nevertheless, the itch came to the surface again with the Florida Republican Party's offer, and Jimmy realized that perhaps his career would not feel quite complete if he passed on the offer for Florida's top political job. After talking about the proposal with his wife, Eleanor, he accepted the party's nomination and hit the campaign trail one more time. To his surprise, the Florida voters had not forgotten Jimmy Diamond and elected him as their governor and then once again four years later. He held the position until December 31, 2012.

When he finally left the governor's office, he was ready to settle down with his wife, four children, ten grandchildren, and two great-grandchildren for as long as God would let him live on this good earth.

Two years had gone by and Jimmy Diamond had not thought very much about politics until he received a telephone call from Leslie Overman in the White House about three weeks ago. The woman, with a young sounding voice, asked him if he would consider becoming the next vice president of the United States and consent to a background check.

For almost a full minute, as he listened to the voice over the telephone, Jimmy thought one of his old political friends was trying to have a good laugh at his expense. Some of them could be real tricksters. However, the calm voice on the other end of the line assured him they were very serious about his interest in accepting the position to replace Jerrod Wyman.

During the next minute, as the woman went through the investigation process, the old itch came to the surface once more to the politician inside James Diamond. After the call ended, he felt the need to talk the idea over with his beloved Eleanor, but she took less than a minute to tell him, "Hell, yes, you old coot. You've been sitting around here for two years complaining about what's going on in Washington. Now go do something about it."

Jimmy reflected on what she had said and realized he had been bitching about Washington and the dumbass politicians up there. He called Leslie Overman back at the White House with the private telephone number she provided and accepted her offer. He told her if she found anything in his background that would disqualify him from the position, he would stand in the middle of Main Street in Fort Myers at high noon with his pants pulled down. Indeed, they had not found anything in his private closet, and now he was in the lobby of the West Wing waiting to meet the president of the United States.

The lobby area was empty except for Jimmy and the Secret Service agent. The man had been polite as he escorted Jimmy earlier from the north entrance to the White House, but he was quietly watching him as he stood by the doorway that allowed further passage into the West Wing.

Jimmy's wait, by his watch, was reaching three minutes when a woman in her mid-thirties hurried into the room. She was dressed in a gray power suit with a skirt and a darker gray blouse, along with a black belt tied in a loose bow around her waist to soften the look. Her long blond hair, well cut by someone who knew how to match the hair cut with the shape of the person's face, reached her shoulders. To Jimmy, her first impression was favorable.

With a bright smile, she walked up to offer Jimmy her hand. "Governor, welcome to the White House. I'm Leslie Overman, and we are delighted you could come in at this late hour to meet with President Miller."

Jimmy at six feet two inches in height towered over the young woman by a good six inches. Her handshake was firm but not overbearing and reflected something of her personality and experience. He had met plenty of men and women who took themselves far too seriously. A bone-crushing handshake was one such sign. Power could easily corrupt many people, and their old friends might not recognize them except for their faces.

Jimmy gave her a sincere smile. "Well, it's nice to finally put a face to a voice. You look a lot like one of my granddaughters, so I think we'll get along great."

Leslie smiled, a little embarrassed by the elderly man's openness. A friendly, open relationship among the West Wing employees was something this White House seemed to lack. Leslie missed being able to sit down with some of her co-workers and just talk about topics far removed from Washington politics.

"Thank you," Leslie said back to the governor. "I look forward to hearing about your family and your time in the Florida governor's mansion. Right now, we need to walk back to the Oval Office."

She stole a quick look at her watch. "The president should be ending his telephone call and will want to meet with you immediately. Warren Fletcher will be joining us and the president."

They walked out of the lobby and turned right down the hallway. The Secret Service agent followed silently behind them. This was Jimmy's first time in the White House, so Leslie called out the rooms as they walked toward the end of the hallway and the Oval Office.

"This is the cabinet room on our left and the Roosevelt Room on the right. The hallway circles around this center room and leads to the vice president's office. This next room, on our left, is the office for the president's private secretary."

As they reached the end of the hallway, Leslie stopped at the large single door set at an angle. Two large men were standing on each side. Jimmy quickly concluded they were also Secret Service agents.

"Here we are," she said with her bright smile. She gave the door a firm rap with her knuckles but opened it without waiting for any reply. She quickly popped her head inside to make sure the president was off the telephone and then opened the door wide enough for her and Jimmy Diamond to enter together.

James Diamond got his first look at the impressive Oval Office. His mind registered Leslie's motion to close the door behind them. The Resolute Desk, set in front of the glass windows overlooking the Rose Garden, was the centerpiece, along with two padded leather-covered chairs in front of the famous desk but sitting at a forty-five-degree angle. There were two off-white leather sofas out from the desk with a coffee table placed in between. A medium size, unlit fireplace was against the wall opposite the president's desk. Several library tables placed against the two sidewalls were displaying small ornaments. Paintings of American landscapes partly covered the curved walls of the office. A professional had obviously decorated the room, but it lacked warmth and personality.

President Harold Miller rose from his desk and came around to meet Jimmy near the center of the room. "Governor Diamond, it's a pleasure to meet you." Both men were shaking hands and sizing each other up. The president was only about an inch shorter than Jimmy, but his body was a little fuller than that of the slender Floridian. Both men had thick white hair and lines at the corners of their eyes.

Miller pointed to the man who was now rising from the right-hand chair in front of the desk. "This is Warren Fletcher. I'm sure your paths must have crossed before."

Fletcher walked over to the governor and shook the offered hand. "Yes, Mr. President," Jimmy replied. "Warren and I have attended a few governor association conferences in the past. The two men broke their handshake. Jimmy now looked back to the president. "I think we met briefly at the last convention, sir, when you received the nomination."

Miller took a quick glance at Fletcher. He wished either Warren or Leslie had reminded him of this previous meeting before he had met with Jimmy Diamond. He recovered quickly. "Well, it was an exciting evening for all of us, and I appreciate everybody who helped to put me over the top in the balloting."

Diamond was not a fool and gave no indication that he realized the president did not remember him. "It was a great night for the Republican Party and for you, Mr. President."

The president waved his hand toward the sofas. "Thank you. Why don't we sit down so the four of us can talk?"

Miller and Fletcher took the sofa on the right. Jimmy and Leslie sat on the sofa putting the fireplace to their left. Leslie asked if anyone would like a cup of coffee but all gave her a polite "No, thanks."

The president laid the closed file containing the personal information about Jimmy on the coffee table. "James, my people have reviewed your public record, and it's very impressive. You've held several important elected positions in your state and were elected with a fairly nice percentage of the vote."

Warren Fletcher added to the president's comment. "The fact the Republican Party in Florida asked you to return to public service after an eight-year absence speaks to your record. I think that's very impressive as well."

Leslie wanted to add her thoughts to the conversation. "I believe it's worth mentioning you won election to the governor's office with a very strong majority. Obviously, the Florida voters had great faith in your ability to run the state government. We need more people in our party like you, Governor."

Jimmy smiled throughout all of the accolades thrown out by the president and his two senior staffers. *Who is selling whom?* he asked himself.

He smiled back at the three people but stopped when his eyes met the president's. "Thank you all for those wonderful comments. I take great pride in the faith the people of Florida have given me. I will always remember their trust." Jimmy sensed Harold Miller was not one to waste time with small talk. "Mr. President, how may I help you, sir?"

The president gave a little bob of his head to indicate it was time for business. "I need a new vice president, and I would like to nominate you, James, to be that person. Would you accept the position?"

James Diamond looked directly at the president. Right this moment, the other two people were not in the room. "Mr. President, I would be happy to accept the position of vice president, but I have one condition. I hope very much, sir, it will not upset any plans you've already made."

The president flashed a look at Leslie, and she in turn wanted to sink into the folds of the sofa cushions. She had not known about any conditions from the governor.

Diamond noticed the silent exchanges between the president and Leslie Overman and came to her rescue. "Now please don't hold anything against this young lady. She must have asked about my personal and private life six ways to Sunday, but I never mentioned this one little condition to her. In fact, I didn't think about it until I was on the plane flight to Washington."

Leslie secretly thanked the older man sitting next to her. The president did not like unpleasant surprises. Should Diamond's "one condition" be more than the president could accept, she would face Miller's temper after the meeting.

"Okay," the president said. There was not quite the same level of friendliness in his tone of voice as had been there before. "What do you want?"

Diamond picked up the subtle shift in the president's attitude but did not allow it to deter him. "Sir, I want to be your vice president, and I will support your policies to the best of my abilities, but I only want the job for two years."

Warren Fletcher did not show the relief suddenly flashing through his body. He had been sure Diamond would ask for something the president was unwilling to grant.

Leslie Overman hid the relief flooding through her body. She was certain this request would not be an obstacle for the president.

Nevertheless, Miller did not let them or Jimmy Diamond off that easy. He only said one word. "Why?"

Diamond knew the job was his but still wanted to answer the question to the president's satisfaction. "Sir, I'm seventy years old, almost seventy-one, and will be almost seventy-three when you take the oath of office for the second time." Jimmy could see the smile starting to form on the president's lips. The reference to the second term hit a hot spot with the man.

"It will be a tough reelection campaign, no matter who runs against you. You need a younger man by your side. I will be glad to support and work for you, but your future lies with someone who can help you win a second term. I will throw in my support for you during the campaign, but I only want the VP job for two years. With me in place, you have plenty of time to find the perfect candidate to be your next vice president. If you can live with my one little condition, then I'm ready to get to work."

Harold Miller quickly rose from the sofa, and everybody else stood to follow the president's movement. He had a big smile on his face as he walked the few steps around the coffee table to reach Jimmy Diamond and offer his hand. "I can live with your one request, James."

Diamond flashed his own big smile and accepted the president's hand. "Good. Let's get things off to a good start. My name is Jimmy."

Chapter 10

The whirlwind event of nominating a new person to be the next vice president of the United States started early on Wednesday morning when the White House leaked the name of the leading candidate to favorite members of the national press. This was to give the news media time to prepare their coverage and background information on Diamond. It would also give time for the American people, outside of the state of Florida, to become more familiar with Jimmy Diamond's biographical information and political record.

At 4:00 p.m. on Wednesday afternoon, at her final daily press briefing, Alison Warden, White House press secretary, announced the president would be holding a special press conference in the White House Red Room the next day at 1:30 p.m. to announce his choice for vice president. She provided some personal information on Jimmy Diamond's family and cited his strong background in domestic politics and his high approval ratings from the voters in Florida.

The Washington press corps had plenty of time to flash the "breaking news" to the American public regarding Governor James Diamond being the president's nomination and to have their reporters reach out to many of the senior members of Congress for their comments.

Section 2 of the Twenty-fifth Amendment to the Constitution outlines the requirements to fill a vacancy in the office of vice president. It states the president can nominate any person qualified by law to fill the position, but both houses of Congress must ratify the appointment by a simple majority vote.

Karen Phillips was the senior CNN congressional reporter and very familiar with the Senate. She was in her early thirties with a slender figure and long black hair. Tina Lewis, recently promoted from producer to full reporter, worked the House side of Capitol Hill. She was married to a third-shift supervisor at the Potomac Electric and Gas Company and had two boys. She was near the same height as Karen Phillips but ten pounds heavier and wore her curly auburn hair styled with a shorter length and framed around her face. They had been tracking down the higher-profile members of Congress to record their comments before the time of the official announcement.

Speaker of the House Larry Frye was full of praise for the president's selection. The Representative from Iowa rattled off several positive points for the nominee and suggested there should be a quick confirmation for James Diamond. Marion Roswell, Democratic House Minority Leader from Kansas, also felt the president had made a good choice. "I've known Governor Diamond for many years. He's a person you can trust and work with."

On the Senate side, Majority Leader Tom Evans of California also voiced support for the proposed nomine. The six-five former professional basketball player was nearly fifty pounds heavier than his basketball playing weight. The contrast between the Senator and the slender Karen Phillips was amusing. She had to extend her arm to the fullest to have her microphone reach the tall senator. "I will support the president's selection. It is an important position as set forth in the Constitution, and we need to have the vacancy filled quickly and by a competent person. James Diamond meets the requirements."

Minority Leader of the Senate Avery Docks echoed Larry Frye's words in his support of Diamond.

Karen Phillips wanted to get to Randy Fisher and catch his comments for the nightly news. She knew the president had no love for the junior Senator from South Carolina, but Fisher would not fall into her little trap. "Senator, what do you feel about the president's selection for vice president?"

Randy Fisher looked at Karen rather than her camera operator standing behind the reporter. "The Constitution calls for the president to select a person and submit his or her name to Congress for confirmation. I spent a lot of time in Florida when I worked in the private sector, and I always heard very positive remarks from Governor Diamond's constituents. I think the governor will bring great honor to the office and provide support to the president."

Karen worked to keep a smile off her face. Senator Fisher had phrased his response in a manner that allowed her to ask to another question. "Senator, you stated Governor Diamond would bring great honor and support to the White House. Are you indicating President Miller needs to bring stability to the White House since there have been several serious problems with previous members of his cabinet?"

Randy Fisher was shaking his head. "I did not mean to make any reference to past cabinet selections by President Miller. Governor Diamond is fully qualified to be vice president, and the president has made a great selection in his nomination. I expect the governor to be confirmed quickly by the Congress."

All the comments from the congressional members were ready for release after the president made his announcement. At the appointed time, the two men walked into the Red Room within the White House. The senior staffers, assembled to support their president, quietly lined up along the outer wall, while members of the press filled the chairs.

Jimmy Diamond's wife, Eleanor, and some of his family members had flown into Washington and were standing off to the side as the president moved toward the podium.

Miller's face showed his pleasure for this event, and he advanced to the podium with a spring in his step. After pausing for several moments to ensure he had everyone's attention, he began to speak. "Good afternoon. The Twenty-Fifth Amendment to our Constitution provides for the replacement of a vacancy in the office of vice president nominated by the president and confirmed by the legislative branch of our government. The position of vice president comes with important responsibilities in respect to the operation of the Senate and to the executive branch. Our history had shown eight times the vice president has been required to step into the position of the president. Therefore, it is prudent we have a highly qualified person to be in position to replace any sitting president in times of crisis."

The president paused for several seconds to gather his thoughts. "I am very delighted today to present the person who was at the top of my short list to fill this important position. Governor James Diamond has proudly served the citizens of the great state of Florida for thirty-four years. He started his career as a city council member in his hometown of Fort Myers and was further elected four times to senior positions within the Florida state government. He decided to retire from public service, but the public would not let him go. After eight years in retirement from public life, he was asked to run for the state's highest office and spent the next eight years as governor of Florida. We have asked him again to step out of retirement and become our next vice president. He brings a wealth of experience that I will utilize as we work together to make this country better for our children and grandchildren. I am very pleased to announce that James Diamond is my selection for the next vice president of the United States. I look forward to his successful and quick confirmation by the Congress."

The president stepped back to meet Diamond as the nominee stepped forward to shake hands with the president. The assembled group in the Red Room began their applause. Diamond moved over to his wife, accepted a kiss on the cheek, and then stepped up to the podium to make his remarks. The seventy-year-old former governor stood tall with a straight back. He projected calmness, competence, and maturity and appeared ready to handle his new responsibilities once confirmed.

"Thank you, Mr. President. With great honor and gratitude, I accept the nomination for vice president of the United States and look forward to the confirmation hearings. I take great pride in my thirty-four years of public service in my home state of Florida and look forward to working with you and the staff members here at the White House. I also look forward to working with the Congress as we move forward with your agenda for reductions in our budget and Federal spending. I also want to assist in any way you direct to continue to bring our brave men and women home from Afghanistan as our successful mission there nears completion."

Diamond stopped speaking for a few moments. "Some people think being a public servant is just to have a job protected by the federal government. That kind of thinking could not be further from the truth. Being a public servant is a privilege, and it also means long hours of work with far too many federal employees never receiving any recognition for their dedicated commitment to making our country better.

"I want to salute every federal employee as I take this step forward to work with this honorable man and make the future of our country better for all of our children. I want to thank you again, Mr. President, for your support in this nomination and God bless our country."

Chapter 11

Washington DC
Thursday—January 15, 2015
7:30 p.m. (EST)

Randy Fisher did not think he would be back at the Philippine embassy so soon after the holiday event. However, on Monday afternoon, June Little, his receptionist, informed him the Philippine ambassador was on the telephone requesting to speak with the Senator. He immediately set aside the pile of never-ending reports he was reading and picked up the telephone.

"Good afternoon, Ambassador Bello. It's very nice to hear from you again."

"Thank you, Senator Fisher, for taking my call. I know how busy your schedule keeps you."

Randy assured him the pleasure was all his and asked what he could do for the ambassador.

"I have a special request from Ambassador An Nguyen from the Vietnamese embassy. He would like to meet with you but realized his conduct at the ASEAN reception was not quite proper and is a little hesitant to reach out to you."

Randy came back with a friendly response, "What could I do for Ambassador An Nguyen that our State Department couldn't handle?"

"I believe he feels your State Department is a little too tied up with your country's efforts to turn all the security arrangements in Afghanistan over to the Afghanistan government to be concerned with Vietnam. He has asked me to host a private dinner with you at my embassy. Do you have any open night this week that would allow you to meet with him?"

Randy was running his schedule over in his mind, and the delay caused the Philippine ambassador to assume Randy was hesitant to accept the invitation.

"Senator, you really didn't have a proper opportunity to meet with Ambassador An Nguyen at our last reception. He really is a very nice man. If it would not be improper for you, I would ask that you meet with him as a favor to me."

Randy had already decided to accept the invitation. "Actually, it would be my pleasure to meet with Ambassador An Nguyen. I'm available this Thursday evening if that would be acceptable to both you and Mr. Nguyen?"

Now he was again approaching the front entrance to the Philippine embassy. There were not as many lights turned on inside the building as the last time, and the weather was about fifteen degrees warmer than it had been on his previous visit.

He had not reached the front door when the same young Philippine woman who accepted his invitation on his last visit opened it. This evening, she wore her thick hair woven into a long ponytail draped down the right shoulder of her three-piece business suit. It reflected a more business situation. "Good evening, Senator Fisher. It is a pleasure to welcome you again to our embassy."

Randy gave her a smile. As she helped him remove his winter coat, he asked her name and position with the embassy. "My name is Raina Bello, and I am the granddaughter of Ambassador Bello. I work directly in his office when I'm not answering the door." She said the last part with a shy smile, and Randy had to chuckle. He immediately liked her smile and the confidence she seemed to radiate.

"Then I guess you must be the very best assistant available."

She smiled again. "I am, but I'm also enrolled in your George Washington University. I will finish my degree in legislative affairs this spring and then will return home to work in the office of our president."

Randy was further pleased with the young girl's deportment. "I hope you were able to learn something of value from GW and working so close to the location of our federal government."

"It was very interesting to watch the progress of your two pieces of legislation this past year and how you were able to win a two-thirds majority vote in the US Congress and prevent a veto from your president."

Randy thought about the victory Tom Evans and he had won over the president. "That was a good example of the separation of power within my government, but I'd rather have the legislative branch cooperating better with the executive branch. It allows the government to be more efficient when we go about the people's business."

Raina was leading Randy toward the elevator at the back of the entrance lobby. They passed several other people heading for the door Randy had entered. Since it was after normal working hours, Randy assumed they were members of the Philippine delegation on their way home for the day.

Randy followed Raina into the elevator, and she pressed the call button for the top floor. After the doors closed, she continued with her comments. "Still, it was interesting to see how your Congress was able to vote over a potential veto from your president. We had, for many years, in my country, the terrible problem with President Marcos. He was abusing his powers of office, and we had no way to control him. Your checks and balances system, between the three branches of your government, works very well."

Randy laughed. "I'm sure it wouldn't be hard to find some Americans who would disagree with you, but it's lasted over two hundred years. I think the most important responsibility I have is to ensure the future success of my country."

The elevator doors opened on the third floor, and the two walked out onto the carpeted hallway. "Yes, I think that is true for any good citizen for both of our countries."

Randy followed the young Philippine woman down the wide hallway with closed doors leading to what he assumed were offices on each side. They were almost back to the front of the building. There was a floor-to-ceiling window, at the end of the hallway that would have allowed him to look down on Massachusetts Avenue, but they turned into the last room on the right, and he discovered Ambassadors Bello and An Nguyen sitting in two oxblood-colored wing-back Queen Anne leather chairs. The chairs were placed to face toward the doorway he had entered but at a 45-degree angle toward each other and straddling a beautiful fireplace made from the same material as the exterior of the building. As Randy approached the two men, they rose from their chairs to greet him. He could appreciate the warmth of the blazing fire as they all shook hands.

Raina stood off to the side as Bello made the introductions between Randy and the Vietnamese ambassador. An Nguyen's head only came up to Randy's shoulders. His black-and-gray-mixed hair was combed straight back, and he sported a trimmed mustache and goatee. The effect on the elderly diplomat reminded Randy of one of his college professors of history from his days at USC in Columbia.

When the official introductions were over, Raina stepped closer to her grandfather. She surprised Randy when she spoke to Bello in a very soft and respectful tone. "Sir, the dinner will be ready in about five minutes if you would like to move across the hallway."

Bello smiled at his granddaughter and placed his left hand lightly on her arm just above the elbow. "Thank you, Raina, dear. We will be there shortly."

Raina bowed slightly at the waist and then turned and walked out of the room. After she left, Randy turned to Ambassador Bello. "You must be very proud of her, Ambassador. I was very impressed with our conversation on the way up here in the elevator."

Bello smiled at the compliment by the US Senator. "Thank you. I am blessed every day with her presence."

Ambassador An Nguyen took a moment, after the exchange between Randy and Bello, to regain control of the conversation with a low sound from his throat. Randy looked down at the distinguished politician. He could tell Nguyen had something to say.

"Senator Fisher, before we sit down for dinner, I want to first thank you for agreeing to meet me here with my good friend Isko and to also once again apologize for my conduct during the holiday event here last month. My conduct was unforgivable."

Randy extended his right hand again to the Vietnamese Ambassador. "I very much understand, and we will have no further need to discuss that evening."

An Nguyen took the offered hand again and bowed slightly at the waist. Isko Bello smiled as well. One of the evening's largest obstacles was now behind the three men.

Bello motioned for them to walk toward the door. "Let's move across the hall to the dining room."

The three men moved through the same door Randy had entered a few minutes ago and into the room across the hallway. In it were a small round table and three chairs. The table setting was less formal than Randy might have expected—only a white tablecloth with the basic dinning utensils. As they approached the table, Raina was instructing a waiter in the placement of several dishes of food on the table.

Bello indicated which seat the guest should take, and Randy moved next to the table. After they had taken their seats, Raina approached Randy with a bottle of wine and filled the crystal glass in front of his plate. She completed a circuit around the table and then placed the wine bottle in a standing cooler. She moved toward the doorway and wished them all a pleasant dinner as she pulled the door shut behind her.

The men were now alone, and each picked up his wineglass as Bello offered them a toast to good health and a peaceful year.

Bello next picked up the large platter in the center of the table and handled it to Randy. It contained a chicken and pineapple entree and smelled wonderful. Randy had not eaten since an early lunch and was famished. Using the large serving spoon, he took two helpings of the dish and then passed the platter to An Nguyen on his left. A cooked carrot dish completed the meal.

For twenty minutes, they ate and discussed several topics. The Diamond nomination for vice president was the first item, and then they moved on to the differences in the weather for this time of the year in the United States as compared to Southeast Asia. The meal was very pleasurable, and Randy was enjoying the company of Isko Bello and An Nguyen. He had been a little nervous before the meeting, as this was his first time with a Vietnamese citizen.

The Vietnam War had ended almost forty years ago. The terrible cost of the war was hard to forget when over fifty-eight thousand names, engraved on the black granite memorial along the National Mall in Washington, represented the American lives lost in the conflict. Randy was too young to have served in that war but had met many men during his four years in military service who had fought and survived the bloody conflict.

Randy could remember an incident in his own life about fifteen years ago. He was back in South Carolina and attending college at USC in Columbia, when he went into a department store at the Columbia Centre Mall off Harbison Boulevard, in search of a lightweight jacket for the mild winter weather normally experienced in the capital city. He had found exactly what he was looking for, and the price was in his budget. He had made the decision to purchase the jacket but looked at the tag to read the cleaning instructions. The "Made in Vietnam" on the label shocked him. He had not realized the United States had any type of trading agreement with its former enemy. He must have stood there for four or five minutes looking at the label, trying to decide if he should purchase the jacket. In the end, he put the jacket back on the hanger, replaced it on the rack, and left the store. Now he was having dinner with Vietnam's ambassador to the United States. Times had really changed. He wondered what Lawton Fields, his friend in Arizona, would say about this. Lawton had fought as a Marine rifleman during the conflict. Randy suspected the old man would have refused the invitation.

When they finished dinner, a waiter appeared with a rolling service cart. He cleared away the dishes, placed coffee cups and saucers on the table, and filled their cups. He left the room without saying a single word. Randy knew the reason for the dinner invitation was about to begin.

To his surprise, Ambassador Bello made the opening comment. "Senator, what do you know about the ASEAN Conference?"

Randy set his cup down on the table. "First, I would like to thank you for this wonderful meal and ask if we could address each other by our given names. I hope that would not be a terrible breach in protocol. My first name is Randy."

Both older men chuckled and agreed to the suggestion. Randy looked at the men, trying to assess their reason for this discussion. "Good, now the name bit is behind us; you asked about ASEAN. I know the organization formed in 1961 from the old ASA, Association of Southeast Asia Conference, and the original member nations were the Philippines, Malaysia, and Thailand. The official birth of ASEAN was in 1967 with the addition of Indonesia and Singapore. Since then, Brunei, Myanmar, Cambodia, Laos, and Vietnam have been added."

Randy turned from Isko to An when he mentioned Vietnam. The little man bobbed his head in recognition.

"You have your central office in Jakarta and hold an annual main conference and several mini-conferences, but I'm not sure of the meeting schedule of those. Your purpose is to promote improved relations and economic conditions, look to the regional security, and improve stability among yourselves."

An Nguyen reached over and laid his right hand on Randy's suit coat sleeve just above the wrist. "Thank you. I do not believe there are more than a small handful of people in Washington who would know half of what you just said." He spoke very good English with only a slight accent.

Randy looked back to the small man. "I thank you for your compliment, but I will tell you that I have a very good staff, and they put together a briefing for me on certain areas the Philippines and Vietnam have in common. I certainly hope my State Department would have more than six people who are fully conversant in ASEAN and the South China Sea. I assume that's why we're here together tonight, to discuss the disputed territorial claims of the South China Sea by the member nations?"

Nguyen was nodding his head. "You are partially correct, Randy. We wanted to discuss the territorial disputes but not between the members of ASEAN. Our concern lies with China. They also claim ownership of the waters and islands within the South China Sea and are continuing to expand their influence in the entire region."

An Nguyen reached inside his suit coat pocket and withdrew a folded paper the size of a letter. He unfolded the paper and laid it in the center of the table. It was a standard map of the South China Sea printed by an ink-jet printer. Randy immediately recognized the large land mass of southeast China and the thumb shape land mass of Vietnam, Laos, and Thailand. Directly to the east were the islands of the Philippines. South of Vietnam and the South China Sea were Malaysia, Brunei, and Indonesia.

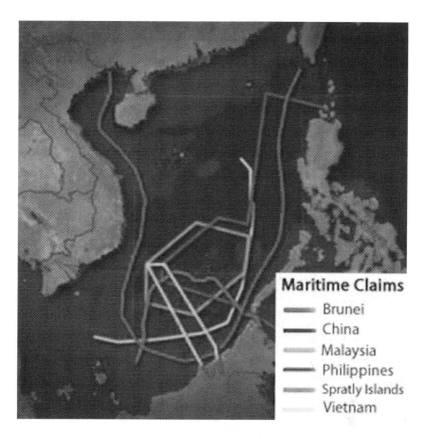

Maritime Claims
— Brunei
— China
— Malaysia
— Philippines
— Spratly Islands
— Vietnam

An Nguyen took a fountain pen from his shirt pocket to use as a pointer and indicated the outer line imposed over the blue waters of the sea. "You can see this line starts from Mainland China and follows the land mass of my country and then south to Malaysia and Brunei. It curves northeast and runs parallel with the coastline of the Philippines and back to Mainland China. This is the area of the South China Sea claimed by China. Within the outer line lies the Spratly Islands, Scarborough Reefs, and the Paracel Islands. They barely acknowledge the twelve-mile limits set forth by international decree for all countries."

Isko Bello pointed his finger at the map of the blue waters of the South China Sea. "In 1974, China seized the Paracels from Vietnam and killed seventy Vietnamese troops. Again, in 1988, they clashed over the Spratlys and sixty Vietnamese sailors were killed."

An Nguyen leaned his body away from the table and sat back

into his chair. "My brother-in-law was killed in the skirmish. He left behind a wife and three children. My oldest nephew is today a captain of one of our newest submarines."

All three men were quiet as they considered the information on the map. Perhaps for Nguyen, it was time spent on recollection of a long-dead relative.

Bello broke the silence. "As you can see, China is trying to control the entire region of the South China Sea even when their so-called territory almost touches most of the shores of these other countries. Plus, they have a history of violence that can't be ignored."

Randy pointed at the Spratly Island and Scarborough Reefs. "I've read the oil and gas deposits in this area are significant. China needs more energy, and these are the closest sources to its mainland except for perhaps the Bo Hai production fields directly to their east."

Bello got up from his chair and walked to the coffee service table. He picked up the carafe and refilled all the cups. "When Marcos was in power in my country and the United States continued to support his regime, it created a lot of ill will between the Philippines and the United States. After his removal, the Philippine people wanted all of the US military removed. Clark Field, Subic Bay, and other installations reverted to the Philippines, and the United States lost a great amount of its military presence in the entire southeast. Now China sees little resistance to stop its expansion program. Each of the member nations of ASEAN has a navy but nothing compared to the size and number of China's PLAN."

Ambassador An Nguyen picked up the briefing from there. "It is not a question of if China will make a military move but when. We receive weekly reports of increased activity from their navy."

Randy set his empty coffee cup down on the table. When Bello reached for the carafe, Randy put his hand over the cup to indicate he did not need a refill. "Gentleman, I am just a Senator in the United States Congress and have little or no influence in the White House. What would you like me to do?"

Bello smiled at his young guest. "It is a tribute to your personal character that you display modesty. Yes, you are just a Senator, but you have the attention of your press and the respect of the country. We understand the strained relationship you have with President Miller, but he will not always be president. We feel Senator Evans will very likely be in the White House after the next election, and you have close ties with him."

An Nguyen leaned his body back closer to the table and Randy Fisher. "We would like for you to come to our part of the world to get firsthand information on the situation. Our next annual ASEAN summit is in March. You would meet with every leader of the member nations, our ministers, like me, who represent ASEAN in other countries, plus our defense ministers. You would receive a full report that could be used to help persuade officials back here in your country of the seriousness of the situation."

Randy was silent as he considered the invitation. He had never traveled to Southeast Asia before. He could use his position on the Select Committee on Intelligence and Armed Forces as a reason to justify the trip.

"What are the dates of your conference in March?"

Chapter 12

Washington DC
Friday—January 16, 2015
4:30 p.m. (EST)

Randy Fisher was early for his appointment with Senator Tom Evans. He thought about stopping in a coffee shop in the Capitol building but decided to continue on to Tom's office for their 5:00 p.m. meeting. Maybe Tom would be free and he could get home early tonight. It was movie night with Annie, and he did not want to be late. Tonight, they were watching one of his favorite movies, *The Quiet Man*, with John Wayne and Maureen O'Hara.

Tom was in the official office of majority leader instead of his normal suites in the Senate Russell Office Building. When Randy was almost forty feet from the entrance to Tom's office, he noticed a large crowd of news reporters and technicians with portable broadcast equipment milling around the entrance. He wondered what was going on inside.

He decided not to fight his way past the journalists, turned around, walked back past two doors, and turned the corner at the hallway. Down fifteen feet was a private entrance to the office that Tom and Randy had used several times when they were going to the leader's office for a meeting.

Randy gave the door a little rap with his knuckles. He waited a few more moments, and when no one opened the door, he used more force to get someone's attention. Finally, the door opened. A very large and unknown man stood squarely in the doorway, staring down hard at Randy Fisher.

The faceoff between the two men quickly became awkward. The man did not speak or give ground, and Randy finally broke the silence. "I'm Randy Fisher, and I've got a meeting with Senator Evans."

There was still hesitation on the man's face, but he finally opened the door enough for Randy to enter. Randy seemed to sense that he should wait before moving forward.

The man closed and locked the door behind Randy. He turned his body slightly and moved past Randy but motioned for the Senator to follow him down the short hallway that came to an intersection. Several other large men were standing outside the closed door to Tom Evans's private office. *Tom must still be in another meeting,* Randy thought, so he turned left to walk out to the reception area to wait until Tom was free.

There, he found two additional large men and a woman with blond hair who looked a few years younger than Randy. The men were standing. One seemed to be watching the main entrance door. Randy could hear the murmuring from the reporters through the door. The other man was simply watching Randy. The woman, seated on the sofa, fingers flying over the keyboard of her Blackberry, seemed completely oblivious to his presence.

Tom's receptionist was seated at her desk but looked up at the sound of his footsteps and recognized the South Carolina Senator. "Oh . . . Senator Fisher." She took a quick look at the computer screen to check her boss's schedule and then turned back to Randy. "You're a little early, Senator. He is still with his three thirty appointment. Their meeting is running a little long."

"That's not a problem. As you said, I'm here a little early," Randy replied. He stepped toward the open end of the sofa, wondering why the two men had not elected to take the available cushions on the open end of the sofa. They were very large. Maybe they would be touching shoulders and would be uncomfortable with their proximity.

As he took the seat, the blond woman suddenly realized she was no longer alone on the sofa and turned toward him. Her face brightened with a pleasant smile. "Excuse me, Senator Fisher, but we've never met. I'm Leslie Overman, the deputy chief of staff at the White House. It's a pleasure to finally meet you in person."

Randy suddenly felt like a jerk. The men were Secret Service agents, and the woman was here with someone from the White House. That could only mean the nominee for the vice president was in with Tom. Jimmy Diamond was making a courtesy call on the Senate majority leader before the confirmation hearings.

"Thank you, Leslie. It is a pleasure to meet you. I assume you are assisting Governor Diamond on his visit to the Hill?"

"Yes. We are calling on the Senate and House leadership. I hope we can count on your support for confirmation."

Randy smiled as he answered, "I've already made my thoughts known about the nominee. Governor Diamond earned the respect of the Florida citizens. Whenever his name came up during my travels in Florida years ago, he received high praise for his fairness and open mind. I see no reason to vote against him."

Leslie was about to thank the Senator when the door to Tom Evans's private office opened and Jimmy Diamond walked out with Tom directly behind him.

At six feet five inches, Tom Evans was still a few inches taller than the slender older man was. He could see Randy over the governor's shoulders. As they approached Randy and Leslie Overman, the majority leader made the introduction. "Governor, you probably haven't met Randy Fisher, our junior Senator from South Carolina. Randy, this is Jimmy Diamond from Florida."

Randy was already standing as the two men approached and offered his hand to the man who would probably be the next vice president. "Governor, it's a pleasure to meet you."

Diamond grasped Randy's hand with a smile on his face. "Mine as well, Senator. You have made quite a reputation for yourself these last few years up here in DC. I hope I can count on your support for my confirmation."

Randy released the big hand that had closed tightly on his own. "I already told Leslie you're probably a sure thing. When a public servant of your caliber comes along, we just get out of their way and let them get the job done."

Diamond continued smiling and responded, "Well, that was nicely said. So are you and Tom here planning any big blockbuster bills this year for the White House to deal with?"

Randy could tell Diamond was playing with him. He decided to go along with the gentle rub. "Sir, our next bunch of bills is what

Tom and I are about to discuss now that you've let him go. We want to look at a few new revenue-raising ideas. We are thinking about a federal sales tax increase on all gun purchases and an annual license fee for all guns registered in the country. Can we count on the support of the White House after you've been confirmed?"

Tom Evans was standing next to the two men facing each other. He could see a twinkle in the older man's eye.

Diamond looked down to the floor and then back up to the young Senator from South Carolina. There was a smile building on Randy's face, and Diamond was having trouble holding in his laughter. "I can at least promise you a spirited response from the White House on those issues."

Randy could not hold the laughter building inside himself. He had seen the distressed look developing on Leslie Overman's face. A confrontation between the two men might not be a good thing to happen with fifty reporters standing outside the door just waiting to catch some sort of rift between the Democratic-controlled Senate and the White House.

Diamond immediately started to laugh and lightly slapped Randy on the shoulder. "If we can't laugh a little about what we do, the job will kill us."

Randy got his own laughter under control. "Governor, I look forward to working with you."

The men all shook hands again, and Tom Evans escorted Jimmy Diamond out of his office to stand beside the next vice president and say a few words to the waiting reporters.

Chapter 13

Lian Wu, Chairman of CNOOC, and his Vice Chairman, Huang Zhao had been meeting at 3:00 p.m. every day starting the week of January 12. It was not by design but simply the urgent need to work together to comply with the orders from the Ministry of Land and Resources.

Every day, they would update each other on their progress. Three weeks after the board meeting, they were still struggling with the enormity of their task. During the first week, Huang Zhao would let fly with his anger and frustrations at the stupidity of the entire situation. Finally, his friend and mentor had to sit him down and urge caution. "We will not solve this by losing control of our emotions. We must focus our minds and bodies on our jobs. I need you, Huang Zhao, but you will do me no good until you get control of yourself."

Huang Zhao promised to stash his emotions in a deep corner of his mind, and they were working as a team once again. Still, the new production schedules were nearly impossible to meet.

An expanded production schedule created many organizational and logistical problems. Perhaps the three big obstacles—money, equipment, and experienced workers—were the main factors.

For any business expansion, the overriding concern is always money, and oil exploration and mining is no exception to the rule. The cost of huge ocean oil drilling platforms is enormous but not the only requirement. The production of oil from underwater wells requires tankers, storage facilities, pumps, drills, piping, and a long list of other equipment.

Before they could determine the financial requirements, they needed to know what the equipment would cost, and before they could estimate that figure, they needed to know what equipment was available. Conventional fixed platforms could cost well over a billion dollars each and take two to three years for construction and additional time for transport to the oil field and erection at the drill site.

They had four conventional platforms on order and paid for with a scheduled delivery time in late first quarter. Huang Zhao had mentioned before the need to threaten the manufacturers with penalties for delayed delivery but hesitated, as he remembered something from his childhood. When he was sick and needed medicine, his mother would mix it with sugar to make the bitter taste easier to swallow. He decided to offer a bonus to the manufacturers if they improved the delivery of the new equipment. The latest report from their supplier now assured a delivery date in the middle of February.

The early delivery date would help, but they still needed eight more platforms, and he knew there were no possibilities to deliver those units with the normal three-year construction cycle. One option would be to purchase platforms from other oil-drilling corporations that had orders in-house with the manufacturers and were near completion, but after several wasted days, they abandoned that avenue.

Finally, Hang Zhao decided to look into drill ships. A drill ship was exactly what it sounded like. A ship outfitted with an oil-drilling platform and a GPS positioning system to maintain the ship over the wellhead. The ships first found life in exploratory drilling for new oil and gas wells or for scientific research drilling. However, over the years, the drill ships were enlarged and capable of drilling wells as deep as 2,500 meters.

Still, the problem was cost and availability. A new drill ship would cost over six hundred million dollars and required a minimum of one year to construct if placed on an existing ship suitable for the purpose. As to availability, there were an estimated ninety-five to one hundred drill ships in operation throughout the world, but most would already be in service.

The final dreaded answer lay on Huang Zhao's office desk. After days of working the phone and running the financial figures with Lian Wu, they had to accept the inevitable. They could not afford the new drill ships even if they could find them ready for immediate delivery. The only solution was to look to salvage companies for used equipment.

From a dealer in Murmansk, Poland, they found two ships that were over thirty-five years old. The seller faxed the ship's papers and maintenance records, and Huang Zhao sent a purchase order and electronically wire transferred the funds. Used equipment dealers in South Korea and Malta each provided a drill ship, but they were thirty and thirty-two years old.

China itself was the second largest manufacturer of all ocean vessels, and he found four used ships ranging from twenty-six to twenty-nine years old available from used equipment suppliers. After being assured of their operational condition, Haung Zhao paid the asking price.

With different ages and operational conditions, the ships came with various price tags. For the ships thirty years and older, the price ranged from forty to forty-five million dollars and seventy-two to seventy-five million each for the ships under twenty-nine years old. By the time he had cut all the purchase orders, the original $4.8 trillion needed for eight brand-new drill ships totaled less than $470 million dollars. This was a manageable figure for Lian Wu. Huang Zhao only hoped that the ships' papers and maintenance documents were true as advertised by the sellers.

Now that he had the problem with the drill ships resolved, he could turn his attention to the workforce. He needed to outfit twelve platforms—eight drill ships and four conventional rigs. He needed enough men for three shifts per platform, and Huang Zhao could not just pick these men from a tree like apples. Oil drilling was a tough business, and people could get hurt. Offshore oil drilling required the crews to live either on board the platform or on a support vessel anchored nearby. The crewmembers would be away from home and family for months at a time.

There were a number of HR companies specializing in the high-quality trained labor required for this hard and dirty business. Huang Zhao sent out the employment notices and alerted the

CNOOC personnel department to start accepting the applications. However, the oil-drilling business was operating at near capacity, and applications were only trickling in. After two weeks, Huang Zhao sent out a second round of emails to employment companies whose standards were not quite as demanding as the first organizations, and the responses started to come in at a heavier rate. For the best-experienced men on the list, they offered sign-on bonuses to the top candidates who would be the shift supervisors. Huang Zhao would not cut his standards for the men hired to be in charge of each shift or have the ultimate responsibility for each drilling operation.

Tankers to transport the oil and gas from the production fields back to the onshore refineries were next on the list. He would need three used ships for oil and gas transport for each platform to prevent the onboard storage tanks from becoming filled and holding up production. Their costs were well below the drill ships, averaging five million dollars each, but still he needed thirty-six ships. For those, he cut purchase orders for $180 million dollars.

In the end, the money was actually the easiest problem for Lian Wu to solve. China was one of the biggest moneylenders in the world, and the global economy was still down. China's Central Bank had cash to spare and knew the CNOOC was operating under the guidance of the Ministry for Land and Resources, so Lian Wu was able to secure a new line of credit for one trillion dollars. The $470 million for the drilling platforms and $180 million for the tankers was just the start of their equipment needs.

Oil—Energy . . . Energy—Oil . . . It was all big business, perhaps generating the largest gross dollars in revenue of any business in the world. Nevertheless, the oil-drilling business was a small world in one way; almost everybody knew everybody else. When CNOOC started buying drilling rigs and tanker ships, along with huge amounts of piping and millions of dollars of other required equipment and materials, combined with hiring men for ships and platforms, the word quickly spread throughout the industry. China was expanding its offshore oil-drilling production capacity. The question everybody was asking throughout the industry was "Where?"

Chapter 14

The original Constitution provided no procedures for the selection of a new vice president of the United States. The Twenty-Fifth Amendment to the Constitution was ratified in 1967 after the assassination of President John F. Kennedy and included Section Two for the purpose of providing a new vice president if required.

Prior to passage of the Twenty-Fifth Amendment, sixteen of the previous thirty-seven vice presidents either died in office, resigned, or succeeded a dead president. Some of the vacancies in the vice president's office extended for long periods.

After the death of Franklin D. Roosevelt on April 12, 1945, Vice President Harry S. Truman succeeded to the presidency. He did not select a new vice president, and the office was vacant until January 20, 1949, when Truman took the oath of office for the second time and Alben William Barkley became the thirty-fifth vice president of the United States the same day for his next four years.

Truman was running very low in the polls during the 1948 campaign when Barkley delivered a rousing keynote speech at the Democratic National Convention. Already having had a good relationship with Barkley, Truman wisely asked the Kentucky Senator to be his vice president running mate. The "Iron Man" from Kentucky set new campaigning precedents during the 1948 election. He flew across the country in a United Airlines DC-3 called the *Bluegrass* remodeled with a bunk bed and seats for secretaries, advisors, and reporters. Truman was famous for his "whistle-stop campaign." Barkley gained popular notoriety with his "prop-stop" campaign. Truman won the election over the favored Thomas Dewey, and Barkley set new precedents for the office of vice president.

Alben Barkley elevated the status for the office of vice president. Other VPs regularly presided over the Senate, but Alben delegated a considerable amount of that responsibility to others. He was the first vice president to attend cabinet meetings and to have an official office either in or near the White House. Truman brought Barkley into his administration in a completely different manner than Roosevelt had treated Truman. The influence of the office of vice president, established under Alben William Barkley, would never be the same again.

Confirmation of all presidential appointments is under the jurisdiction of the United States Senate with one exception—the vice president. Section Two of the Twenty-Fifth Amendment states the nominee will take office after both houses of Congress have confirmed him or her by a majority vote.

The Senate and House have the right to conduct hearings and hear testimony from the nominee and any other witnesses they deem necessary. In the present case of considering Governor Diamond, the Speaker of the House Lawrence Frye and Majority Leader of the Senate Thomas Evans decided to form a committee of seventeen members comprising members of both the House and Senate. The two leaders also agreed they would select the committee members but would abstain themselves from serving on the committee. They decided the chairperson for the committee would be the longest serving member in Congress regardless of party affiliation. The other sixteen members, divided equally by party, would come from both houses of Congress.

The longest-serving member of Congress was also the oldest member of Congress. Republican Congressman Ralph Peters was ninety years old and just reelected for the twenty-second time and starting his twenty-third term. He represented a Texas district that bordered Mexico and Arizona. His office website described the congressional member as active and honest and attributed his longevity to daily walks for his body and watching the television game show *Jeopardy* for exercising his mind.

Using their powers of office, the speaker of the House and the Senate majority leader quickly selected the names for the members of the committee. Larry Frye chose five Republicans and three Democrats and Tom Evans completed the group with his choice of five Democrats and three Republicans to balance out the numbers. The chairperson, as normal, would have the deciding vote if the other members split their votes down the middle.

The committee had only one responsibility—to determine if James Diamond was qualified for the office of vice president. Their vote would be a recommendation of approval or disapproval to the full House and Senate body. Once the committee sent the nomination back to the House and Senate, the entire Congress would take a vote. Normally, the opinion of the committee would reflect the eventual outcome of the voting process.

Senator Randy Fisher was a little surprised to see his name on the committee roster. He had not discussed this with Tom Evans nor had the majority leader broached the subject with the young senator. Still, like any good soldier, he would follow the orders of his leader and participate in the process.

Chapter 15

Jasper Lawrence was the Democratic Senator from Wyoming and had campaigned for a seat on the committee to advise the Congress on the qualification of Governor Jimmy Diamond to be vice president.

He was in his fourth year of his second term and would be facing reelection in 2016. His last campaign for reelection to the second term in 2012 had cost nearly eight million dollars to defeat the Republican challenger. He had used almost one million out of his own personal funds as his PAC money had not been enough to pay for the television ads he needed to broadcast over the local networks in his state. He was, by all standards, a wealthy man, so using his personal funds had not impeded his lifestyle, but Jasper knew that money alone did not ensure reelection. He remembered a Senate campaign in a neighboring state many years ago where the incumbent had chosen not to run for reelection so both parties put everything into their candidate. The Democratic candidate outspent the Republican by almost a five-to-one margin but lost the election. Money was a big help but did not guarantee success.

In 2016, Lawrence knew he would again be facing another strong challenge from the Republicans and needed to get more time in front of the public. The nomination of Jimmy Diamond could be the ticket and stepping off point for his reelection bid. The C-SPAN network would broadcast the hearings, and he planned to be the most prominent member of the committee and the one everyone would be watching. Once completed, the nomination process would die quickly in the national press, but his part would play a long time in his home state.

He planned to use the 1994 court case *Florida v. Tanner* to fight against Jimmy Diamond. Diamond had been in his second term as the Florida attorney general when he tried to stop an abortion by a young woman in her second trimester.

Both the pro-choice and right-to-life political groups viewed the case as a challenge to the 1973 landmark decision by the Supreme Court, *Roe v. Wade*. There was huge press coverage within Florida, and the national press was beginning to follow the case too, when the Florida Supreme Court ruled against the state's request for an injunction to stop the abortion. Then Attorney General Diamond argued they needed the injunction, as he wanted to take the case further up the judicial ladder. When the Florida Supreme Court ruled against him and the abortion had taken place, he stopped his pursuit of the case.

With the outcome of the case quickly decided, the national attention fell away before if really got started so very few people in the country knew how Jimmy Diamond tried to challenge *Row v. Wade*.

Jasper knew any discussion about abortion and *Roe v. Wade* would bring him the attention he needed for his reelection. Wyoming was a pro-choice state, and the hearing, once the abortion case came to the public's attention, would play well in his home state.

His staff was working hard to dig up all the old testimony from the 1994 Florida case, and Jasper Lawrence planned to bring it all out during the committee meetings. The committee schedule called for the hearings to start on February 3.

Chapter 16

Zhanjiang, China
Friday—January 27, 2015
10:15 a.m. (CST)

In 1950, regional naval forces were consolidated under the General Staff Department command in Jiangyan and later moved to Taizhou, Jiangsu Province, marking the beginning of the Chinese Navy. It was mostly a run-down collection of ships and boats acquired from different fighting groups. The naval air force, organized several years later, and the PLAN operated with about 2,500 Soviet advisors. With additional Soviet assistance, the navy experienced several more reorganizations during 1954-1955, and three main naval forces were established. They still exist today with the North Sea Fleet, East Sea Fleet, and the South Sea Fleet.

During this time of expansion, the PLAN purchased all new ships directly from the Soviets or built their own with Soviet assistance. Then the Chinese started building their own ships copied from Soviet designs and finally graduated to constructing ships from Chinese designs.

During this same period, the Chinese army was the dominant branch of the Chinese military. When the relationship between China and the Soviets began to cool, the huge army took defensive positions along the joint border to repel any possible invasion by the northern Communist country.

When the collapse of the Soviet Union occurred, the Chinese government decided to shift additional resources from the army to

75

the navy, and a series of increases in new construction and naval personnel began within the Chinese Navy.

In 2008, the official English-language Chinese state media stopped referring to the People's Liberation Army Navy but instead used the term Chinese Navy and the prefix "CNS" as a Chinese Navy Ship.

Up until that time, the other nations of the world considered the Chinese to own a "brown" and "green" water navy used to patrol the coastal area of China and to be no threat to any world power like the United States with its own massive "blue" water navy. Starting in 1989, the Chinese Navy emerged from its territorial waters and conducted missions to far-off ports of call. Chinese naval vessels visited ports in Hawaii, Thailand, Pakistan, and India.

In 1997, a four-vessel convoy consisting of three warships and one replenishment oiler began the first circumnavigation of the Pacific Ocean. During the period of May 15 to September 23, 2002, the guided missile destroyer *Qingdao* and the replenishment oiler *Taicany* completed the PLA Navy's first circumnavigation of the world. They conducted exercises with the French fleet and the Peruvian navy.

Between 1985 and 2006, PLAN naval vessels visited thirty-six foreign countries and conducted joint naval exercises with eight countries, including the United States.

In 2009, during the sixtieth anniversary celebration of the PLAN, fifty-two vessels conducted maneuvers off *Qingdao*, including several previously unknown nuclear submarines. Afterward, several major newspapers from other world capitals stated that only the United States Navy had the power to confront the Chinese Navy.

In late 2012, the People's Liberation Army Navy took ownership of their first aircraft carrier, the *Liaoning*, able to project power for a thousand miles in any direction.

The Southern Fleet, headquartered in Zhanjiang, Guangdong Province, and selected for the organizational meeting today, was located on the very southern tip of the Chinese mainland. Admiral Fang Li, the commanding officer for the Southern Command, was quietly sitting at the head of the table facing the large wall-mounted projector screen. He was watching his senior operations officer, Admiral Deshi Yang, review the planned deployment of forces for the upcoming expansion into the South China Sea.

Admiral Yang had selected the largest conference room in the building for the meeting. Besides the two admirals, ships' captains and executive officers of lesser rank were present to learn their assigned region within the South China Sea and the rules of engagement each ship would operate under during the extended assignment. These officers, with their destroyers and frigates, would have the responsibility to protect the twelve new drilling platforms and their support ships.

In addition to the naval officers, Huang Zhao, vice chairman of CNOOC, sat at a table in the back row of the room with his senior geologist and several staffers. Their position in the room was a direct indication of their hierarchy within the organizational structure for the mission.

The CNOOC geological department and mining experts had known about the thirty-eight new production fields, but the company had avoided the locations because of the close proximity to Vietnam, Malaysia, and Brunei and their territorial claims. The potential rewards for new and cheaper oil and gas so close to the Chinese mainland represented a dangerous risk from other countries with cross claims of ownership.

They would now be moving into these contested waters with oilrigs and warships. This was an explosive combination, and Huang Zhao feared the worst possible incident could happen.

The junior naval officers did not share his concerns. Before the meeting started and the admirals were in the room, they were acting more like members of a sports team inside their locker room before a big game. Their excitement and energy filled the room. Despite the normal quiet decorum associated with the conduct of naval officers, Huang Zhao felt like the men were preparing for war rather than the protection of his ships and men.

The production fields were scattered throughout the Spratly Islands and Scarborough Reefs, but the fields expected to be the most productive were in Spratly Island, very close to islands occupied by military forces from Vietnam, Malaysia, and the Philippines. The navies of the other countries could react quickly to their incursion.

For over an hour, Huang Zhao listened to Admiral Yang assign the ships to each drill site and state which officer would be in charge of each squadron of warships. The action plan called for a destroyer and frigate, working in tandem, with each drill ship and its support ships. This would provide protection at the drill site and an escort warship for the tankers as they traveled back to the Chinese mainland with their precious cargo. The captain of the destroyer would be in command of the squadron and have overall command of all the ships in the group, civilian and military.

As Admiral Yang droned on, Huang Zhao was quietly stewing over in his mind the command structure. Civilian ships did not operate in the same manner as a warship. Huang Zhao had never been in the military or navy and was hesitant to speak out about the subject, but he knew his senior geologist was thinking the same way as he was. The young man had been writing notes and drawing figures on his writing tablet since the meeting started. Huang Zhao could read some of the notes. At first, they were just a record of the meeting, but as the operations officer started describing the assigned warships and command structures, Huang Zhao could see large written questions like, "Are they serious?" scrawled across the page. The younger man was squirming in his chair and looking at the other members in the CNOOC staff. Huang Zhao knew he had to speak up before the geologist attracted the attention of Admiral Fang Li or his operations officer.

The lesser-rank Chinese officers had concealed their earlier anticipation from before the meeting and not spoken a single word once the admirals had entered the conference room, nor had Admiral Deshi Yang opened the meeting with an invitation to bring up questions. Huang Zhao was not certain if he needed to raise his hand or just speak out. He decided to err on the side of caution and raised his hand to get the attention of the operations officer.

Admiral Deshi Yang noticed the raised hand in the back of the room but continued with his plan for the upcoming event. As a student of naval history and a graduate from China's war college, he had felt from the very first instructions he had received from Admiral Fang Li that they were planning for war rather than the protection of oil-drilling ships. It made no difference to him. He would follow any order from his superior officer.

Deshi Yang had not indicated this was a presentation opened to questions and planned to ignore the intrusion. When Huang Zhao persisted and did not lower his hand, the admiral finally stopped his presentation to address the question from the senior representative from CNOOC. Every officer in the room snapped his head toward Huang Zhao. Who would dare interrupt a briefing from the chief of staff of the Southern Command? Everyone continued to stare, except for Admiral Fang Li, who slowly looked over toward one of the few people in the room not in a naval uniform.

"You have a question, Mr. Zhao?" Deshi Yang asked from the front of the room. The look of annoyance on his face could not be missed by Huang Zhao.

Huang Zhao silently cleared his throat. He did not want to show any disrespect to the officer, but he also did not want to show any fear. His people in the room, outnumbered by a ratio of twenty-five to one, were still his responsibility. Moreover, once the drilling operation commenced, he would have additional employees to worry about besides those in this room. "Thank you, Admiral Yang, but I'm concerned with the overall command structure. I certainly agree with your organizational chart for the People's Navy, but I am concerned with your officers' lack of experience with the operational structure of civilian ships and specifically offshore oil-drilling platforms. There are many differences between these vessels, and to have someone not experienced with the many functions of oil-drilling platforms may cause a problem that will degrade efficiency."

Huang Zhao thought he had described the situation in a manner not to offend the naval officers, so the response was not what he expected.

Admiral Deshi Yang laid down the wooden pointer that he had been using during his presentation in front of him. He looked at Huang Zhao for almost fifteen seconds without speaking. When neither man blinked their eyes as a sign of caving in, he finally asked his own question, "Have you every served in the military or navy, Huang Zhao?"

Huang Zhao realized he had erred in questioning the admiral's plan; it was too late now. He kept his eyes locked on the admiral's face as he gave a one-word response, "No."

Deshi Yang's face did not change as he spoke again. "There is only one commander, and it will be the assigned squadron naval commander." Without another look at Huang Zhao, Admiral Deshi

Yang picked up his wooden pointer from the table and continued with his presentation as if Huang Zhao had never spoken.

Huang Zhao continued to listen to the presentation, but nothing would ease the terrible concerns boiling within his mind. In two weeks, the drill ships having the furthest distance to travel from the sellers would be arriving in Zhanjiang to match up with the other drill ships from China and the other support vessels with the naval task force. Of the twelve new platforms, eight had final destinations in the Spratly Islands, and the other four to the Scarborough Reefs. The tankers would stay in port until drilling operations commenced and their empty hulls needed to bring the crude oil and gas back to shore.

Huang Zhao looked at the ocean chart illuminated on the projector screen. With the drills ships, service vessels, and naval warships, there would be over seventy ships leaving port. Once the thirty-six tankers put to sea, the total count would be over one hundred ships. The South China Sea contained 1.4 million square miles within its boundary, and one-third of the world's shipping passed through its waters. The presence of this flotilla of ships would suddenly make the sea seem a very small body of water.

Chapter 17

At 10:00 a.m., Committee Chairman Ralph Peters brought the heavy gavel down twice on the wooden base next to his right hand to signal the commencement for the confirmation hearing to begin for Governor James Diamond. The schedule called for three days of testimony with the governor to appear on Wednesday afternoon or Thursday morning. The weather outside was chilly but mild for the season with bright sunshine. The room's atmosphere was calm. The news media had their first-string reporters jammed into the room, and all expected an easy confirmation process.

Chairman Peters selected the Rayburn Office Building with its fifty-one committee-meeting rooms because it was the largest of the House office buildings, and his own office was located in the same building. After all, the position of chairman had a few benefits. Those lucky enough to get one of the highly coveted passes filled the room and slowly settled down to listen to the long list of witnesses scheduled to testify before the committee.

The Rayburn Office Building received its Certificate of Occupation in 1965 and contained within its walls almost 2.4 million square feet of space. It provided office space for 169 representatives and was connected by both subway and walking tunnels to the Capitol Building. One little known fact was the fully equipped gymnasium in the lower level designated for use by the representatives. A well-known fact was the final cost of eighty-eight million dollars for the building.

The committee room was large enough for the seventeen members and their support staff as required, a table with three chairs for the witness and his or her support staff, if required, and additional rows of chairs for the press and visitors. The television coverage, provided by C-SPAN, Cable-Satellite Public Affairs Network, would provide the viewing public gavel-to-gavel coverage.

Congressman Peters made his opening statement on the legality behind the committee's authority and the procedures for the confirmation process. He announced the tentative schedule for the witnesses and the rules to govern the question-and-answer process. Any member could ask questions but his or her time was limited to fifteen minutes per witness unless the person requested extra time from the chair. In all, Ralph Peters took his fifteen minutes plus another ten for his opening remarks. The nonagenarian knew this would probably be his last time to be in the bright public spotlight, and he wanted the public to see he was still qualified to handle the responsibilities as a member of the House of Representatives.

The first witness to appear before the committee was called by the chairperson himself, but really, the work had been done by one of his staffers. The witness, first secretary for the confirmation committee, took the witness table and was administered the oath. For over an hour, this person read into the official record information gathered by the committee staffers on the background and personal history of James Watson Diamond. All of the committee members were present for the opening event and stayed for the entire time. Before C-SPAN, some committee members would no doubt leave the room to tend to other business or sneak a smoke in the days before cigarettes were taboo. They would leave one of their staffers to suffer through the dull reports and call them back when another more important witness came before the committee to testify. Today, under the eyes of the television camera lenses, they stayed at the table with their staffers lining the wall behind them.

The next witness called to testify was concerned with the financial background of the nominee. For another thirty minutes, there were no surprises, and with the competition of their testimony, Chairman Peters called for the lunch recess until 1:30 p.m.

Randy Fisher hurried from the room. He needed to make some phone calls and answer a call of nature. The urination process was the first order of business, and he was not the only member of the committee to hurry to the nearest facility.

When they reconvened in the afternoon, the members again took the same chairs. The prearranged seating floor plan called for the members to appear equally arranged around the tables with the Democrats and Republicans sitting in an alternating pattern. Chairman Peters sat in the center of the U-shape of tables and chairs.

Now was the time for various committee members to call their own witnesses. All the people called to testify were on the schedule, so no surprises were expected.

These witnesses were mostly character witnesses arranged by Leslie Overman and the White House and were called by the Republican members of the committee at Leslie's request. Their questions from the committee members appeared perfectly scripted for the most part. The Democrats had their opportunity to question the witnesses, but again, there were no surprises. When the clock on the wall rolled around to 3:30 p.m., Chairman Ralph Peters looked at his witness list and made the biggest announcement for the entire day. "Since we have completed all the testimony of the witnesses except for two, I will call for Governor Diamond to present himself in front of this committee tomorrow at 1:30 p.m. This committee is adjourned for the day."

Chapter 18

Washington DC
Wednesday, February 4, 2015
10:00 a.m. (EST)

The committee for the confirmation resumed the next day on schedule. The news media reporters, filling the available chairs once again, eagerly waited for the main event when the governor would make his first appearance.

The morning session, consumed by the last of Leslie's Overman's list of star witnesses, went as planned, and Randy Fisher had to admit the White House deputy chief of staff knew how to run a smooth show. He had seen her several times talking with her staff members and on her Blackberry. She presented a confident and professional outward appearance. He decided maybe all the people President Harold Miller had working for him were not as bad as the president himself.

After lunch, it was time for the highlight of the day. Every seat filled again in the committee room, and Chairman Peters warned the visitors that he demanded absolute quiet throughout the proceedings. He reminded them they were here as guests of the committee and needed to act accordingly. Finally, using a long bent forefinger, he indicated for the committee secretary to call Governor James Diamond before the committee.

Jimmy Diamond walked through the rear double doors of the room with a straight back and a smooth, confident stride. Every eye turned and followed his progress to the witness table. The dark-blue pinstripe suit offset his snow-white hair. He took the center chair at the table but reached to the chairs on both sides of his own and pulled them forward. He was flying solo, with no assistants or legal representation. He carried no notes or material for reference. He was going to do this from the hip.

Ralph Peters ask the governor to take the oath. Standing at his chair, right hand raised, Jimmy Diamond gave the appropriate reply to the committee clerk. Once the preliminary procedures were completed, Peters ask the governor if he had any opening remarks.

"Thank you, Mr. Chairman," Jimmy begun. "I will reserve my time at the end of my testimony for my closing remarks."

"That is your privilege, Governor. Now I have several representatives who have express their desire to ask a few questions. Let me again remind the committee members that you are limited to a fifteen-minute question-and-answer session unless the chair approves an extension."

The softball questions from House Republicans allowed the governor to get comfortable before the committee and the cameras broadcasting his testimony to the country. Randy Fisher again was just a spectator. He had made up his mind on the governor, and his opinion was already on the record. He settled back into his chair for the duration of the afternoon.

It appeared President Miller was going to have an easy path for his nominee. The questions were routine, and Jimmy Diamond answered them with ease. His lack of notes or reference material spoke volumes for his mental capacity. In general, it appeared the members of the committee were looking favorably toward the governor.

As the last House member finished with his questioning, Chairman Ralph Peters looked at his schedule and the wall clock. One last person, Senator Lawrence from Wyoming, waited at the end of the table with a list of questions for the governor, and it was only 2:30 p.m. With luck, they could complete the questioning to allow Diamond to make his closing remarks and recess at 3:00. Perhaps in executive session behind closed doors, they could take a vote to recommend confirmation, and the Congress could vote tomorrow. That would please the president, and it would look like Ralph Peters knew how to run a committee hearing in a very efficient manner.

At 2:30, Chairman Peters looked over to Jasper Lawrence and

informed the committee members the senator from Wyoming would have the floor.

Lawrence was waiting and ready for his opportunity. The forty-seven-year-old senator was sitting straight up in his chair to make his five-ten height appear a little taller. His reddish-blond hair, parted on the left with the sides combed back over his ears, projected a dignified older look. A notebook and small stack of papers lay in front of his place at the table. He appeared organized and started to speak in a calm and clear voice.

"Thank you, Mr. Chairman, and I want to thank you, Governor Diamond, for being here today in front of the committee."

Jimmy Diamond gave a little nod of his head and a small smile toward the senator.

"Governor, I would like to go back to your time as the attorney general in Florida. I believe we heard previously and entered into the record that you were the attorney general from 1988 to 1996. Is that correct?"

"That is correct."

"Good . . . thank you for the answer. Now, do you remember a case from 1995, *Florida v. Tanner*, in which you represented the state in your capacity as attorney general?"

There was only a slight hesitation from Diamond before he answered the question. "I do."

"Good . . . thank you for that answer." The room had gone deadly quiet as several reporters were sensing Jasper Lawrence's softball questions were building up to something more important.

"Now, Governor, my research indicates this was a court case about a sixteen-year-old pregnant young lady who wanted to get an abortion, but you were attempting to prevent the abortion. Governor, we all know your record as a Republican and your firm stance on right-to-life. The papers following the story suggested you were using this court case as a stepping-stone to challenge *Row v. Wade*. Were you trying to set a precedent against the 1994 hallmark case that you would later use to try to get the Supreme Court to overturn *Roe v. Wade*?"

Suddenly, the confirmation hearing of James Diamond took on a different tone. The committee members were sitting up a little straighter in their formerly comfortable chairs. The press awakened from where the dull testimony had lulled them and started warming up their smartphones, and Chairman Peters knew there would be no vote today to recommend confirmation of the appointee.

As soon as the question was out of Jasper Lawrence's mouth, two members of his staff started handing out to each committee member a file with copies of the written press coverage of the 1995 court case along with copies of official court documents.

Diamond took the question in stride. He certainly was not prepared to discuss the case, but he would not let the little senator rattle him. "There was no attempt on my part to prepare for any future case again *Row v. Wade*, Senator Lawrence."

The press was now texting messages out to their producers. Abortion rights were now before the committee members, and the seemingly routine confirmation process and questioning they had been hearing had taken a different turn.

Randy Fisher opened the file folder handed to him by a member of Senator Lawrence's staff. He quickly scanned the few pages it contained. There was a photocopy of the form for the filing of the case with the court, additional photocopies of press articles that had appeared in the local papers, and finally a copy of the court ruling. Randy had never gone to law school, but it seemed the file was a little thin. However, he knew it did not take much for the press to hang someone. He closed the folder, picked up his own Blackberry, and sent a quick text message to Tim Smith, his own chief of staff. He kept the text brief. "Are you watching this? Stop everything. Dig into all available info on the court case and this Tanner girl." Randy knew Tim kept three television sets in his office tuned to CNN, Fox news, and C-SPAN.

Leslie Overman's fingers were flying over the keyboard of her own Blackberry as she sent her own message to her staffers back at the White House. "Where did this come from? Find out everything."

Lawrence barely let the governor finish his answer when he fired another question back. "Well, I'm not sure I understand, Governor. The filing papers indicate the young woman wanted the abortion. It appears the parents were in favor of the abortion and the law allowed for the abortion. So why did you try to prevent the abortion with your request for an injunction?"

Diamond continued to sit with his back straight and his arms resting comfortably on the edge of the table. He kept this hands lightly clasped together with his finger intertwined. His outward appearance remained calm, and he appeared to be in full control. "The girl's pregnancy was determined by her doctors to be in its twenty-second week. *Roe v. Wade* allows that if the fetus is viable, then the courts can rule against an abortion unless there is a danger to the mother. In this case, there was no danger to the mother."

Jasper picked up a thin stack of papers stapled together at one corner and held it up for the committee members to see and, more important, for the press to view and C-SPAN to broadcast. He was secretly enjoying his time in the bright lights. "Governor, I have here the ruling on viability as set forth by the US Supreme court. The court ruled a fetus to be viable as being potentially able to live outside the mother's womb, maybe with artificial aid. Viability, as determined by the court, is at twenty-eight weeks and as early as twenty-four weeks. This girl wanted an abortion, and you were trying to prevent it when she was clearly within her rights as stated by our Supreme Court. I do not understand your actions unless you were trying to set up a future court case to try to reverse *Roe v. Wade*. Can you help us understand your decision?"

The room's noise level had escalated, and Ralph Peters took the gavel and pounded the base to restore order. "All right, people . . . let's settle down." He gave the heavy wooden base a few more raps and then laid the gavel down on the table. When he was satisfied with the noise level, he told the witness he could continue with his answer.

Diamond used the moment to show respect to the chairman. "Thank you, Mr. Chairman. I want to answer Senator Lawrence's question to his complete satisfaction."

He directed his answer back to the left of the chairman where Lawrence was sitting. "The Tanner girl was in her twenty-second week of pregnancy, and I wanted to see the child brought to full term. As you stated, Congressman, she was only two weeks away, by the law, from having the abortion prevented. I told the girl as the AG for Florida I would see the child was put up for adoption and the baby would go to a good home. I simply needed the injunction to allow the baby to reach twenty-four weeks. At that time, if she decided to induce labor, the baby would have a 50 to 70 percent chance to survive. This was in no way an attempt to reverse *Roe v. Wade*."

Lawrence was ready for his next attack question when Chairman Ralph Peters spoiled his opportunity. The gavel came down hard once again. "Senator, your fifteen minutes are up, and we have reached the end of today's session. Testimony will continue tomorrow at 10:00 a.m., and this committee hearing is recessed for the day."

Jasper Lawrence's complaint against the chairman's interruption fell against deaf ears over the commotion within the committee room. Jimmy Diamond was up from his seat and heading for the room's exit with Leslie Overman at his side, attempting to keep the members of the press away from the nominee. This did not stop them from hurtling questions at Diamond as he worked his way out of the hearing room.

Some of the reporters raced to the table where Jasper Lawrence was sitting and in no hurry to leave the room. He continued to discuss his concerns about the fitness of the nominee saying Diamond would use his position as the vice president to work for the overturn of *Roe v. Wade*. He promised more information in the next day's testimony. The members of the press were recording everything the senator said.

Randy Fisher left the committee room by a back entrance to avoid the press. He wanted to get back to his office to see what his staff had discovered about the Tanner case.

Chapter 19

Washington DC
Wednesday, February 4, 2015
4:30 p.m. (EST)

Jimmy Diamond and Leslie Overman walked into the Oval Office to meet with President Miller and Warren Fletcher. They were in their SUV caravan, and on their way back to the White House under Secret Service escort when Leslie's Blackberry received the call from Fletcher instructing her to bring the nominee back to the executive mansion.

She kept a brave face on as she approached the Resolute Desk where Harold Miller was sitting. His face showed his displeasure with the new and unexpected development.

"All right, Leslie, let's have it. This nomination was to be a slam dunk. How could you not know about this? Are you competent or not to handle this nomination?"

Leslie stood her ground and faced the president squarely. "I apologize for this mistake on my part, Mr. President. We overlooked the court case. It just never came up in our background research."

"Well, you certainly let us look like fools in front of the committee and anyone who was watching C-SPAN, which was half the damn country."

Jimmy Diamond felt compelled to step in to help Leslie. "Sir, I remembered the case, but it was a long time ago and it wasn't a case with a jury. The judge heard our arguments *in camera*. It was just an attempt to get the injunction. It only got the attention of the local press because the judge was out of town and we had to use extraordinary measures to get him back for the hearing. The press noticed that, and they were there to cover the event. The case was over and done with before any of the national press even found out about it."

Warren Fletcher had been looking at his deputy, but he now directed his question to the governor. "Jimmy, were you trying to set up a case to overturn *Roe v. Wade*? Did you say anything that was not the truth in front of the committee?"

Diamond answered immediately. "No. Everything I said was the truth. Yes, I wanted to prevent the termination, and I was working with a state adoption agency, but the fetus was terminated."

Warren wanted to deflect the conversation away from what happened and to tomorrow's testimony. "Mr. President, I think we can ride this out. I will work with Leslie and the governor, and we can prepare a statement to take the sting out of today's testimony. After all, right-to-life is in the Republican Party's political platform."

The president looked first at Fletcher and then at the two people standing before his desk. "All right. Get it worked out tonight. I want to see Jimmy walk in that committee room tomorrow and put that bastard Lawrence in his place."

Chapter 20

Washington DC
Wednesday, February 4, 2015
6:00 p.m. (EST)

By the time Randy Fisher made it to his suite of offices in the Senate Russell Building, Tim Smith was going at a full gallop into the background of the Tanner case. Randy knew if anybody could get to the reason behind Jasper Lawrence's attack on James Diamond, it would be his own chief of staff.

The tall, slender African American from Cleveland, Ohio, was still looking as fresh in his Savoy Row suit as when he first arrived to work early this morning. He had already pulled the "Dynamic Duo" off their current work assignment to help in the investigation.

Randy found Brad and Tim working in the conference room next to his own office with their laptops open and surfing the Internet for information. When he asked about Renee, they informed him the young woman was in her office and would join them as soon as she finished following a lead she had discovered.

Brad Guilliams and Renee Stockli were Randy's legislative affairs associates. When he first came to Washington, he wanted someone to investigate every piece of legislation he would have to consider before it reached the Senate floor. Tim Smith selected the two young staffers because they were always at the opposite ends of the political spectrum.

Brad Guilliams, tall and slender with a brown hair cut very short, was the ultraconservative member of the office. He had been considering leaving when the change from Robert Moore to Randy

Fisher had occurred. He had felt that he did not fit in with the other members of the Democratic senator's staff. Tim asked him to stay on until the new senator had arrived and settled in.

Renee Stockli, nearly a foot shorter with shoulder-length naturally blond hair and bred to be a party line New York Democrat, was always at odds with Brad and his conservative opinions. Tim and Randy felt if these two could come to some sort of agreement on an issue, then Randy could use the same thinking with the Democrats and Republicans in the Senate. To everybody's delight, the plan worked and the "Dynamic Duo" made an excellent working team. They still did not agree on many issues, but as a team, they made their relationship work and were a valuable asset to Randy's office. Frequently, he purchased tickets to a sporting event, concert, or gift certificates to the hottest new restaurant in Washington and gave them to the two associates as a reward for their hard work. For the last several months, he had thought perhaps the two young and single adults had been getting a little closer outside the office.

Now, after several hours since Randy's text message to Tim Smith, the team was putting together a better picture of the Tanner case and the legal details.

Tim moved his laptop off to the side and pulled his yellow lined notepad over to review the notes he had written from his research. Randy Fisher walked in and took a seat at the end of the table away from Tim. Renee Stockli entered the room after the senator and took a seat across the table from Brad.

Without waiting for Randy to speak, Tim started to call out what he knew so far. "This case was so small it didn't come up on the Internet. I finally went into the State of Florida attorney general's website, accessed their archives for the cases for 1995, and found the Tanner case. The court records indicate they received the papers for the injunction on May 4 of the same year. The girl's name was Roberta Tanner, as listed on the court documents. She lived in Ocala, Florida. She was sixteen years old, and her parents were Robert and Mary Tanner. Robert Tanner owned a swimming pool company at the time with six sales offices around the state. That was when the housing market was still booming, and he was making a lot of money. I did not check on the status of his company today. It might not still be in business."

Brad now spoke up. "I found the case listed in the *Ocala Morning News* for May 5, 6, and 7. After those dates, I could not find any mention of the case again. May 5 just lists the case as filed with the rest of the court news for that day. On May 6, there was real news of the case and lots of coverage since the attorney general for Florida was personally handling it. There was also the part about the state judge being called back from a fishing vacation, which got some attention, but that is all for the sixth. On the seventh, the paper carried the story about the hearing and that the judge ruled in favor of the girl and her parents." Brad dropped his notepad down on the desk and looked up at the assembled group. "That's it for the newspapers and Internet."

Renee Stockli let a little snort escape from her large roman nose above thick lips as she picked up the trail from there. She flipped her blond hair off to the side behind her right ear as she looked at Tim and Brad. "Men . . . you guys need to get better sources than the Internet and newspapers. I found her listed in the 1996 Ocala High School graduation class and called down to the school to see who might remember her. I was able to talk with the guidance counselor before she left for the day. I talked with a Nancy Travis, who was and still is the school guidance counselor and remembered the time of the hearing and when the Tanner girl was going through all the problems. In fact, it was Travis the Tanner girl first confided to about her pregnancy.

"It took some woman-to-woman talk, but I found out Roberta Tanner left home immediately after her graduation when she was only seventeen and married Jeffery Brown, the father of the terminated fetus. She left Ocala and moved to Starke, Florida, near Camp Blanding where Brown was a private in the army. Nancy told me the boy, who was just eighteen, avoided prosecution for having sex with a minor by enlisting in the army and agreeing to stay away from Roberta Tanner."

Brad interrupted Renee's lecture to the three men. He let out a little laugh of his own. "Right. Your woman-to-woman talk? I bet the counselor must have twenty or thirty years on you."

Renee stuck out her tongue at Brad. "Laugh all you want, big boy, but I got the girl's telephone number from Nancy Travis."

"What?" Tim said. "Is the number still good?"

"I don't know yet. I just hung up with Nancy before I came here. She said it was good about three years ago, but she hasn't talked with Roberta since then."

Renee was quiet for a few moments. Sensing she was not sure how to proceed with the last of her information, Randy spoke up first. "OK . . . what's the problem? I can tell you're concerned about something."

Renee looked at the men sitting around the table starting with Randy on her right and then moved to Brad across the table from her. She moved her head left toward Tim Smith and back to her notepad. "None of this is in any of the papers or on the Internet. Roberta Tanner is white. The father of her baby was black."

Chapter 21

Tim Smith muttered a barely audible sound from his throat. "Well . . . that certainly means Diamond is not a bigot. If he were, he would not have tried to stop the abortion. Maybe it is as Senator Lawrence said in the hearings. Diamond was using this to set up a challenge to *Roe v. Wade*."

Randy spoke up now. "If there's a bigot in this mess, it just might be my fellow senator from Wyoming. Some of the strongest militia groups are in that part of the country, and I've heard my *friend* speak out for them at times."

"You think he's after the governor because Diamond tried to stop a mixed-race baby from being aborted?"

Randy moved his hands up from the armrest of the chair. "It just might be the answer. We never know what thing will set someone off. Jasper seemed to take delight in the attention he was getting after the recess. Diamond made a beeline out of there and tried to avoid the press. Jasper was still talking with them and going strong when I walked out of the hearing room."

While they were talking with the senator, Tim was searching his websites. He made a little sound of triumph and flipped the laptop around for the other people to see. "Look here. This is from his own senate website where he files his annual financial disclosure reports. Senator Jasper Lawrence owns a second home in Ocala, Florida."

Renee Stockli moved forward and laid her finger on the laptop screen. "What do you want to bet the good senator from Wyoming has a big swimming pool in his backyard built by Robert Tanner? He's probably known all along about this case, and now he's using it to sandbag the governor's nomination."

Randy was shaking his head. "He's known all about this case and has been waiting for twenty or twenty-one years to get revenge against the governor? I think that's a bit of a stretch even for Jasper."

Tim thought he had the answer. "I think Lawrence knew about the case from his buddy Tanner, but that's not why he's brought this up now." He looked at Randy. "You said he was sucking up to the press after the recess. I think the senator is using this to portray the governor as an opponent to *Roe v. Wade* and use all the attention as a springboard for his reelection next year in Wyoming where *Roe v. Wade* makes headlines every day. Plus he shows the Democrats in his state he's willing to go against the president."

Brad Guilliams added his thinking to the discussion. "The senator is playing up to the Republicans and the right-to-life people but also making marks with the Democrats in his state by embarrassing the president and his selection for VP."

Randy made the next decision. "We need to see if the phone number for the Tanner girl is still good."

Chapter 22

Roberta Brown was just entering her home in Stark, Florida, when the phone in the kitchen started to ring. She was hoping it was Jeffrey calling. He was due back from a two-week training mission tonight and had promised to call when he was back on the base.

Roberta Brown was thirty-six years old and had put on fifteen additional pounds since the court case that ended her relationship with her father. At that time, she possessed a slender body built on a frame less than five feet tall. She had been well into her second trimester before she started to develop any type of a "baby-bump" and hid the pregnancy from her parents for as long as she could.

She had witnessed her father's anger many times before. When he learned of the pregnancy and the race of the baby's father, his rage reached a new level. Only her mother placing her own body between father and daughter prevented Robert Tanner from striking his child.

He immediately started preparations for an abortion, but he made one mistake. He called on an old friend with a legal background to obtain advice. Jimmy Diamond was delighted when he heard his close friend's daughter was going to have a baby. Of course, he had wished the girl had waited until she was older, but the Tanners were well off financially and the family could provide any support the young couple would need.

To his surprise, Robert Tanner wanted to know the legality for having the pregnancy aborted. Jimmy Diamond tried to reason with his friend but to no avail. When it became apparent the decision was final, he refused to assist the father.

Diamond had been a right-to-life proponent his entire life and decided to look into the situation on his own. Jimmy reached out to the high school Roberta attended as a student and persuaded a guidance counselor to talk with him. He discovered the truth about Roberta wanting to keep the baby. He tried to act in the young girl's defense, but the court ruled against his injunction, and Robert Tanner forced the abortion onto his daughter.

Jeffery Brown received only one option. He could enlist in the army and agree to never see Roberta again or face criminal charges. Roberta received strict instructions to break off all communication with her boyfriend. However, the two lovers refused to accept her father's instructions. Roberta used the cell phones of friends and called Jeffrey almost every day. The abortion put her into a depression, and only the secret conversations with Jeffrey stopped her from going insane.

She never let her mother or father know she was still in contact with Jeffrey. Immediately after her graduation, she packed several suitcases with her belongings and left her home for the last time. She sold the car given to her by her father after the abortion. It had been his peace offering to his daughter, but now the money would go to start a new life.

Jeffrey arranged for a three-day leave from the army base and picked her up in Ocala, and they left the city together. She never returned to Ocala or had any contact with her parents again.

They had found a small apartment to rent off base and started a family soon after they were married. Jeffrey Jr. was born almost ten months after she left Ocala and was the pride of her life. He was an only child, and Roberta and Jeffrey Sr. were determined to raise him to accept their principles. To them, race was not even a consideration when there was lots of love in the home.

After she set the two grocery bags down on the kitchen table, Roberta Brown grabbed the handset from the wall-mounted telephone. However, it was not Jeffrey on the phone. The man's voice identified himself as a United States senator from South Carolina. He wanted to know if she had heard the news today about the confirmation process for the nominee for vice president. He also asked if she remembered a man named Jimmy Diamond.

Chapter 23

Washington DC
Thursday, February 5, 2015
1:00 p.m. (EST)

The notice from Representative Ralph Peter's office that the third day of the confirmation hearings would not start until 1:00 p.m. took nearly everyone by surprise. Jasper Lawrence was ready to deliver his final remarks to the committee and once again live in the bright spotlight of the news networks' cameras. Already, the local papers back in Wyoming were asking for interviews and he had appeared on the early editions of both CNN and Fox News. Other national news services were calling his press secretary with requests for more interviews. His reelection campaign was going to start with a big bang.

Ralph Peters was glad for the delay. It gave him time to get an early morning walk around the Capitol Building and a workout in the basement gymnasium.

Jimmy Diamond spent the morning hours in his hotel room with his wife, who had flown up from their Fort Myers home to attend the third day of testimony. Eleanor Diamond paced the hotel room as she suggested they should just return to Florida. The attack against her husband was unjust. Jimmy had provided many years of dedicated service to the citizens of Florida. He wrapped his long arms around her shoulders, drew her close, and provided needed comfort. He would face the committee today, and if the decision went against him, they would be on the first flight back to Fort Myers.

Leslie Overman had spent all of the evening and most of the night preparing a defense proving that Diamond had not broken any laws. She called Jimmy late in the evening to update him on her progress and was surprised when Jimmy told her not to bother with any more research. He would answer the Wyoming senator's question and let the cards land where they may.

At 1:00 p.m., Ralph Peters called the committee to order and again admonished the visitors to keep silent during the testimony. He reminded the governor, sitting again at the witness table, that he was still under oath.

Governor Diamond was back dressed today in a black suit. He looked rested from yesterday's grilling and ready to face more questions. He looked toward Ralph Peters and smiled, nodding his head in understanding.

There were no empty chairs today in the committee room except for one beside Eleanor. Reporters who had thought the proceedings might be too dull before had changed their minds and filled every available spot. Some lined the walls and the committee room clerk had to enforce the legal limit for the number of people in the room allowed by the local fire marshal.

Jasper Lawrence was ready to renew his questioning of the witness. He looked toward the chairman to ask permission to begin. This was a new day, and he had another fifteen minutes. The allotted time would be enough to move forward with his argument that Jimmy Diamond was not fit to be the vice president.

Before he was able to speak, Chairman Peters made a statement. "The reason for the delay in today's committee meeting was due to Senator Fisher from South Carolina. He has requested to bring a new witness to testify. Senator Fisher, you have the floor and the first fifteen minutes." Jasper immediately wondered whom Fisher had brought to testify. He did not have to wait for long.

Randy adjusted the microphone to be closer to his mouth. "Thank you, Mr. Chairman. I appreciate the chair's indulgence in granting the delay. The time allowed me to bring our next witness to Washington from her home in Florida. At this time, I would like to call Roberta Brown to the witness table."

The committee clerk walked up to Jimmy Diamond and asked if the governor would take a seat next to his wife in the visitor section. Diamond had a look of confusion on his face as he stood up but moved to the empty seat by his wife. It was a surprise to him as much as to every other person in the gallery. He had not requested a seat held in reserve and demand for seating had exceeded availability.

He looked over to Leslie Overman, who was next to Eleanor. From Leslie's own facial expression, it was clear that Overman had no clue as to the identity of the new witness. She was looking between him and Randy Fisher and wondering what new problem the South Carolina Democrat was going to give her. She had been counting on his vote for confirmation. Now it might be in doubt.

The door opened in the back of the committee room, and every head turned to see who was entering the room. For the committee members themselves, they simply looked to the back of the room they were already facing.

Roberta Brown entered the room. She was dressed in a dark-blue suit coat with a red blouse. Next to her walked a US Army private dressed in a class "A" uniform. He was taller than the woman, and his skin tone indicated a possible ethnic mix between African American and Caucasian. As they reached the witness table, the private pulled out the chair for Brown, and then he took a second chair for himself.

The clerk asked her to stand and give her name.

Rising from her chair and in a clear voice everybody could hear, she spoke for the first time. "Roberta Tanner Brown."

The clerk administered the oath. "Do you solemnly swear or affirm that the testimony you shall give to the committee in the matter now pending before the committee shall be the truth, the whole truth, and nothing but the truth? So help you God."

Roberta needed to swallow to bring needed moisture to her throat before she could answer. "I do."

Randy Fisher looked toward Roberta Brown. The thirty-six-year-old woman was still pretty, but there were a few lines at the corners of her eyes. She appeared to be nervous and was holding the closest hand of the young service member next to her under the table and out of sight of the television cameras.

Randy looked over at Jasper Lawrence. The Wyoming senator was looking pale and seemed to be nervously working the corner of his papers, which, no doubt, contained the questions he was prepared to ask the star witness.

Randy turned his attention back to the witness. "Thank you,

Mrs. Brown, for taking the time to come all the way from Florida today. Your testimony will help clear up some confusing information brought before the committee. Mrs. Brown, are you the person referred to in the lawsuit of *Florida v. Tanner?*"

"Yes. My maiden name was Roberta Tanner."

"Thank you. Do you know Governor Jimmy Diamond?"

"Yes, sir, I have met the governor, but he was the Florida attorney general at the time."

Senator Fisher's surprise witness brought a higher level of whispered conversation from the press and visitors. Their interest level was at a peak as they waited for the testimony to continue. Many were assuming he was going to drop a smoking gun on the nominee. Leslie Overman knew her job at the White House would end today if Senator Fisher brought forth more damaging information against her candidate.

"Was Mr. Diamond the man who tried to get an injunction to stop the abortion you wanted for your unborn baby?"

Robert Brown had a few tears in her eyes as those terrible days replayed in her mind. "Yes, he tried to obtain the injunction but not against my wishes. He was working for me to prevent the termination of my baby. My father forced me to consent toan abortion. He is the Tanner listed in the name of the court case."

Suddenly, the room was alive with conversation. The testimony had taken a completely different path from what the press and visitors had expected. Leslie Overman was sitting with her mouth open. Jimmy Diamond was sitting with his hands in his lap and looking down at the floor. His wife had leaned over to place both hands on his right bicep. Jasper Lawrence knew what was coming in further testimony and wanted to leave the room, but he was unable to move.

Ralph Peters banged the gavel down several times to restore order in the room. When silence returned, he spoke again. "Continue, Senator Fisher."

"Mrs. Brown, did Jimmy Diamond tell you he was going to use your case as a stepping stone to build a case against *Roe v. Wade?*"

"No, sir. He said we would have a weak case. I was still a minor, and the law favored my father's position."

"According to the court papers, Jeffrey Brown was the father of your unborn child. Can we assume by your name that you married Jeffrey Brown?"

"Yes, sir. We were married just as soon as I graduated from high school and turned eighteen."

Randy Fisher looked directly into the face of Roberta Tanner. "Can you tell us why your father was so adamant that you abort the baby conceived by you and Jeffrey Brown?"

Roberta Tanner sat quietly for several moments. The young army private brought his left arm behind her back and across her shoulders. He placed his right hand lightly on her right arm just below the elbow. She turned her hand over to allow them to intertwine their fingers. "My father objected to the baby because I was a white women and Jeffrey was black."

The television sound equipment could almost pick up the sudden inhalation of air by almost every person in the committee room. Again, the room broke out into small pockets of conversation.

Ralph Peters had to bang his gavel a half-dozen times to restore order within the hearing room. Finally, he was satisfied with the level of silence in the room and looked toward Senator Fisher. "Continue, Senator."

"Where is your husband now? Are the two of you still together?"

"Jeffrey was forced to join the army to avoid prosecution for having sex with a minor person. He was eighteen at the time, and he served for nineteen years in the United States Army, rising to the rank of master sergeant. His vehicle struck a roadside bomb in 2013 while he served in Afghanistan. He is buried in Arlington National Cemetery."

There was more talking in the visitor's gallery, and again, Peters banged his gavel and admonished them to be silent.

Randy waited for the room to be quiet. He only had one more question to ask but needed to provide some additional information about Master Sergeant Jeffrey Brown. "Mrs. Brown, please except my condolences for your loss. Mr. Chairman, for the record, Sergeant Jeffrey Brown served nineteen years in the United States Army. He received the Silver Star and two purple hearts. He is a true hero to this country."

Randy now looked again at Roberta Brown. "Mrs. Brown, one last question please. Do you have any idea why Senator Jasper Lawrence from Wyoming would try to use your case against Jimmy Diamond?"

Roberta looked at the Wyoming senator. She had never seen him until this day. "No, sir. When he called me to ask questions about the case, I told him the governor had been trying to help me save my child. He asked if I would testify in front of this committee. I told him no. I knew he was a friend of my father because my father had built a big swimming pool for Senator Lawrence at his home in Ocala."

Chapter 24

Arlington, Virginia
Thursday, February 5, 2015
7:00 p.m. (EST)

Randy Fisher walked in the back door of his apartment in Arlington, Virginia. He could hear the television playing in the living room. He found Annie watching the news broadcast on CNN and leaned down to kiss her.

She gave him a big smile. "You could have given me a little advance notice that you were going to make a US Senator looked like the biggest fool on Capitol Hill. I would have liked to watch my man put the little prick in his place."

Randy flopped down beside his bride. They had been married now for over a year, but she was still his bride. "My, my, how your language gets when you see a little man like the honorable senator from Wyoming try to hurt a decent person like Jimmy Diamond."

Annie was looking at the television but talking to her husband. "How did he ever get elected to office?"

Randy shook his head. "I don't know, but it'll be interesting to see if he gets reelected."

The news coverage was replaying the final minutes of the confirmation committee hearings. The committee chairman was going to order a recess and then go into executive session to try to get a vote by the committee, but several members called for an immediate vote. A show of hands ruled in favor of the motion. Every committee member raised his or her hand in favor except Senator Lawrence, who abstained.

Chairman Peters then called for a vote by the committee members to recommend or deny that both the House and Senate confirm James Diamond for vice president. All members of the committee raised their hands once again for recommendation except Jasper Lawrence, who remained motionless in his chair.

Larry Frye and Tom Evans had both been following the testimony during the hearings and the quick vote by the committee. Their own chiefs of staff quickly arranged a telephone call between the two congressional leaders, and later, they each issued a press release that the vote to confirm James Diamond by the full Congress would be the next day. The news reporters scrambled for interviews. Everyone willing to go on camera indicated confidence in Diamond's confirmation as vice president by both chambers.

Randy Fisher tried to avoid the press as he made his way back to the Russell Senate Office Building after the committee adjourned, but he was not so lucky. The press gathered around the senator and bombarded him with more questions about his investigation. He just kept replying with "no comment" until one reporter asked why he would take on a member of the Senate who was also of the same political party.

He waited until the other reporters calmed down enough for him to speak above their noise as they jockeyed for a better position. "This was not about politics or that Jimmy Diamond was a Republican. This was a good and faithful servant of the people of Florida unjustly smeared. He simply did not want to reveal the name of the person he was trying to protect. I also feel my fellow senator from Wyoming was a little weak in his preparation."

Randy paused for a moment and then continued, "We need more people in Washington like Jimmy Diamond. I was just trying to correct the record and allow the committee to make the right decision."

Back in his office, Randy handled a few calls screened by his staff. Calls came from Tom Evans and Larry Frye, thanking him for making sure the committee did not make the mistake of railroading Diamond. Several other senators called to offer their thanks as well.

Tim Smith had just returned to the office. He had arranged for Roberta Brown and her son Jeffrey Jr. to visit the grave site of their husband and father at Arlington National Cemetery and then transportation to Reagan National Airport for their flight home. He joined Randy in his office and listened in to the one-sided telephone call from the next vice president.

Diamond spoke in a quiet voice into Randy's ear. He thanked Randy for the work on his behalf and promised to help the young senator someday if he could. "I hadn't seen the Tanner girl since her father led her away from the courthouse. He and I have never spoken since. I'm glad she seems to have a good life even though she's lost her husband."

Randy spoke just as quietly back in reply to the next. "I'm sure her husband lives on in her memory and the life of her son. She has made peace within herself and with God over the loss."

Just before leaving his office, Randy saw a new email pop up on his computer. It was from Leslie Overman thanking him for his efforts. "There are not too many times the Republicans in this White House are thanking a Democrat. Maybe I can help you someday." Randy noticed the email did not come from a White House computer but from a private Yahoo address.

Chapter 25

The vote on Friday to confirm James Diamond as the forty-ninth vice president of the United States went as expected. The House passed the vote by 325 to 20. The Senate followed with almost a matching percentage with a vote of 94 to 5 with one abstaining. Jasper Lawrence was notability absent from the Senate chamber.

With both houses of Congress casting their votes before noon, it was expected Jimmy Diamond would be sworn in that same day. However, White House Press Secretary Alison Warden announced the vice president designate would take the oath of office on Monday with the information as to time and location to follow on Saturday.

In the late afternoon on Friday, Senator Tom Evans received a call from Leslie Overman at the White House. Jimmy Diamond had requested to take the oath of office in the Senate chamber on Monday morning. Would that work with the majority leader?

Tom was quick to reply with an affirmative answer, and Leslie thanked him and added she would be coordinating the event from the White House side. Tom said someone from the office of sergeant of arms for the Capitol Building would contact her very quickly. He would notify the speaker of the house as a courtesy.

The press received their notification on Saturday at the 9:00 a.m. press conference from Alison Warden. The swearing-in ceremony would take place at 10:00 a.m. Monday in the Senate chamber. The chief justice of the Supreme Court, Arnold Allen Lansdale, would administer the oath of office.

The sun shone brightly on Monday morning, and Washington looked beautiful for the event. The weather was still cold, but there had been no snowfall for several weeks and nothing was going to delay the ceremony. The Senate chamber and visitor gallery filled with the press and high-ranking members from the House of Representatives as the time neared 10:00. All the senators, including Jasper Lawrence, were at their respective benches for the swearing-in ceremony. The presence of a large contingent of Secret Service agents indicated the president was in the building.

At 10:00, the president pro tem of the Senate called the chamber to order and announced that several special guests of the Senate were welcome to enter. From the back doors to the side of the podium, President Harold Miller and James Diamond walked in together. The members of the Senate rose from their benches and offered a loud round of applause for the chief executive and the next vice president.

The two men stepped up on the podium as the president pro tem stepped down to make room for the two men and other people needed for the swearing-in process. Eleanor Diamond followed behind along with the chief justice. Arnold Lansdale was in his eighties and walked with his signature wooden cane without any other assistance. He maneuvered up the several rows of carpeted steps with Eleanor Diamond beside him. The three men and one woman arranged themselves as Jimmy Diamond prepared to become the next vice president of the United States.

With the aid of the microphone, the chief justice asked Governor Jimmy Diamond if he was ready to take the oath of office. Jimmy smiled and replied he was ready. Diamond placed his left hand on the family Bible held by his wife, raised his right hand, and prepared to repeat the oath of office.

Less than one minute later, James Watson Diamond was the new vice president of the United States and received a round of handshakes from the president of the United States and the chief justice and a kiss from his wife.

The entire Senate now added their applause to the festivities as they welcomed their new leader. The president pro tem of the Senate handled the gavel to Vice President Diamond. Jimmy turned to the presiding office's desk and announced the entire Senate would recess until 1:00 p.m. to allow an extra-long lunch and celebration as his guests. He brought the gavel down on the wooden base to confirm the statement.

Many members of the Senate worked their way toward the front of the chamber and offered their congratulations to the new vice president. The vice president and his wife slowly worked their way out of the Senate chamber, stopping many times along the aisle as Jimmy received more well wishes.

They finally reached a large meeting room off the Senate chamber to a light lunch of finger food and Florida orange juice. It would have been natural to assume President Miller would have stayed for the celebration and to visit with his former Senate colleagues. However, he left immediately back for the White House after his own congratulations to his new vice president. He shook Jimmy's hand and whispered he wanted Jimmy to receive all the attention from the men and women present in the Senate. He stopped briefly to deliver a peck to Eleanor's cheek.

The two hours were nearly up, and members were drifting back into the Senate chamber. A large Secret Service agent approached Randy Fisher near the chamber entrance. The man asked if Randy would follow him to a nearby cloakroom. Never wanting to offend a man with a gun, Randy followed the agent. Inside the cloakroom, Leslie Overman was waiting.

"Good afternoon, Senator. I wanted to take this opportunity to thank you again for your help in person. I was not prepared on Wednesday for Senator Lawrence's questions, and I'm afraid I let the vice president down."

Randy smiled at the White House deputy chief of staff. "I think the vice president would have received enough votes without any special help from me. He is a good man, and most of the members of Congress would have seen the truth before they cast their vote. You should enjoy working with the VP at the White House. He might help soften their appearance and bring a little warm blood to its veins."

Leslie smiled back at Randy and accepted his gentle jab at the president. "I will be working with the vice president a great deal. He asked me to be his chief of staff, and I have accepted."

Randy was going to ask if that was a promotion or demotion from

White House deputy chief of staff, but more Secret Service agents entering the cloakroom interrupted their conversation.

The vice president of the United States walked in with his wife at his side. "Ah, there he is," he said as he walked up to Randy and offered his hand. "I wanted to thank you again in person for your help on Thursday and to introduce you to my wife, Eleanor."

Randy accepted the beautiful elderly women's hand, and she stepped up and gave him a little kiss on the cheek. "Thank you. I should have known a Southern gentleman would be the one to help bring out the truth about my Jimmy. We will always appreciate your kindness."

Randy looked at the older woman. Her fine facial bone structure had aged well. She kept her own white hair cut in a shorter style. "I was glad to help in my little way," he said. "I was telling Leslie that Jimmy would have won confirmation without my help. Not everybody in Congress is lacking in intelligence."

There was a gentle round of laughter to the reference to Jasper Lawrence. Randy took this opportunity to follow up on Leslie's earlier comment. He addressed his comment to the vice president. "I understand Leslie is going to work for you full-time."

Jimmy was standing between his wife and Leslie Overman. "Yes. I am a very lucky man. I have two beautiful and smart women to keep me on the right track. I asked the president for Leslie's services, and he graciously agreed to allow her to be my chief of staff."

Randy was smiling at the trio, but Leslie's smile was not quite as full as Jimmy's and Eleanor's smiles.

Chapter 26

Huang Zhao was standing on the helicopter deck of the first drill ship to arrive in the South China Sea. The sun was high above his head, and the wind was a light breeze from the south at about twelve knots. The temperature was at a comfortable 80 degrees. At any other time, he would have enjoyed the sunshine on his face and breeze rippling through his hair. He had started his career in the offshore oil-drilling business on a ship very much like the *Lou Chuan*. It was an old vessel, but so far, its condition was as advertised in the ship's papers and maintenance records.

They had received the needed maintenance report from their onboard representative while the ship was still in transit from Poland and had a full repair crew waiting to board the ship when it docked at Zhanjiang. For ninety-six hours, the alternating crews had covered the vessel from stem to stern as they worked to make as many repairs as possible in the time allowed by the Chinese Navy.

Admiral Fang Li and Vice Admiral Deshi Yang made their inspection of the vessel and renamed it the *Lou Chuan* after an ancient castle ship from the Han Dynasty. They stood at the very spot he was now standing and watched as the repair crews tackled the list of major and minor repairs.

The *Lou Chuan*, anchored now over the wellhead for almost two weeks, barely swayed in the gentle rhythm of the waves. The ship's GPS system remotely held the vessel in position with drilling operations underway for only a few days. From his elevated position on the deck, he could see the haze in the distance marking Sand Cay Island about six miles to his west.

When he turned around, Taiping Island was only about one mile from the drill ship. Taiping Island was the largest of the Spratly Island chain. They were twenty-two miles south-southwest from Loiata Island, which was under the protectorate of the Philippine military. That was close and a constant worry to Huang Zhao, but not near as worrisome as Sand Cay Island to his west. He wondered if, with powerful binoculars, he might see the flag of the Vietnamese military garrison flying in the breeze above the island.

Now his oil-drilling crews were working with the constant threat that the Vietnamese navy might attack them at any time. Once already, a small Turya-class Motor Torpedo Boat, capable of speeds near forty knots in smooth to medium seas, had made itself known by approaching the drill ship. Mostly, the Vietnamese Coast Guard for border security used the war vessel for island perimeter patrols.

The Chinese frigate assigned to the drill ship and its support vessels had moved in and positioned themselves between the Vietnamese MTB and the drill ships. The Chinese Navy destroyer stayed back but to the port side of the drill ship to allow for maneuvering if the Vietnamese MTB tried to get around the frigate. There had been no exchange of gunfire, and the Vietnamese vessel had quickly moved off. Probably its mission was to scout the area and take pictures of the Chinese Navy ships.

The first dangerous incident of gunfire had occurred on the *Lou Chuan* only two days after the vessels had arrived on station. It was not from the Vietnamese navy as Huang Zhao had worried but Chinese marines.

Crewmembers of the drill ship had failed to recognize the authority of the captain from the destroyer. He had made an unscheduled inspection and demanded a progress report. Several of the wildcatters had ignored the naval officer or simply dismissed him out of hand. The Chinese captain's warrant officer—class 4, equal to a chief petty officer in the US Navy, had slapped the offending wildcatter, and a small fight had started. The captain had drawn his sidearm and fired two rounds into the air. The fight had quickly gone out of the wildcatters, but now there was a squad of Chinese Navy marines stationed on each vessel.

That was why Huang Zhao had flown by helicopter to this drill ship. He met with the captains of each vessel within the local CNOOC command and tried to reduce the tension already near the boiling point. The quickest fix was to offer premium pay for what he was calling "hardship duty."

He knew he should make similar trips to each drill ship platform. The captain of the Chinese Navy destroyer would pass the information about the little skirmish back to his commander, and the armed marines would appear on the other vessels before Huang Zhao could get to them all. He had no choice but to communicate by cell phone to the senior CNOOC representative for each group and inform him of the possible development and the new pay structure.

Huang Zhao walked down the steps from the helicopter pad. He stepped through a bulkhead door and into the interior of the ship. He immediately felt the reduced airflow inside the interior spaces as he walked past familiar pieces of equipment and control panels. This drill ship was his life, and he normally loved being back at sea. Today, he was looking forward to returning to Beijing. At least inside their corporate headquarters he would feel like he was still in some sort of control.

Chapter 27

The Red River forms at the base of the Hengduan Mountains south of Dali, China. It flows generally southeast, enters Vietnam at the Lao Cai Province, and forms portions of the international border between China and Vietnam. In the northwestern region of Vietnam, the river's name changed to the Thao River. As it continues to flow, other tributaries, *Da River* and *Lo River,* add their volume to broaden the Red River. At the provincial capital of *Viet Tri*, the river's name changes to the *Hong River* and the water flows further southeast to the national capitol of Hanoi before emptying into the Gulf of Tonkin.

The Cam River has its beginning from the Red River as it passes through Hanoi. The river is less than five miles in length but ends at Haiphong, the third largest city in Vietnam and the second largest port in the Communist country.

The history of Vietnam has its beginning in the first millennium BC. The main rivers and tributaries have provided access into the interior of the country and have been used heavily for trade and invading forces that fought to control the country.

In the tenth century, the national Vietnam Navy was born with three regional commands to enlist and train the fishermen along the rivers and coastal waters. They became experts and constituted a seasoned naval force ready to protect the country. The navy, through the many years, was involved in many wars and battles primarily with Chinese forces. The largest battles were three navel engagements called the Battle of Bach Dang waged against the Chinese Southern forces in AD 938 and resulted in the death of over one hundred thousand Chinese sailors.

The current Vietnam People's Navy has its headquarters located in Hai Phong and commands a navy of seven frigates, six submarines, forty corvettes and missile boats, and various transport or logistic ships. The forty-two thousand officers and sailors of the People's Navy are under the command of Admiral Binh Huy Pham, Political Commissar Vice Admiral De Thuc Ho, and Chief of Operations Rear Admiral Trieu Thanh Le.

Admiral Binh Huy Pham was standing on a balcony outside his office on the third floor of the headquarters for the Vietnamese navy as he looked out toward the port waters. The temperature was near 95 degrees, and the breeze brought the smell of salt water to his nostrils. The admiral was nearing the mandatory retirement age of sixty-five as set forth by the People's Navy regulations and enjoyed the few precious moments he could find to watch the activity in the harbor. The three-story command building provided for only one balcony, and for Admiral Binh Huy Pham that allowed him privacy to reflect on the past and consider plans for the future. It provided some solitude similar to when he stood at the helm of one of the ships he had commanded during his almost forty years in the service.

Bing Huy Pham had been a very young member of the People's Navy when the war ended with the American military in 1974. During his time in the naval service, he had seen plenty of combat with the neighboring countries as they tried to steal the valuable natural resources that his growing country desperately required. Today, the demand placed on his naval forces meant the war vessels docked at the four naval bases at Da Nang, Cam Ranh, Nhon Traob, and Rhti Quoc would be very busy.

The executive branch of the Socialist Republic of Vietnam in Hanoi had declared the modernization of the People's Navy to be a priority to repulse unauthorized foreign vessels from intruding into Vietnamese waters. The required monetary expenditures for a country of over ninety-one million people had been a terrible drain on the thirty-nine-billion-dollar annual budget.

Bing Huy Pham had been the architect for the modernization program, having been chief of staff for the navy for four years and in his current position for the last three. He had one more year until his own chief of staff would move into the higher flag rank and Bing Huy Pham would be retired.

The latest additions to the navy's arsenal were the four new Lada-class diesel-electric submarines. When submerged, the 2700-ton warships had a speed of twenty knots and were capable of a sustained cruise of forty-five days. The ship's complement of thirty-five officers and sailors were responsible for the eighteen torpedoes and antisubmarine or anti-ship missiles. All four submarines, having completed their sea trials, were available for duty. The meeting scheduled to begin very soon might determine their first assignment.

The sound of throat clearing behind Bing Huy Pham brought him back to the present. He took one last look at the Vietnamese flag of solid red with a large golden star in the center flying from the staff beside the balcony and reluctantly turned from the harbor view to acknowledge the presence of Captain Thanh De Bui, his administrative aide.

Thanh De Bui bowed slightly at the waist. "The group is assembled, Admiral, in the secure conference room."

Bing Huy Pham simply nodded his head and followed the younger officer out of his office and down the hall to the high-security conference room. He passed through the overly thick doorframe and entered the room. The large conference table was able to accommodate fourteen sailors and officers from his fleet and they filled all the chairs except for the two reserved for him and his aide.

He took his place at the head of the table. The admiral's aide closed the door and sealed the room. The interior of the door and walls, constructed with a variety of special materials, prevented any mechanical-electrical listening devices from eavesdropping on their conversation. The armed guards stationed outside the room would deter the old-fashioned type of intelligence-gathering by humans trying to listen in to the secret meeting.

To Bing Huy Pham's left sat Rear Admiral Trieu Thanh Le, his chief of staff and his replacement in one year. On his right was Vice Admiral Dc Thuc Ho, commissar for the navy and the direct representative to the People's Central Government in Hanoi. The three admirals controlled all levels of the navy under the purview of the Central Government.

Today's meeting was to discuss the latest intelligence report from the South China Sea. Vietnam did not possess a space-based satellite photoreconnaissance system like the United States and other major foreign powers. Instead, they relied on a series of digital photographs taken from the deck of a patrol boat or plane.

Commodore Hau Le Dung, senior officer for the People's Naval Intelligence Service, was prepared to begin his presentation. He waited until Admiral Bing Huy Pham made a slight motion with his right index finger and then activated the remote control for the overhead projector. The first picture taken from the patrol boat in the South China Sea of the new Chinese drill ship and support group filled the screen.

"The Chinese drill ship is called the *Lou Chuan*, and it has been on station for nearly fourteen days near Taiping Island in the Spratly Island Chain. It has the normal complement of support vessels for a sustained drilling operation. No tankers for oil transportation back to the Chinese mainland have arrived, but they would not be needed for several weeks at the earliest."

He activated the remote again to scroll slowly through several more frames showing a long-distance photo of the support vessels and then more close-ups of the *Lou Chuan*. When he stopped activating the remote, the screen filled with a long-distance photo of a Chinese destroyer. He allowed the group to get a good look at the warship and then brought up the Chinese frigate in the next photo. The following image was a split screen showing both warships. The Vietnamese naval officers sitting at the table looked closely at the two ships. They might be warships from a foreign country in their waters, but to sailors with a love of the sea, their trained eyes could appreciate the majesty of a vessel afloat on the open waters.

"The 052C type destroyer pictured on the left is the *Yu Yuen*. It has a displacement of seven thousand tons with a top speed of thirty knots. It normally has a crew of 280 men with an estimated cruising range of 7500 nautical miles. It's armament consists of forty-eight HHQ-9 long-range surface-to-air missiles, eight C-805 anti-ship or land attack cruise missiles, one Type 210 100-millimeter dual-purpose gun and two 30-millimeter Type 730 close-in weapons systems. It also has six torpedo tubes and can accommodate a Kamov KA-27 or Harbin Z-9C anti-ship helicopter."

The briefing officer paused to allow the men at the table to fix the magnitude of the destroyer's weapons in their minds. He continued with his description of the second warship pictured on the screen. "The frigate on the right is the *Yang Wei*. It displaces 4,300 tons with a top speed of twenty-seven knots. Crew strength is 128 men with an estimated cruising range of eight thousand miles. Its armament is less than that of the *Yu Yuen*, but it is still a formidable warship. It has anti-ship missiles, SAM (surface-to-air missile) launchers, Type 210 100-millimeter gun and four AK-630 6-barrel 30-millimeter CIWS (close-in weapon system) capable of firing four thousand rounds per minute at an extreme range of four thousand meters."

"We estimate the Chinese Navy has twenty-five of the Type 052 series destroyers and forty-seven of the Type 054 frigates."

Le Dung flipped to his last picture showing the entire Chinese flotilla of warships and the CNOOC vessels. "When our patrol craft approached the drill ship, the frigate moved in to intercept. The destroyer reacted by staying back to protect the drilling platform."

Commodore Hau Le Dung turned the projector off, and the light level in the room was reduced. Captain Thanh De Dui rose from his seat and activated the ceiling light fixtures. The men in the room took a few seconds to allow their eyes to adjust to the brightness. Several lit cigarettes and inhaled deeply. The room quickly filled with the smoke.

Hau Le Dung continued with his briefing. "The group of ships in our waters was two warships, the drill ship, and three support vessels. We have reports but no pictures yet of more flotillas moving into the South China Sea near the Spratly and Scarborough Reef area. We believe there could be as many as ten to twelve of these oil-drilling groups. The preliminary reports indicate a major escalation by the Chinese government in offshore oil drilling in our territorial waters."

The men were silent for several moments. Vice Admiral Dc Thuc Ho broke the silence. "Is the Chinese Navy deploying warships with each drilling operation?"

Le Dung nodded his head in an affirmative motion. "Yes. Information gathered to this point seems to confirm that two Chinese warships protect each drill group. If the count of drilling platforms is twelve as we suspect, then the Chinese are flooding the South China Sea with twenty-four warships and forty-eight commercial ships to support the drilling operations. When they deploy the required tankers to transport the oil and gas back to their mainland, the number will increase by another estimated thirty to forty vessels."

The men in the room shifted in their chairs, and they whispered their thought to others sitting beside them. Again Vice Admiral Dc Thuc Ho was the first to speak. "I need to immediately inform the Central Government of this new development, and we need to immediately issue a protest to the Chinese government."

Admiral Trieu Thanh Le leaned forward to look at the commissar sitting on the other side of Huy Pham. "We have warned them many times in the past, but they ignore our complaints and steal vital resources our country needs. We need to show them how they will pay a heavy price for the oil they steal."

Admiral Bing Huy Pham had not spoken through the entire presentation. "We need to remember a very important fact. The Chinese Navy is the second largest in the world. We must move carefully with any response we propose to make."

Trieu Thanh Le countered with his own words of advice. "Large or not, if we do not respond, they will continue to expand their influence in the South China Sea. Every day, they attempt to limit the passage of our commercial fishing fleet and force us back closer to our shores. They claim sea territory hundreds of miles from their own coastline and up to the twelve-mile limit of the Philippines, Malaysia, and Brunei."

A middle-aged captain from the furthest end of the table raised a hand in a request to speak. Bing Huy Pham motioned for the officer to proceed. Captain Cam De Ho stood at the table. The forty-one-year-old was one of the captains of the new Lada submarines. "My brother owns a small fishing fleet that operates in the South China Sea. He writes to me nearly every week, and in each letter, he describes how the Chinese Navy harasses his ships. Sometimes, they will stop and board his vessels looking for weapons or demanding transits fees from the boat captains. I agree we must move carefully, but we need to protect what is rightfully ours."

Admiral Bing Huy Pham sat quietly looking at the table. His eyes locked on the wood grain in the table's smooth surface, but his mind was thinking about the ships and men under his command and the new danger they faced. As he got older, he was more cautious than the young officer he once was when he walked the bridge of his first command.

As he considered the orders he needed to issue, he could hear the discussions taking place around the table. This time, he cleared his throat to get their attention. He looked first at the young submarine captain and then to his chief of staff. "Issue orders for two Lada submarines from the fleet to put to sea. Assign them to the South China Sea near the Spratly Island and Scarborough Reef. They are to observe and report. They are to take no action without direct orders from this command center."

He paused for a moment as he considered the next order. This one could result in the loss of life if the ship's captain was not very careful. "Order the Turya-class Motor Torpedo Boat that took the pictures to make several approaches to the drill ship. We need to discover the response they will receive from the Chinese warships. What are their rules for engagement with our fleet?"

He brought his left hand, palm open, down firmly on the tabletop. "Make sure the MTB captain understands this is not to be an attack. He is not to use any weapons against the Chinese unless he needs to save his boat and crew. This is an intelligence-gathering mission. The captain must clearly understand the operation. I want no loss of life from his crew."

Admiral Bing Huy Pham looked around the room. "We will not let the Chinese Navy encroach any more into our territorial waters, but we will not risk war until we know the facts. There is still time for us to observe and make our plans."

Chapter 28

Life in Washington DC and for members of Congress is not always a nonstop roller-coaster ride. Most of the time, their working days are filled every minute with committee meetings, time spent on the Senate or House floors, or fast trips back to their regional offices to meet with their constituents. There is not a vote to confirm a vice president every week.

After Jimmy Diamond had taken the oath of office on February 9, Randy Fisher was able to work his normal twelve-hour day and then go home to spend time with Annie. In the thirty days since the new vice president had taken office, Randy had made two weekend trips home to South Carolina and given three paid speeches to fill the campaign coffer for the next election in six years. He could not count again on the Republicans forgoing a fight for his seat on the next go-around.

He had been pleasantly surprised to receive a telephone call from Leslie Overman at 5:00 p.m. the previous Friday with an invitation from the vice president for Randy and Annie to join Jimmy and Eleanor Diamond for a private dinner at their new residence. What evening did Senator Fisher have open the following week?

Randy checked his schedule, and they set a preliminary date for the ninth with Randy to confirm the date after he checked with Annie and her schedule. There were no conflicts in their calendars, and the dinner was set.

Most people can easily answer the question: where does the president of the United States live? Ask the same question about the vice president and you will probably receive many different responses. The White House sits on sixteen acres in Washington DC, in the most exclusive location in the city.

The vice president's residence resides on seventy-two acres on the US Naval Observatory. The white, three-story Victorian mansion, built in 1893, was originally used as the home for the superintendent of the observatory. It was such a beautiful home that in 1923, the chief of naval operations claimed the home for his own use and kicked the superintendent out.

In 1974, Congress agreed to provide funds for a renovation and decided to make the 9,150 square-foot mansion the official residence of the vice president. The two first vice presidents eligible to live there were not able to use the home or not willing to live there. Gerald Ford was only vice president for a short time and did not have time to move into the residence. Nelson Rockefeller already had a beautiful home in Washington and only used the residence for parties and other official functions. Walter Mondale was the first vice president to live in the home.

Randy and Annie Fisher arrived at the residence for their private dinner fifteen minutes early. They approached the front gate entrance, saw the uniformed members of the Secret Service, and stopped the Ford Explorer for the security check. After passing through the iron gates, Randy drove up the paved driveway past a long, oblong-shaped flowerbed and pulled under the portico where he stopped the car. The interior lighting from inside the home helped to offset the darkened sky. There was very little moonlight this evening, and most of the home's outward appearance and the nearby grounds were not visible.

Several members of the house staff were immediately at the car and opened their doors. Randy walked around the front of his car and took hold of Annie's left hand. Together, they walked up the front steps to the porch. It was a short walk to the front entrance, but the porch opened to the right and a large veranda wrapped around the entire corner of the home. They were not able to see exactly where it ended. Annie wanted to explore the porch, but Randy kept a firm hold on her hand. They had not reached the front entrance when Jimmy Diamond opened the door instead of a servant or butler.

"Come in. Come in. Don't stand out there in the cold. The taxpayers are paying the heat bill," he said with a big smile on his face.

They walked into the entrance, and Eleanor Diamond entered the reception hall from the dining room. Randy shook hands with both of the Diamonds and introduced Annie to the vice president and second lady of the United States.

Annie felt an instant warmth from the older couple. They seem to fit together as a couple like her own parents did. A butler was standing off to the side and offered to take Randy's and Annie's overcoats.

Eleanor walked around her husband to take Annie by the arm and offered to show the home to her guest.

"We've only been here about ten days, so we're still learning things about the house ourselves," she informed her guests.

Annie looked around the Reception Hall. The focal points were the fireplace in the right back corner and the doorway on its left side leading into a small foyer and the wooden staircase to the second and third floors. A light cream area rug partly covered the hardwood floor, leaving about a two-foot border of the highly polished wood showing beyond the outer edge of the rug. The yellow-painted walls and cream-colored wood trim supported a twelve-foot ceiling, and the large chandelier hung in the center of the ceiling provided a warm glow to the room.

From where she stood, Annie could see to her left through the wide double glass doors with small window frames into the dining room. Off to her right was another set of double doors allowing access to the living room. "It a lovely home from the outside, and I can't wait to see the rest of the downstairs," she said.

Eleanor Diamond led the party on the home tour. They walked to their right and entered the living room. The fireplace in the reception room was back-to-back and identical to the other unit in the living room and shared the same chimney. The room was square except for the rounded far-right front corner, which matched the shape of the wrap-around veranda. The wall-to-wall carpet matched the color of the area rug from the reception room.

The doorway to their left brought them to the sitting room and the garden room through another connecting door out from the sitting room.

The flowers and ferns in the garden room captivated Annie's attention immediately. "I can see how this room is named!" she exclaimed. The two men stood just inside the doorway to the flower room while Eleanor and Annie walked around the glass-sided room softly touching the flowers and stopping to smell their fragrance. Annie's eyes were wide open in delight. "I must see this room again someday when the sunlight is coming in through the glass outer walls. It must be simply breathtaking."

Eleanor stopped at a blooming jasmine. "They tell me there is some sort of plant from every state in the union within this room. I am afraid I have not had time to learn them all. Thank goodness, we have a trained horticulturist here one day each week to assist the gardener with the plants." She stopped by a beautiful planter of hollyhocks with pale-pink pedals.

"These are just so beautiful," she said.

Annie looked around the room. The floor-to-ceiling windows would allow plenty of sunshine into the room. At the far end of the room, two small exhaust fans near the ceiling would help to remove excess humidity. "This would keep me busy all the time. I might not want to ever leave this room."

From the sitting room, they could see into a lounge with a television set, comfortable chairs, and a sofa. The tour led back into the foyer and past the stairway and then again into the reception room. The butler was waiting and announced dinner was ready.

The downstairs tour completed, Eleanor allowed Randy to take her arm, and together, they walked into the dining room. Jimmy Diamond acted as escort for Annie.

The dining room had a similar area rug as the reception room and a fireplace in the front wall located between floor-to-ceiling windows framed in drapes. A wooden hutch stood against the sidewall, and next to it were two doors, an in and out, allowing entry into the pantry/kitchen. The centerpiece of the room was the wooden dining table.

The cloth-covered table, capable of seating ten diners, was set with only one table leaf and could easily seat six, but tonight it contained chinaware for only four. Randy walked Eleanor to the end of the table and helped her with the chair. He walked around the side of the table, stood by the chair with his back to the fireplace, and remained standing until Jimmy Diamond settled Annie on the other side of the table. When Jimmy reached his own chair at the other end of the table and made to sit down, Randy finally took his seat.

Jimmy Diamond looked around the table. "We didn't take time for cocktails, so we must make up for our lack of etiquette. What would everybody like?"

For the next two hours, Randy and Annie enjoyed a dinner of baked chicken with a mild mustard sauce, boiled new redskin potatoes, and a green bean dish with a unique seasoning Annie could not identify. Warm Dutch apple pie and vanilla bean ice cream followed the meal and complemented perhaps the best coffee Randy had ever tasted.

The dinner conversation had begun with the confirmation hearing and Jasper Lawrence's attempt to embarrass the vice president. From there, it branched out to how Annie and Randy had met. The revelation of Energy Secretary Raymond Cleveland and his assistant, Thomas Dean, were stealing millions from their own department sparked an interest in the Diamonds. Talk of relatives and Randy's Aunt Francis Ward in California followed. In all, it was a pleasant dinner for the two couples.

As the staff cleared away the few remaining dishes, the vice president looked across the table toward Annie. "May I borrow the senator for a few minutes to discuss something in private?"

Annie looked at Randy and then back quickly to the vice president. "You may borrow him anytime, sir. Just make sure to always return him in the same condition."

With a little laugh, the vice president rose from his chair and motioned Randy to follow. The two men walked out of the dining room, leaving the two women talking about living in Washington, and passed through the reception room and foyer into the sitting room.

"Would you like another cup of coffee or some sort of after-dinner drink?" the vice president asked.

"No, sir. I'm fine," Randy replied.

The vice president took a padded leather-covered chair next to the fireplace, and Randy sat down on a sofa next to the wall and at the end away from the VP. He waited until Jimmy was ready to discuss whatever was on his mind.

"Were you surprised I requested to take the oath of office in the Senate chamber?"

Randy thought for a few moments. "Not really surprised. Previous vice presidents have taken the oath there when they came from the Senate. I was surprised you waited until Monday instead of Friday afternoon after your confirmation vote."

Jimmy nodded before he spoke. "It was to be in the afternoon, but when I requested you be invited to the ceremony at the White House, the idea seemed to disrupt their well-laid plans." He looked at Randy as if waiting for some sort of comment from the senator.

When Randy remained silent, he continued, "It seems you're not too welcome at Sixteen Hundred Pennsylvania Avenue."

"The president and I don't run in the same circles," was all the VP could get from Randy.

He nodded with a slight smile on his face. "So I've heard. That's a shame because I like what I see in you." Randy continued to sit quietly. "All right. Let me ask you another question. "What do you think of Leslie Overman?"

Randy felt on safer ground now. "I really don't know her well except what I've heard and read about her. I met her for the first time the same day I met you. I've heard she's competent, and I've not seen anything to make me think otherwise."

Diamond nodded his head. "I think she's a fine person and was an excellent deputy chief of staff in the White House." He paused for a few moments. "She was demoted to my chief of staff because she failed to pick up the little news blip about the Tanner case. Hell, I had forgotten all about it myself, but the president wanted her fired from his staff. I jumped in and asked for her to be my chief of staff."

Randy just shook his head. "He's got a quick temper and will not accept any failure. I think it was very nice of you to take care of her."

Diamond looked directly at Randy. "Is it true you had a run-in with the president in the Oval Office a while back?"

Randy remained silent as he contemplated the question. He decided someone in the White House needed to know the truth. "Yes. As I mentioned at dinner, I was certain Raymond Cleveland was stealing from his Department of Energy research fund. I decided to inform the president before the press discovered it. I went to the White House and met with the president and William Olinger. They accused me of trying to steal the money. We exchanged some words, and I am proud to say I kept my temper and just explained what was happening and walked out. The crap hit the fan the next week when Cleveland stuck a forty-five automatic pistol in his mouth. I've never been back again to the White House, and as long as Harold Miller occupies the Oval Office, I'm not missing a whole lot."

Randy had to take a few breaths to get his breathing back to normal. He had not thought his recollection of the events on that day would affect him so much. Well, it was out, and Diamond could make use of the information in whatever way he decided to.

"Thank you for confiding in me. Your information, along with some other things whispered in my ear over the last week, will help me in dealing with the president. Mind you, I'm a Republican and proud of it, but I'm an American first." They looked at each other for several seconds, and Diamond broke the silence. "I will not repeat what you just told me. Why don't we rejoin the ladies?"

Chapter 29

Sand Cay Island, South China Sea
Monday, March 9, 2015
7:00 a.m. (CST)

Sub Lieutenant Huynh Tan Phat could feel the throbbing motors of *Ly Nam De*, a motor torpedo boat, as his men made ready to set sail from the People's Navy port at Sand Cay Island. Today, the Vietnamese warship would approach the Chinese drill ship operating near Taiping Island until they drew fire from one of the Chinese Navy warships. His orders were to determine their battle plan for defending the drill ship and the support vessels. How close could they get before the enemy would fire to defend themselves?

He looked back toward Sand Cay Island. Vietnam had claimed the island for many years and in 1974 placed a military force on the island to defend their rightful claim. Sand Cay was the ninth largest island in the Spratly Island chain and the fourth largest island occupied by Vietnam. Trees and scrub bush covered most of the fourteen acres, and the only buildings were those hauled by navy transport vessels and erected by previous sailors. Not a single square inch of the island surface possessed any value to his country. Only the oil and gas beneath the waters that surrounded Sand Cay and the other Spratly Islands made the otherwise mass of sand and rocks worthwhile. It was hard for the naval officer to judge if the natural resources were worth the lives of his men.

Huynh Tan Phat had explicit orders not to fire his own weapons but to be the target for the Chinese Navy. His instructions were to pilot his vessel directly at the drill ship and wait until the Chinese opened fire. The Iranians had done this to the Americans in the waters close to their territories. He was certain the reckless tactic would provoke a reaction from the Chinese Navy. The orders did not tell him what to do if the ship could not pull away before the Chinese were able to target their weapons accurately enough to blow his ship apart.

The *Ly Nam De* was a Turya-Class Motor Torpedo boat named after a sixth-century Vietnamese emperor hailed as a hero for repelling an invasion of the Liang Dynasty in the To Lich River. The fast warship had three M503 B2 diesels engines with a combined 15,000 horsepower and a top speed of forty knots—well above either of the Chinese ships. He would need every knot of speed the ship's engineer could produce.

The ship normally carried a complement of forty, but today, he would operate with a minimum crew to reduce the possible loss of life if his plan deviated from the expected.

His petty officer walked up to the pilothouse and informed Huynh Tan Phat the ship was ready for sea. The captain took a last look at the dock and the crewmembers who were not a part of the day's mission. They lined the dock yelling and cheering for their comrades. Each one would gladly take the place of another man on the mission. He could not have been more proud of them.

He turned his back to the dock, ordered minimum forward speed, and piloted the ship into the narrow channel connecting the South China Sea. Within seconds of clearing the dock, he increased power and allowed the warship to build speed until they were at twenty-five knots. He would maintain this speed until he was in the initial edge of the estimated danger area. At that time, he could expect to draw fire from the Chinese warships. If they reacted as before, one of the ships would move from their patrol position to place itself between the *Ly Nam De* and the drill ship. His plan was to approach the unprotected side of the drill ship and its support vessels and force the Chinese warships to move from their protecting positions to screen the drill ship. He would maintain the twenty-five-knot speed until the first weapon fired at his ship. Then he would call for maximum speed and hope the extra fifteen knots would prevent the Chinese guns from locking onto his vessel. If the Chinese decided to use one of their ship-to-ship missiles, another Vietnamese naval ship would have to make the next mission.

They had traveled two-thirds of the six-mile distance to their target. Using powerful binoculars, he could see the drill ship was lying inside the perimeter of the three support ships. The bow of the drill ship was facing north as before and the frigate was off to the port side and slightly ahead of the drill ship also facing north. The destroyer was on the senior side of the drill ship heading north as well but lying motionless. The layout could not be better for Huynh Tan Phat.

When protecting ships and transports, the navy's best plan called for the ships under escort to move at top speed inside the protection screen of the warships. However, drill ships have to maintain their exact position at all times unless they disengage from the drill and possibly lose all equipment connected to the ship and entrance of the wellhead. The Chinese could not have a more exposed position or be more open to an attack.

As he drew within the two-mile mark toward the Chinese ships, Huynh Tan Phat steered the patrol craft 45 degrees to starboard and then straightened out the vessel for three hundred meters before turning back 90 degrees to line up for the port aft of the drill ship. Now the destroyer was on the opposite corner of the drill ship and farther away from his approaching vessel. The frigate was on his side of the drill ship but facing away. He could see men on the civilian vessels pointing at his ship and making wild gestures. Heavy smoke appeared from the stacks of both warships, and their engines provided power to their propellers, slowly moving the warships from their positions toward his own craft. He called down to the engine room and alerted them to be prepared to deliver full power at any moment.

He was near enough to the drill ship that only the destroyer's radar mast could be seen from his position. The bow of the frigate was swinging to port and slowly cutting through the blue water of the sea. For the Chinese, it would have been too late if this had been a real attack.

In fact, Huynh Tan Phat was amazed he had caught the Chinese warships off guard. Neither ship was in the position he would have chosen to protect the drilling vessels. One of the support ships lay aft of the starboard side of the drill ship and would require the destroyer to maneuver around it before it could turn to starboard to bring itself around and block his path.

The *Ly Nam De* was within three hundred yards off the drill ship itself. If Tan Phat had wanted to bring the vessel under fire, there was nothing to stop him. The frigate was moving but still needed several minutes to clear the other two support vessels and bring itself in a firing position.

Huynh Tan Phat's vision pulled away from the frigate to the puff of smoke from the destroyer. A few seconds later, he could hear the "whistling" sound of a gun shell as the weapon passed over his patrol boat. He risked a look back in time to see the shell impact at least two hundred yards beyond his own craft.

Incredible! The captain of the destroyer had ordered his ship to open fire at the Vietnamese motor torpedo boat by targeting his enemy over top of the drill ship. The Vietnamese warship was too close to the drill ship, and the destroyer's four-inch deck gun could not be depressed enough to target the approaching Vietnamese patrol boat without hitting their own civilian ship.

What an unbelievable risk by the Chinese captain! *A potential disaster,* Huynh Tan Phat thought, should the shell pass to closely above the volatile gas floating from and around the drill ship.

His ship had drawn fire, and the action from the Chinese had provided him important information he needed to send to his superiors. He yelled for full power, and the engineer below deck was quick to respond. He immediately felt the three engines feeding more power to the ship's propellers, and *Ly Nam De* nearly leaped out of the water. He pulled the wheel hard to starboard and put the craft into a 270-degree turn. He would leave the area in a different direction from his approach to the ships.

Now that he was farther away from the destroyer and the frigate had cleared the two support vessels, he commenced a zigzag pattern to make his ship a more difficult target. He could feel the full power of the engines through the soles of his shoes as they reached their maximum speed of forty knots. The destroyer fired several more rounds, but they splashed off to starboard in the area where he had first approached the drill ship.

They were safe, and his men on the ship were yelling at each other and laughing about how they had caught the Chinese unprepared for an attack. Sub Lieutenant Huynh Tan Phat had an interesting report to prepare as soon as they reached the docks. He had been very surprised by the ease with which they had been able to approach the enemy. That information would figure heavily in his report.

Chapter 30

Randy Fisher approached the outer security perimeter to the Central Intelligence Agency main headquarters building in Langley, Virginia. He pulled his Explorer to a stop at the first security gate. A uniformed armed guard approached his vehicle while a second man stayed within the protective guard shack.

Randy rolled down the window and opened his ID folder to show his driver's license and Senate ID card with photo. The guard took a careful look at the two photos and ID cards and then compared them to the information on the clipboard in his hand. Apparently, Randy satisfied the guard at this first security checkpoint. The driver informed him to proceed to the next gate.

Randy shifted his foot from the brake to the gas pedal, and the Explorer moved forward. He increased his speed and a minute later entered the concrete barriers set at sharp angles to force vehicles to slow down to below ten miles per hour. He stopped again at the next checkpoint. Here, reinforced steel poles would need to drop into a recessed cavity to allow his car to pass. After another close examination of his credentials, the guard motioned for him to proceed toward the visitor parking lot close to the seven-story building named after George H. W. Bush.

Randy entered the lobby of the building and approached the final security inspection point. For a third time, he showed his various forms of identification to the two men and one woman behind the bulletproof security screen. They finally accepted him for who he was and asked that he take a nearby seat and make himself comfortable. His escort would arrive in a few minutes to take him to the seventh floor of the building.

Ten minutes later, the senator entered the office of his friend and the DDO, Deputy Director of Operations, Marion Bellwood.

"No chance a reporter will ever get past your security procedures to write any kind of embarrassing exposé on how they walked into the CIA building and discovered all the secrets about Area 51."

"If they did, I and a lot of people would be out of a job real fast," Marion said as he met Randy at the room's halfway point and shook his friend's outstretched hand.

Randy looked around the room. It reflected his friend's disposition for a no-frill decor. The wall covering was a plain taupe-color paint. Randy remembered his aunt once saying, "If you do not know what colors to use, go with taupe. You never can be too wrong with that color." Apparently, the interior decorator must have agreed. The taupe walls did seem to go with the black carpet, but appreciating the decor was not the reason he was inside one of America's most secret locations.

"I saw your notice informing the State Department of your overseas trip," Marion said.

Randy had filed the appropriate notification form to let the State Department know he was planning a fact-finding trip to the South China Sea. It was a courtesy gesture, and it made sense in case they needed to contact him or he encountered any unexpected situations.

"I'm leaving Thursday after the Senate recesses for the early spring break. I will be gone about twelve to fourteen days. It's the first time Annie and I have been apart for more than a just a few days since our wedding. I am not sure she's happy about the idea. I think she's going to discover our little apartment is bigger than she remembered when she lived there alone before we got married."

Marion Bellwood simply nodded his head in understanding. His career had required him to be away from his wife and family for months at a stretch. Sometimes, he could not even communicate home for weeks on end.

"Get used to it, buddy. These overseas trips get more frequent the longer you stay in the Senate."

Randy hoped his friend was wrong. He enjoyed his life with Annie and hated to be away from her for more than a few days.

"Okay, you got me through your security obstacle course and up here on the executive floor. What's the important information you think I needed to know?"

Marion reached back to his desk and picked up a remote control for the sixty-inch flat-screen TV attached to the wall opposite his desk. He brought up the first picture showing a line of vessels moving out of a seaport. Randy was not knowledgeable enough to determine what exact kinds of vessels he was looking at on the TV.

Marion used the built-in laser pointer in the remote control to highlight the lead ship. "That's a drill ship used for offshore oil drilling." He used the red laser to draw disappearing circles around three of the other ships. "Those are support vessels for the drill ships. They carry drill pipe, lubricants, repair parts, and maybe sleeping quarters for the crew of the drill ship. Everything they need when they arrive on station to begin their drilling operation and maintain themselves for weeks or months at sea."

He flipped the projector to another picture showing two warships. Again, Randy could not identify their exact type. "Those are their escorts—a Chinese destroyer and frigate assigned to each group of oil drilling ships. The Chinese are taking their security very seriously with their expansion into the South China Sea."

Randy walked closer to the TV to try to pick out more details of the warships and their armaments. The forward-mounted guns were impressive, but the missile launchers were scarier.

He pointed toward the screen. "How many groups has the Chinese launched into the area?"

"We are not quite sure yet, but it appears there are ten to twelve groups. Our people down in photo analysis are working to identify all the different vessels by their name or hull number so we have an accurate count. We do know they are going into the South China Sea, and it appears they are heading to the Spratly Islands and Scarborough Reef. Some left port more than four weeks ago and the others only a few days ago."

Marion flipped to the last picture he wanted to show his friend. Randy's eyes focused on an aircraft carrier sitting at a port dock.

"That's the Chinese aircraft carrier, the *Liaoning*. This photo shows the carrier was in Zhanjiang. By now, it probably has already set sail. We will have a better idea of its destination with our next satellite pass. The Chinese Navy christened the *Liaoning* several years ago, but it was another year before they had pilots trained for at-sea flight operations. The warship has been used, until now, as a show of force as it moved around the South China Sea and up near Taiwan. This might be the first time it's been deployed for actual duty and to respond to any negative reaction from the other countries claiming portions of the waters where the oil drilling operations are being conducted."

"Have the drill ships started any actual operations?" Randy asked.

"Yes, in several locations in the Spratly Islands. The Scarborough Reefs are a little farther sailing distance."

Randy walked away from the screen to stand closer to his friend. "This is what the members of ASEAN were worried about. China is expanding into these waters for the oil and gas. The situation is as volatile as the products the drill ships are bringing up from beneath the ocean."

Marion walked back to his desk. "That's what I wanted to show you and let you know what you might be getting involved with."

Randy followed his friend's movement to the desk. "Do you have any information to indicate there's some sort of planned military operation to go along with the Chinese expansion?"

"No," Marion answered. "But this many warships moving into those waters is a dangerous situation. It would only take a small miscalculation on somebody's part to ignite the whole area."

Marion moved behind his desk and opened one of the drawers on the credenza behind his chair. He removed a small box and laid it on the desktop. "I thought you might need to take this with you." He removed a Blackberry device from the opened box.

"Thank you, but I've already got a Blackberry," Randy said.

"Not like this one," Marion replied as he walked back around his desk and handed the communication device to Randy. "It's got the ability to scramble your cell phone signal and to create a small field around you to prevent any electrical equipment from tapping into your conversation."

Randy took the offered device. It was a little thicker and heavier than the phone in his right pocket but otherwise looked the same.

"Listen, I'm not going over there as a spy for your organization. I am a United States senator on a diplomatic mission. It might raise some serious questions if they discovered I had a scrambled telephone with me."

Bellwood could not keep all the frustration from his voice. "You listen to me, MP. You are going into a dangerous area with lots of warships and men with short tempers. There have been many military skirmishes with people killed on both sides. I want you to be able to call out of the area just in case our worst-case scenario might happen to occur when your butt is over there. The last thing I want is to be the one to make a condolence call on Annie."

Randy felt the weight and thickness of the device in his hand. "All right, Mr. Spymaster. How does this scrambling device work?"

Marion took the phone from Randy's hands. "It operates by pressing the convenience button on the side against close attempts to listen in on your conversation, but the signal will not be scrambled unless you're talking to another person using a telephone similarly equipped. In your case, the other phone will be mine. If you talk to anyone else on the phone, then someone else might intercept your conversation. The signal-blocking device will work with any call, but the scrambler only activates if you're talking to me."

Randy took the device back from Marion. "Will your people be able to monitor my calls?"

Marion Bellwood could not prevent a shit-eating grin from spreading across his face.

"No more than any other cell phone conversation. Come on; we need to go down to tech services to have them transfer all the data from your old phone into this new unit. That way, all your contact information will be available. The numbers will be the same, but you'll just have a few new features."

Chapter 31

Hai Phong, Vietnam
Wednesday, March 11, 2015
8:30 a.m. (CST)

Admiral Binh Huy Pham lit his fifth cigarette of the morning and frowned at his cup of tea. The liquid had gone cold, and he needed a fresh brew. He pressed the buzzer on the telephone that would signal his orderly to bring a fresh cup. He decided to postpone the morning task he had assigned for himself and stepped out onto his balcony.

The harbor was busy with fishing vessels, commercial freighters, and his warships. More Vietnamese warships were preparing to set sail for the South China Sea. Vice Admiral Dc Thuc Ho had returned from his meeting with the People's Party in Hanoi. The navy was to make ready to resist any further expansion by the Chinese into Vietnam's territory within the South China Sea.

He had truly hoped to avoid any conflict with their giant neighbor to the north. The lopsided number and composition of their respective naval fleets heavily favored the Chinese in any prolonged engagement. His fleet, impressive as it was for a country the size of Vietnam, would be no match for the second largest naval fleet in the world. Still history was full of naval engagements in which the underdog came out the victor. Even in his country's history, there were many such cases. However, those engagements took place long before the invention of aircraft carriers and their ability to project power for hundreds of miles in any direction.

His orderly rapped his knuckles on the doorframe and entered with a new cup of hot tea. Huy Pham turned reluctantly from the harbor view and resumed his seat at the desk. The report on his desk was from the commanding officer of *Ly Nam De* near Sand Cay. It would provide the details of the Chinese rules of engagement toward his ships if they needed to launch an attack against the Chinese.

He took a sip of the hot, sweetened tea. The taste was perfect to his liking. After a moment, he set the cup on its saucer, opened the folder, and began to read the report from the action at Sand Cay. The commanding officer's report, extensively detailed, allowed Admiral Huy Pham to envision the approach taken by the commanding officer of the *Ly Nam De*. As he read the words, he could almost feel the throbbing engines and the hard bounce of the hull across the waves of the sea. He missed those younger days now gone forever.

When he finished the report, he sat back in his chair and without thinking, lit another cigarette. He agreed with the warship's commanding officer. The Chinese had not been on alert yesterday morning. He could not always count on surprise, but sometimes the superior force thought they were so strong in their position, they just assumed victory would be theirs. Huy Pham knew he would need to order more missions to test the Chinese—perhaps to the point where their enemy would assume the Vietnamese navy was just going to harass their ships. All bark with no bite.

Another knock on his doorframe and rear Admiral Trieu Thanh Le entered with a folder in his hand. "This just came in from our people in Zhanjiang. The Chinese Navy's aircraft carrier, the *Liaoning*, has set out to sea. We do not have a known destination, but we can safely assume it will be the area around the oilrigs. With its aircraft, the carrier can establish a protective umbrella over the entire South China Sea where they appear to be expanding their drilling operations."

The presence of the *Liaoning* added another new worry to the senior admiral's thoughts. This decision would not be easy. "Contact the commanding officer at the Da Nang naval base and have him issue orders for two of the Lada submarines to pick up and shadow the carrier. We need to know where she is at all times."

Admiral Thanh Le nodded his head and left the room to issue the order. Now Huy Pham would need to add the Chinese aircraft carrier into any plans he needed to formulate.

Admiral Dc Thuc Ho entered Huy Pham's office. He did not

knock on the door to request permission to enter. Without asking, he planted his plump frame in one of the chairs facing Huy Pham's desk. "I just heard from Hanoi. The Chinese Foreign Ministry is refusing to respond to our accusations that their fleet and oil-drilling ships have trespassed into our territorial waters."

"That is what I expected," Huy Pham replied. "By not responding to our foreign ministry, they prevent us from developing any dialogue with them."

Thuc Ho pounded his fist on the wooden arm of the chair. "I think we need to initiate our own dialogue. You should order our fleet into one of the oil fields and force them to remove their ships. When the Chinese Central Committee sees that we mean business, they will remove the drill ships and their fleet."

Huy Pham looked into the face of the political commissar. "And if they decide to stand and fight and bring in more warships? Do I need to remind you the Chinese Navy has a superior number of warships by almost seven or eight to one over our fleet?"

Thuc Ho stood from his chair and looked down at the fleet admiral. "You need to find backbone and face these bastards. These are our territorial waters, and it's our oil and gas they are stealing." His voice was full of fury as he pointed his stubby index finger at the senior admiral.

Huy Pham come out of his own chair and stepped around his desk to stand face-to-face with Thuc Ho. "Do not forget your position here, Admiral Thuc Ho. I am the commanding officer of the People's Navy. I will order in the ships and put the lives of our sailors in jeopardy when I think we have no alternatives."

The two men continued to stare at each other for several more seconds. Huy Pham wanted to reduce the tension between himself and Thuc Ho. He walked behind the desk and resumed his seat. In a calm voice, he spoke to the political officer. "You must not forget those maps and miniature wood ship models are real ships in the South China Sea. They contain men with blood running through their veins. I do not want their ships to be unnecessarily painted red from blood."

Thuc Ho sat down again in his seat. "Then what do you propose to do? We must make some sort of statement to force them to respect our territorial waters."

Huy Pham looked at Thuc Ho. He knew the political commissar had highly placed friends in the Central Government in Hanoi. He would have to placate the vice admiral until the situation developed into a clearer picture. Otherwise, Thuc Ho would notify Hanoi of his indecision and attempt to have Huy Pham removed and himself installed as the fleet admiral.

He looked to his left at a stack of papers he had set aside earlier to read, including the after-action report from the captain of *Ly Nam De*. The thick, stapled bundle on top of the stack was the travel and meeting itinerary for the ASEAN summit in Brunei for next week.

"Next week, I will be at the ASEAN summit in Brunei. Their countries' leaders will represent all the member nations. They will have with them their senior military officers to advise them on this situation. With our alliance with ASEAN, I will force them to confront China as a unified organization. With the combined naval fleets, we can force the Chinese to reconsider their position in the South China Sea."

Thuc Ho was shaking his head. "Maybe the Philippines and Malaysia would side with us, but the other member nations have little or no interest in a fight with China, or their respective navy is too small to be of any assistance. It's a waste of time and you'll only allow the Chinese to get a stronger presence in the South China Sea."

Admiral Huy Pham looked back at his junior officer. "That is my decision for now. I am not willing to urge war with China until we have exhausted all possible paths to a peaceful solution to this situation."

Thuc Ho rose from his chair and walked toward the door. He turned back just before he reached the doorway. "You worry about those sailors. If we wait until the Chinese bring in their carrier and an overpowering force, then you will lose even more lives. In addition, our country will be forced to maintain our economy without the natural resources we need."

Chapter 32

Admiral Fang Li, commanding officer of the Chinese Navy Southern Command, was in the map room reviewing the current disposition of his fleet and the CNOOC oil drilling vessels. The schedule, as laid down by Minister Chen of the Ministry of Land and Resource, for the first quarter was near completion. Eleven of the twelve groups were on-site. Only one of the new drill ships had required extensive repairs when it arrived from the supplier. The dock master at Zhanjiang had committed to have that ship ready for sea duty in a few more days.

He was pleased with the situation as shown on the map. Nearly all of his warships were on station and prepared to protect the civilian vessels. The little foreign naval commands that cruised the South China Sea and dashed in close to his warship were only a mild annoyance to the vessels under his command.

He liked the expression "under his command." When the transport tankers started to arrive and attached themselves to the drill ships to take on their precious cargo, he would command the largest fleet of Chinese vessels in the history of the modern Chinese Navy. To top off the picture, the pride of the Chinese Navy, the *Liaoning* was under his command. To date, the aircraft carrier had been a symbol of Chinese naval strength, but now it was in actual operation to protect the ships in his command area. He could only imagine the jealous faces of the commanders of the Northern and Eastern Fleets.

Fang Li walked from the map room down the hallway to his office. He walked past the men and women working at their desks in his outer offices and entered his private domain. After closing the door, he removed his hat and walked to the luxurious office chair behind the desk.

His office decor reflected his role and command of the headquarters for the Southern Command of the Chinese Navy. Ship models and paintings of ships at sea charging through the water all projected an image of power. A large map of the world covered one entire wall—not like the detailed maps in the room down the hall, but one he could still use to envision his ships expanding the influence of the Chinese Navy. There were 250,000 members of the People's Liberation Army Navy, and the bulk of the navy was currently under his command.

Fang Li favored the new shortened name, Chinese Navy. In recent years, the navy had received priority funding over the army, and the trend would continue. Fang Li knew if this mission was successful, his ultimate goal, far beyond the Chinese Navy, would be within his grasp. For some time, he had had his eye on the office of minister of defense, and with the importance of the oil and gas reserves in the South China Sea, he was one step closer to his objective.

He looked to the stack of reports from various ships under his command. The one of most interest was from the captain of the destroyer guarding the Taiping Island oil production area. The Vietnamese navy had made their first approach toward his warships and their protected oil vessels. The captain reported he had taken preventive action and had fired on the Vietnamese patrol vessel and forced it out of the area.

Fang Li was pleased with this officer's response to the enemy patrol boat. He wanted officers who were not afraid to take the initiative and enlarge their area of command. Fang Li had always been the first to react when he faced the enemy.

From the report, he could deduce that at the first sign of danger from one of his warships, the Vietnamese had turned tail and run for their homeport. He was secretly hoping to see the aircraft of the *Liaoning* involved in some interaction with the warships from the other nations claiming territorial rights in the South China Sea. What was the purpose of maintaining these warships and their weapons if they were never used?

A firm knock on his door interrupted his thoughts, and he gave permission for the intruder to enter. It was his chief of staff, Vice Admiral Deshi Yang, who opened the door and walked to Fang Li's desk.

"Sir, here is the information on next week's summit meeting with ASEAN. You are scheduled to fly into Bandar Seri Begawan on Tuesday, the seventeenth, and meet with the leaders for the ASEAN Plus Three conference the next day. There is to be a reception the evening before."

Fang Li grunted at the stupidity of the ASEAN summit. As the commanding officer of the Southern Command, he was responsible for representing China to this organization of the countries surrounding the South China Sea. The "PLUS Three" conference meeting included China, Japan, and South Korea. These three nations were not member nations of ASEAN but were referred to as "dialogue partners."

Fang Li grunted again. "To waste my valuable time with these worthless meetings. They will use the opportunity to issue their complaints against our mission, and I'll have to pretend I'm concerned and try to placate them."

Admiral Yang was in full agreement with his commanding officer. "It's too bad you can't sail into Brunei Bay on one of our Type 052D destroyers. The sight of our newest destroyer might make them think twice before they complain about our expanded presence in the South China Sea."

Fang Li laughed at the idea. "Yes, it would be an impressive display of our superior military power." He was going to set aside the papers with the agenda for the ASEAN summit but then brought the papers back to the center of his desk. A new idea had formed in his mind.

He looked up at his assistant. "Will the *Liaoning* be on station by next week when I am due to fly down to Bander Seri?" He used the shortened name for the capital city of Brunei.

Deshi Yang looked at the wall map and then out the window behind his admiral to put the map of the South China Sea into his mind and picture the location of the aircraft carrier by next week. "Yes, Admiral. It should arrive twenty-four to thirty-six hours before you would need to leave."

Fang Li leaned his body back into the heavily padded swivel

chair. He thought about the plan forming in his mind. Maybe there was a way to impress these people.

As he looked up at Admiral Yang, a large smile was forming on his face. "I was planning to fly out to the *Liaoning* next week until you reminded me of this damn meeting. Now I will have to fly to Brunei instead."

He got up from his desk and walked to the window. He stood there for a few moments to finalize the plan still forming in his mind. He turned around to face his chief of staff. "I think as the commanding officer of the Southern Command, I need a military escort to fly with my command plane. I want two armed fighters from the *Liaoning* to rendezvous with my plane on the southern flight down to Bander Seri and continue with us. They will land after my plane and remain at the airport until I am ready to leave. I will then take one of the fighters to transport me to the *Liaoning* for my inspection of the carrier. I think the sight of two armed fighter jets from the only aircraft carrier in the entire region will make a very suitable impression on our friends from ASEAN. Yes, let them watch me bring in two armed fighters and then complain about our new role in the South China Sea."

Chapter 33

Brunei! The smallest member nation of ASEAN was the host for this year's summit. The Southeast Asian country, divided into two landmasses, found itself bordered by Indonesia to the south and on three sides by the South China Sea. The total land mass was almost 5300 square kilometers and slightly smaller than the state of Delaware.

The government of Brunei is a constitutional sultanate called the Malay Islamic Monarchy, ruled by one man with the title of sultan and prime minister. The sultan's family has ruled Brunei for over six hundred years. To help in that endeavor, the sultan appoints a council of ministers to deal with executive business. He also appoints a religious council, which advises him on spiritual matters. There is a privy council dealing with constitutional matters and a council of succession to determine who should succeed the throne when the need arises.

The sultan's influence peaked between the fifteenth and seventeenth centuries when his control had extended to northwest Borneo and east to the southern Philippines. Internal fraction over royal succession, colonial expansion by European powers, and piracy contributed to a period of decline. In 1888, Brunei became a protectorate of the British Empire and finally received its independence in 1984.

Brunei has a population near 410,000 people, consisting of a variety of ethnic groups with the largest being Malay at 66 percent followed by Chinese at 11.2 percent, followed with the indigenous people composing only 3.4 percent. The balance is a hodgepodge of various people who have integrated into the Brunei society. Because of the country's abundant petroleum and natural gas fields, the Bruneians enjoy one of the highest per capita GDPs in Asia.

The capitol of Brunei, Bandar Seri Begawan, is located on both sides of the Sungai Brunei River, which allows access to the South China Sea by way of Brunei Bay. Over twenty-two thousand people live in the city with a quarter of the country's population settled in modern housing developments north of the city. Until 1970, the city was simply know at Brunei Town. Today BSB, the "Town of the Seri Bagawan," takes its name after Sultan Omar Ali Saifuddien, who took the title of Seri Bagawan after he abdicated his seat of power in favor of his son in 1967.

Any first-time visitor to BSB can't avoid being impressed with the modern buildings, including the twin malls of the Yayasan Sultan Haji Hass and Bolkiah shopping complex and the magnificent Omar Ali Saifuddien mosque, which is the dominant building seen from almost any location in BSB.

The balcony connected to the guest room of the Empire Hotel and Country Club provided United States Senator Randy Fisher an unobstructed view of the South China Sea. He looked out toward the brilliant-blue waters while thinking that all the tension in the area was due to the abundant reserves of oil and gas under its surface.

Randy had made the trip from Washington DC over a period of several days. On Friday morning, he had taken a flight from Regan National to New York City. From there, the plane flew fourteen and one-half hours to Seoul, South Korea, where he spent the evening with James Carmichael, US ambassador to South Korea, and Lieutenant General Lyle Sherman, the commanding officer of the US Eighth Army.

The next day, local military authorities provided a private tour of certain US military installations, including Camp Boniface in the DMZ (demilitarized zone). There, on a raised platform, he was able to look into North Korea and see for the first time one of the darkest countries on the Earth. Very little information passed the exterior borders of the small Communist country, except it seemed to spend a very high percentage of the national budget planning for war with their neighbor to the south. Even their protector, China, grew weary of the saber rattling from their little neighbor.

The number of troops wanting to meet him and shake his hand surprised Randy. He mentioned this to his guide to the forward defense position, General Hollis McCormick. The officer smiled at him. "Senator, the troops don't often meet a real hero from Washington. Just politicians. We might be thousands of miles away from home, but we all know you took a bullet and saved our country several years ago. That makes you very special in their eyes. We are here to prevent another Korean War, which is very possible considering the constant tension between the North and South. These young men and women know the call to arms might come at any moment and they might have to pick up a weapon to defend this country. You have already proven you are willing to risk your life to protect our country. They want to let you know that you're really one of them."

Randy had felt the general's words deeply. It had been years since he had worn the uniform and felt the pride of belonging to the best military force in the world. He vowed to remember the importance of the individual men and women who worked every day to protect their country. Too many people back in Washington said the words but sometimes forgot the meaning.

On Monday, March 16, he took an early flight on Asian Air to Manila in the Philippines and arrived at the Manila Ninoy Aquino International Airport. The airport handled over twenty-five million passengers every year, making it one of the busiest in the Philippines.

The airport was named in honor of Benigno "Ninoy" Aquino Jr., who was assassinated on August 21, 1983, after returning to the Philippines from his self-imposed exile in the United States. His premature death prompted his wife, Corazon Aquino, to run for president of the Philippines, an office she held from February 1986 to June 1992. On August 1, 2009, she succumbed to colon cancer.

After he quickly passed through the airport arrival procedures, a small contingent from the Philippine government met Randy and whisked him off to the Malacanang Palace on the Pasiq River, the official home to the Philippine president. The Pasiq River flows northwest to southwest and connects Laquna de Bay to Manila Bay. Most of Metro Manila lies along the banks of the river.

Isko Bello met Randy at the Malacanang Palace. Bello had

returned from the United States to act as one of his two hosts at the ASEAN summit. Vietnamese Ambassador An Nguyen would be the other one and would meet them at the hotel in Bandar Seri Begawan.

Bello walked Randy into a small dining room for lunch with a table set for three people. From another doorway, the president of the Philippines entered, and Bello made the introductions.

"Senator Fisher, may I present the Most Honorable Bayani Limbaco, the president of the Philippines. Mr. President, this is United States Senator Randal Fisher representing the state of South Carolina."

Randy smiled and shook hands with the Philippine President. Limbaco was nearing sixty-two years of age. His height of five feet six inches was about an inch and a half above the average for the Philippine people. He still sported a thick head of salt-and-pepper hair, and the smile on his face seemed genuine.

"Thank you for this invitation and for allowing me to accompany you to the ASEAN summit," Randy said as he looked down at the shorter man.

President Limbaco smiled and indicated for Randy to take a seat at the dinner table. "It is our pleasure to have such a distinguished visitor here in Manila. We cannot remember when an American citizen has risen through your political system so quickly and earned the respect of your compatriots and other countries throughout the world. No government official who must deal with the threat by terrorism can over appreciate your action. Even in the Philippines, I must always be concerned with the terrorist elements in our country."

Isko Bello now entered the conversation. "Today, we are faced with an old threat once again raising its ugly head. The expansion by China into the South China Sea is a threat no nation in this area can ignore. As founding members of ASEAN, we work together to avoid territorial disputes between our fellow member nations, but China sits alone. They are expanding their influence into the South China Sea hundreds of miles beyond their land borders and the international twelve-mile limit. Even if you accepted the two-hundred-mile limit some countries try to impose, they are well beyond those limits in the South China Sea. Here, they are claiming territory right up to our twelve-mile limit."

A side door opened, and a man dressed in white cooking attire entered, pushing a stainless-steel serving cart. Stacked on the cart were three covered hot serving dishes containing their lunch, and the waiter requested permission of the president to serve their meal.

A few minutes later, Randy and the two Philippine government officials were again alone. President Limbaco picked up the conversational thread. "China is expanding its influence in all areas of Asia. Their campaign to modernize and build a large naval force has allowed them to spread well beyond their borders. They are in the Sea of Okhotsk east of Russia and further east toward your Aleutian Islands. Now, they are pressing further south into the South China Sea and even more south into the Solomon Islands."

Randy had been silent for the entire time since the three had sat down for lunch. "When the United States pulled its navy and other military forces out of Southeast Asia, that eliminated any counterforce to China's expansion. Once the Soviet Union was no longer a threat, the Chinese could redirect defense resources from the northern area toward South East Asia and their expansion program. Their thirst for energy and other natural resources has forced them to look toward the ASEAN member nations."

Randy did not bring up the fact that the current US military presence in Southeast Asia was at the insistence of countries like the Philippines. For many years, the US Seventh Fleet, based at Subic Bay, was the second most active facility next to the US Air Force base at Clark Field in the Philippines. Together, these two US military installations were the largest American facilities outside the United States. When the US military left, there was nothing to slow the growth of any foreign power with a larger military strength than that of the Philippine military or any other nation member of ASEAN. Now, the results of the decision by the Philippine Government and other ASEAN member nations were coming back to haunt them.

President Limbaco seemed to be reading Randy's thoughts. "It was our decision to ask the United States to turn over their military installation to us and pull their forces out of our country. Over the years, Japan has been just as insistent for a reduced US military presence, and they, too, are facing the same threat from the Chinese government."

Ambassador Bello looked to Randy. "If we are going to check the advance of China into the South China Sea and other parts of Southeast Asia, then we're going to need the assistance of the United States. Your position on the Senate Armed Forces Committee is important, and it is why we wanted you to attend the ASEAN summit. You'll meet the leaders of the member nations and their defense ministers."

President Limbaco laid his hand on Randy's arm. "You will also meet the other two representatives from the ASEAN Plus Three group. China, Japan, and South Korea will be there. Japan and South Korea will side with us and against China in these discussions."

He removed his hand but kept his eyes focused on Randy's face. "From all of these leaders, you will hear their concerns about China. It will be the prevailing topic of discussion in the public meetings and in their private conversions that you will be a party to."

Isko Bello added his own words of advice. "You've got to pay close attention to everything that's said during the next few days. Please listen closely to the Chinese government representative. You might be surprised our old friend Admiral Fang Li will be representing the Chinese People's Government during the summit. It's the first time he has attended the summit as the senior Chinese delegate and the first time a military officer is representing China in lieu of a member of their civilian government."

Now, a day later, Randy was looking at the view of the South China Sea. He could not see the modern Brunei International Airport but knew it to be off to his right. He had arrived this morning with the Philippine delegation including President Limbaco and Ambassador Bello.

After his check-in at the Empire Hotel, he had lunch with Ambassador An Nguyen and Vietnamese President Tran Van Huong. The forty-nine-year-old president was a slender man at five feet seven inches. He was dressed in a navy-blue business suit and welcomed the senator to his three-room suite for their private luncheon. This was only the second Vietnamese person Randy had ever met. The two previous times he had met An Nguyen, the meeting had been at the Philippine Embassy in Washington. He could not stop from playing the old news clips from the Vietnam War within his mind. The two men he had dine with did not reflect the dress and character of the Vietnamese soldiers and citizens in their loose-fitting shirts and pants. Along with his ambassador, President Van Huong repeated most of the same warnings Randy had received from the Filipinos yesterday at lunch in Manila. To those, they added the latest developments from the reports obtained from their navy and the gunfire from the Chinese destroyer near Taiping Island.

An Nguyen went on to explain the complexities of the largest island in the Spratly Island chain. "The island is administered by the Republic of China (Taiwan), and the Taiping Island Airport has a four-thousand-foot-long runway. There's a regular flight of C-130 transport planes providing the food and other materials the inhabitants require.

Vietnam occupies the island, but China and the Philippines also claim ownership. This was the first of the new drilling operations the Chinese have started and the first to be protected by Chinese warships."

Randy was silent for a moment as he digested this new information. He looked at the Vietnamese president and spoke carefully so as to avoid showing any disrespect to the leader. "With the tensions running so high in the South China Sea, do you think it is wise to have your patrol boats running a simulated attack against the Chinese warships? The slightest miscalculation could precipitate a major military conflict between your two countries."

The Vietnamese president spoke softly back to Randy. "I was but a very young man when the war ended between our two countries. The combined loss between the North and South was nearly two million Vietnamese people. We do not risk conflict with China recklessly, but we must not allow them to further their expansion efforts. They will consume all of the natural resources available in the South China Sea, starve us into submission, and force their way upon my country.

"If we allow that to happen, who will be next? Laos? Cambodia? Thailand? These countries have land routes connected to the Chinese mainland and are dependent on the free passage through the South China Sea. You already know a very large portion of the world's shipping passes through our part of the world. How soon will China put restrictions on other countries unless we face them now?"

An Nguyen now spoke up. "This evening's reception and dinner will be for the leaders and other representatives of the ASEAN member nations. You will be there as our guest, but tomorrow morning, we have a breakfast meeting scheduled and you will meet with our fleet commander, Admiral Binh Huy Pham. You will learn that he is most aware of the risk involved with the close-up action of our navy with the Chinese naval forces. He'll be able to provide a very clear picture of the most current event."

Randy had about three hours until the evening's dinner. After his lunch with the Vietnamese president and their US ambassador, he had taken some time to see parts of the city. He was impressed with the beauty of the modern buildings. The valuable income from Brunei's gas and oil production provided the necessary funds to construct the new buildings and homes for the people. He knew from some of his reading that the Brunei River still received untreated sewage from the capital city. For the continued construction of the required infrastructure in Brunei, the funds from the oil and gas reserves must continue.

He noticed the Brunei flag hoisted from the poll on the grounds of the hotel. The yellow flag contained two diagonal bands. The top one was white, and a black band was below. They started on the high hoist side of the flag and ran to the lower opposite corner. The red national emblem lay superimposed at the center. The flag was moving from the warm breeze off the South China Sea. As he continued to watch the flag fluttering in the breeze, he heard from overhead the sound of aircraft. He turned to see what type of plane was making the high-pitched noise, which was different from the low rumbling sound of a standard passenger jet. Suddenly, two fighter jets appeared from the backside of the hotel. They were low enough for Randy to make out the missiles attached to the weapon pods under the wings of the jets. He could easily see the painted flag of the People's Liberation Army Navy on the fuselage of the jets.

The jets were flying side by side but suddenly spilt apart and each altered its flight path to both port and starboard as they gained altitude and circled away from the airport. Then Randy heard the deeper sound of a heavier and slower moving aircraft. Turning back to look toward the hotel roof above his head, he saw a Chinese military jet transport appear from over the hotel. It moved quickly past the hotel and on toward the BSB airport where Randy had landed earlier. He was able to make out the same flag that was on the fighter jets painted on the transport jet.

It appeared Admiral Fang Li had arrived, and he wanted to make an impression on everyone in attendance at the ASEAN summit. Randy shook his head as the transport jet slipped down below the surrounding buildings and from his sight. Fang Li had made an impression on the young senator. It was not one of Chinese naval or airpower though; it was the recklessness of the admiral having two fully armed fighter jets fly demonstration patterns over the populated capital city of Brunei. This was a dangerous man—not because he commanded a large naval fleet, but because he would risk portions of it simply for show.

Chapter 34

The evening reception was held in an open-air courtyard, and dinner took place in the grandest public room the Empire Hotel could provide. The hotel featured an eighteen-hole golf course surrounded by scenic landscaping and lagoon pools and was built next to the world's oldest rainforest in Borneo. Tennis courts, bowling alleys, exercise rooms, and other sport activities were available for the hotel guests. After all their physical activities, guests can opt for a sauna, spend their money at the shopping arcade, or use the private cinema for additional entertainment.

For food, the Empire Hotel offers seven dining options from a casual setting to the most elegant restaurants. The outside venue, for tonight's reception, provided a magnificent view of the waves coming in from the South China Sea. The patio area was large enough to hold the entire assembly and still allow ample room for small groups to meet and discuss the events most pressing on their minds. Some had brought their wives or husbands with them, and their presence was to help keep the atmosphere low-key. The patio area was of stone construction with a railing around the balcony overlooking the bay. There were two groups of ten flags located on each end of the patio area arranged in alphabetical order of the countries. These were moving softly in the warm and gentle breeze off the water.

Randy was thankful for Annie's insistence he purchase a custom-made evening dinner jacket and pants for such an occasion. The rays from the setting sun highlighted the outdoor patio. Along with the men and women wearing their countries' traditional dress, gowns of many different colors all added to the evening's atmosphere. It was to be a celebration, but Randy could hear snippets of conversations and the appearance of two Chinese fighter jets was dominating the talk among the attendees. Some were urging that a formal protest be made against the Chinese for the dangerous stunt using armed fighter jets.

Isko Bello and An Nguyen approached Randy together, escorted him around the reception area, and made introductions. To all, he was a new person, but everyone knew of his history with a terrorist and a nuclear device coming close to almost destroying a large portion of the Mid-Atlantic area of his country. Some of the guests simply wanted to question him about October 17, and others wanted to know more about what his thoughts were now.

For his part, Randy attempted to turn the conversation away from himself and asked questions about the member nations of ASEAN. How did they view China's recent movements further into the SCS? Were their governments in any discussions with China? The answers to these questions were the reason he had traveled thousands of miles to come to the summit. To learn!

The reception was to start at 7:00, conclude at 8:00, and then move into the connected dining room. When it was apparent almost all the representatives had arrived, the last invited guest chose to make his entry.

Chinese Admiral Fang Li, commander of the Chinese Navy Southern Command, walked into the patio area. He was in the company of three officers outfitted in their dress uniforms of a white open-neck coat with picked lapels and square laps. Their long gray pants came down over black shoes. The two men and one woman wore white shirts and black ties. They removed their uniform peaked caps of white with a black band at the base and placed them under their right arms.

Admiral Fang Li was not in his navy's dress uniform. Rather, he was wearing a typical spring/autumn uniform for daily use. It was all gray for the navy with the same peaked cap worn by his subordinates. He had yet to remove his hat as he stood just inside the patio entrance to allow everyone to witness his arrival. Finally, he put an overly large smile on his face as he removed his cap and stepped forward to meet the other guests.

The volume of the conversation had noticeably diminished with Fang Li's entrance, so he received the attention he desired. China was to be the center of the discussions for the next few days, and he was to be the center of his delegation.

He moved around the patio shaking hands with the various leaders and their military aides. His own officers made sure that he had a full glass of champagne and that no one could approach the admiral without his permission.

Most of the delegates spoke with Fang Li until he reach Randy, who was still with Ambassadors Bello and Nguyen. Bello offered his greeting to Admiral Li, but Nguyen remained silent. Fang Li looked down at the smaller Vietnamese delegate.

"Good evening, Ambassador Nguyen. We have not seen each other since our meeting in Washington. I hope you are still not harboring any hard feelings against me for my intrusion on your party."

When Nguyen failed to respond Isko Bello introduced his guest. "Admiral Li, I do not think you have met Senator Randal Fisher from the United States. He is here as our guest to the ASEAN summit."

Fang Li's attention remained on Nguyen several more seconds before shifting his view to the American to his right. He had to look up slightly to the taller and younger man.

"So the Americans are back in Southeast Asia," he said in near-perfect English. "We have not seen very much of the US Navy since you were forced to pull your warships back to Pearl Harbor and Japan after the Philippine government ordered them out of their waters."

Randy smiled politely at the Chinese admiral. "Oh, we still break the waves in the South China Sea from time to time. When you have a world-class navy capable of sailing all the oceans, some people might mistakenly think we are not able to project our naval power back here in this part of the world."

Fang Li looked at the younger man. The American had not fallen for his little insult, so he would ignore the same jab from the US senator. Instead, he opted to speak to the man as an equal.

"I think you understand the Chinese Navy a little better than most politicians I meet. We each need our massive navies to protect ourselves from aggression."

Randy looked back at the admiral. He knew the other people standing within hearing distance were waiting for his reply. "I like to think we use our navy to prevent aggression against countries that do not have the ability to completely defend themselves."

Fang Li continued to show his smile. "So, you are still the policeman of the world. Perhaps your nightstick is not quite as capable against the more modern weapons the world must face today?"

Randy let a little laugh escape his lips. "I'm a former policeman myself. I would never underestimate the experience of an old beat cop walking the streets of his neighborhood. Many criminals are behind prison bars who thought they were smarter than the old cop."

Chapter 35

Bandar Seri Begawan
Tuesday, March 17, 2015
8:00 p.m. (CST)

The Empire Hotel had selected their best dining room for the leaders of the ASEAN group. Randy joined the other diplomats as they walked into the huge facility from the outdoor reception area. The room had fifty-foot ceilings with the interior surface painted an antique white. The outside wall, next to the reception area and the two end walls, were floor-to-ceiling glass windows. In the center of the room were four sets of four columns arranged in a large square. The columns had golden bands at various heights until the halfway mark. At that point, each of the four columns had a rectangular box with clusters of lights on all four sides to illuminate the room. Above the light fixtures, the columns were all white. The placement of the columns and the arrangements of the tables and chairs provided a sectional look to the space even though the floor plan allowed easy movement around the room.

There were two large round tables within the four columns. In each of the four corners outside the center columns were two more matching tables. Each table had place settings for eight people, and the head maître d' and his staff used their skills to help the leaders of the ASEAN countries find their proper chairs. To Randy's surprise, he found himself at the same table as Admiral Li. It appeared he would be subject to the admiral's wisdom for the entire evening.

The meal arrived by way of white-suited waiters, and the food was excellent. Randy noticed some guests received a red meat and others a fish. Somebody in the kitchen had researched their guests' various preferences and religious beliefs very well.

Throughout the evening, Admiral Fang Li regaled his table companions with stories from his youth and when he was a young officer serving on his first Chinese warship. He dominated the conversation sometimes by answering his own questions. In every story, he was the hero or the person who needed to correct an officer of higher rank. Occasionally, other guests tried to start a conversation with the person sitting next to them, but Fang Li would notice and ask them a question or make a comment about their country to pull them back into his conversation.

Randy Fisher sat quietly through the dinner, watching and listening to the Chinese commander for their Southern Command. He watched as the admiral showed arrogance and poor manners. He planned to avoid participating in the man's conversation until Fang Li seemed to realize the younger American had been silent during most of the meal.

He trained his next comment and questions toward Randy Fisher. "My young American friend, I seem to remember from my reading of your heroic efforts from several years ago that you earned a history degree similar to your mother. Certainly, you must have studied your famous naval victory at Midway Island during the Second World War. No doubt, the value of the aircraft carrier was never more obvious. Neither side brought their warships within sight of the enemy. Neither side was able to bring the huge guns of their battleships against the enemy. Truly, it was an amazing day for your carrier fleet."

Randy nodded in agreement. Others at the table were awaiting his reply. "It was a great victory for all American Naval forces, both those at sea and the staff personnel at Pearl Harbor and Washington."

For the first time since the start of the dinner, Fang Li did not know where the conversation was heading. "What did your people at Pearl Harbor do? Land-based personnel do not fight sea battles on aircraft carriers."

Randy shook his head. "Victory is not won by one man alone or even an aircraft carrier. The American fleet at Midway consisted of three aircraft carriers: *Enterprise, Yorktown,* and the *Hornet.* The *Yorktown* had sustained heavy damage at the Battle of the Coral Sea just four weeks before Midway. The ship's captain notified Pearl

Harbor by coded message the ship's engineer's damage assessment. The *Yorktown* would need four to six weeks in dry dock for repairs before being able to return to sea duty, perhaps even sent back to the mainland for repairs beyond what the specialists at Pearl could provide.

"Instead, Nimitz ordered the damage repair specialists at Pearl Harbor to work around the clock for seventy-two hours, and *Yorktown* put out to sea to join up with *Enterprise* and *Hornet*. That increased the attacking force at Midway by fifty percent against the enemy."

Randy was just warming up, as he looked Admiral Fang Li in the face. Maybe his history degree would be of some help. "Then there was the invaluable assistance of Commander Joe Rochefort and his twenty-five code-breakers at Pearl Harbor and the naval intelligence division in Washington. Some of them were ordinary enlisted men, and they were able to break the Japanese naval code. Without them, Admirals Fletcher and Spruance might not have been in the perfect location to intercept the Japanese carriers and take a far superior force by surprise."

Randy paused for a moment. "Admiral, it takes more than guns and ships to win battles. The Japanese were overconfident with their superior naval force before Midway, and they never were able to recover from their loss at that battle. After their four carriers were sunk, over two hundred of their most experienced pilots were lost at sea because their flight decks were lying on the bottom of the Pacific Ocean."

Chinese Southern Commander Admiral Fang Li had no reply to the young and insolent American. Luckily, the other table guests, bored by the admiral's dominating and boorish manners would not hear any more words of wisdom from the Chinese officer. One of his staff officers approached the table and whispered a few words into his ear. Without offering a reason to excuse his sudden departure, the Chinese admiral rose from his seat and left the dining room with the officer.

Some of the other table guests breathed a sigh of relief. All of them were experienced diplomats and trained to display proper manners at all times, even when faced with such a boor as Admiral Fang Li.

The president of Cambodia looked at Randy. "I'm afraid our admiral will not listen to the advice coded within your words."

The Philippines chief of naval operations was sitting two chairs to Randy's left. "I must agree with the president. I don't believe I have any commanding officer who would have promoted that *gentleman* beyond mess boy."

The table filled with laughter for the first time since the dinner had begun. For the balance of the evening, the conversation turned to more pleasant topics.

Chapter 36

Bandar Seri Begawan
Tuesday, March 17, 2015
11:45 p.m. (CST)

Randy heard the ringing of the phone he was calling. Finally, the connection completed, and he heard the most beautiful voice in the world say his name.

"Randy, is that you?"

"It's me, Annie." He could hear a lot of confusing noise in the background. "Where are you? I can hardly hear you."

Annie Fisher looked at her lunch companion and mouthed the words, "It's Randy. I'll be right back." She got up from the restaurant table and walked out to the reception area where the noise level was much lower.

"Is that better?" Not waiting for his reply, she went on, "I'm glad you called. Our bed is too big with me alone, and I miss your feet to keep my toes warm."

Randy laughed as her voice came in loud and clear through the Blackberry Marion Bellwood had given him. "We need to plan on a vacation out here next year at this time. The temperature is in the low eighties here at midnight. How are you? I miss you like you can't believe."

Annie laughed back in response. "I'm okay. You'll never guess who I'm having lunch with." Annie did not wait for Randy to answer. "Eleanor Diamond called me up yesterday and wanted us to get together. We're over at National Harbor where we had our first date."

Randy smiled back into the phone. "You're at McLoone's by the river?"

"Yes," Annie replied. "She came with her Secret Service detail to pick me up at the apartment. I happened to mentioned I rode over on the ferry to meet you the first time so she said that is what she wanted to do today. I thought the senior Secret Service agent was going to have a stroke. He told her it would be too risky. Eleanor asked him if he could swim, and he never said another word." They both laughed as Annie finished her story.

"Boy, do I miss you," she continued. "How are your meetings?"

Randy knew he could not discuss anything he'd heard at the meetings over the phone, and he did not call his wife to talk work. "They're interesting. So what else is happening back there?"

"Just more work. We got two more projects in this week. If we keep getting more projects, they're going to have to hire another electrical engineer."

Randy knew the workload must be heavy for Annie to admit she needed help. She loved her job and worked more than sixty hours per week. Luckily, most of the time was at their apartment.

"When are you coming home?" Annie's question brought Randy's mind back to the moment.

"I'm not sure yet. The main summit meeting is starting tomorrow. I'll have to let you know."

"Okay. Listen, I had better go. I love to hear your voice, but I had better not keep the second lady of the United States waiting. She might eat my dessert." Then she whispered into the phone, "Do they call her SLOTUS like they call the First Lady FLOTUS?"

Randy laughed again. "I don't know, but I'll bet she'll tell you if you ask. I'll talk to you again tomorrow."

Chapter 37

Vietnamese Captain Cam De Ho of the *Da Nang*, a Lada-class submarine, was drinking a cup of hot tea this morning as he made his way through his command. He started every day with a walk-through of the submarine.

The Lada-class warship was the newest Russian-built diesel-electric submarine designed to replace the aging Kilo-class submarine that the Russians produced for many years. The first Lada-class vessels began sea trials in 2005, but the Russian navy determined the vessel had flaws in the propulsion system and considered pulling the plug on the program. By mid-July of 2012, the designers had worked out the flaws and production resumed. Vietnam placed orders for four of the submarines, and Hull 229, the *Da Nang*, arrived in the fall of 2014. Hulls 231, 232, and 233 followed in early 2015. The ships' names came from major cities in the Communist country, *Ha Noi, Hai Phong*, and *Khonh Hoa*.

Da Nang was the first submarine Cam De commanded as captain. His first sea duties were on surface ships, but he always dreamed of commanding a submarine. With the support of his commanding officer, his request for underwater warfare service came through, and he returned to the Vietnam Naval Academy at Nha Trang for three years of training. After the training was completed, he served on two Kilo-class submarines. His first assignment was as an engineering officer for eighteen months, and then he did a two-year tour as an executive officer.

His life's ambition reached fulfillment with his assignment as captain to the first Lada-class submarine to arrive at Hai Phong. Admiral Binh Huy Pham had pinned the new epaulets on his shoulder boards when he had received his orders for command.

For years, the Russian-built Kilo-class submarine was the stock vessel used mostly by China, Vietnam, and certain other countries aligned with the old Soviet Union. The Kilo class had gone through many upgrades and models, but now the Lada class was its replacement.

With a crew of thirty-eight highly trained sailors, the seventy-two-meter submarine displaced 2,700 tons when submerged. Its two diesel air independent propulsion (AIP) systems produced power for a surface speed of ten knots, but the top speed doubled when submerged. It would slide through the water on a single shaft with a seven-blade propeller. Cam De Ho had taken the *Da Nang* on her sea trials and confirmed the manufacturer's claim of a forty-five-day submerged endurance performance and a depth of three hundred meters.

The Lada featured a new anti-sonar coating for the hull, resulting in a low acoustic signature and sophisticated sonar equipment with bow and flank arrays along with the towed sonar array. The submarine was faster and quieter than the older Kilo submarines.

De Ho entered the forward torpedo room. They still referred to the weapons rooms as the "torpedo room," but the Lada carried a combination of eighteen torpedoes and antisubmarine or anti-ship missiles. He found his weapons officer supervising a weapons crew working to ensure one of the torpedoes was properly tuned and ready for deployment.

With his morning inspection completed, De Ho returned to the control room to check their location. Together with *Ha Noi*, a sister Lada-class submarine, they had been shadowing the Chinese aircraft carrier for three days. Captain Cam De Ho was the senior officer and in overall command of the two navy warships.

They had sailed from the Vietnamese Naval Base at Da Nang and traveled southeast into the South China Sea. Vietnamese navy search planes had maintained track of the carrier group as it sailed south from Zhanjiang, China, and provided updated location reports to fleet headquarters. They continued to relay the information to De Ho. The reports informed De Ho the carrier was with a screen of three destroyers and a tanker ship for refueling.

When the carrier group entered the waters near the Mischief Islands, it reduced speed and began to sail in a roughly rectangular box with the southwest point about fifty miles from Taiping Island to their southwest and the northernmost point about two hundred miles from the Scarborough Reef to the northeast. It appeared the carrier was taking station to create a circle of protection to include all the new drill sites.

When the two Lada submarines arrived in the same area as the carrier, he had ordered the *Ha Noi* to take station on the port side of the carrier and brought the *Da Nang* to a position on the starboard side. Both submarines were maintaining a five-thousand-yard distance from the carrier. With the carrier's speed reduced to fifteen knots to conserve fuel, his subs were able to maintain their positions.

The control room was quiet when Captain De Ho entered the command space. He went first to the chart table where his executive officer, Lieutenant Le Van Hoach, was updating their position.

Van Hoach looked up from the map and smiled at his captain and friend of many years. "Good morning, Captain. How did you find the ship this morning during your tour?"

De Ho slapped his friend on the back. "It was in perfect condition, my friend. I would not have expected anything else from the best executive officer in the fleet."

De Ho took a moment to look around the control room and then settled his eyes on the map. "So where is our friend this morning?"

Van Hoach moved a half step to his right to allow the captain a better view of the map. The new submarine had a beam of only seven meters, and space was always a premium. "The carrier is nearing the end of its northeast limit of travel if it is to remain in the established pattern. We should see them altering their course in about fifteen minutes for their run to the northwest unless their captain decides to think outside of the box." Van Hoach made the last comment with a full grin on his face.

De Ho looked over the map to fix the positions in his mind. "Yes.

Our friend seems to lack any imagination. They just keep sailing the same pattern. Where are Captain Cam Le and the *Ha Noi*?"

Van Hoach moved his marking pen over the map to the port side of the carrier. "The *Ha Noi* is here. He has decreased his distance from the carrier to 3,500 yards. I didn't see an order in the log book where you authorized the change in distance."

De Ho did not say anything in response to Van Hoach's unasked question. Captain Cam Le was five years junior to Cam De Ho and two years behind Van Hoach in service time. De Ho would not publicly say that Cam Le had used his family's political connection to get command of the Lada submarine before other more qualified officers. On this current mission, De Ho would be more comfortable having Van Hoach in command of the *Ha Noi*, but such a call had not been his to make.

De Ho glanced at his wristwatch from habit, even though he knew the time. "It's too late to surface and radio for him to back off to the five-thousand-yard position. As we get close to dusk, we will maneuver our ship over toward his and try to contact him with the underwater telephones."

De Ho started to move away from the chart table but stopped and turned back to his XO. He had a little grin on his face. "Please record in the log the current time and our position and indicate the *Ha Noi* is out of position against orders. Let's see how the little bastard responds to the official record after we return to port."

Chapter 38

Mischief Reef
Wednesday, March 18, 2015
9:30 a.m. (CST)

Military organizations and private enterprises the world over experience the same problems with their personnel and promotions. It is not always what you know but whom you know that allows people with less experience and fewer qualifications to get the better jobs. For Vietnamese Captain De Ho, it resulted in Cam Le's promotion to the new Lada class submarine over the executive officer of his own ship. The Chinese Navy had similar problems within its organizational structure.

Commodore Jin Wang was the commanding officer of the Chinese aircraft carrier *Liaoning*, and his appointment had come about from his uncle's powerful position on the Chinese Central Committee. The forty-two-year-old commodore had commanded a destroyer prior to taking command of the *Liaoning* but had no flight experience, nor had he ever before been in command of a flotilla.

The man designated to be the commanding officer of China's newest warship had spent the last ten years of his career involved in the rebuilding of the carrier only to die from lung cancer before the sea trials were completed. Jin Wang had known of the officer's terminal condition long before death actually claimed the officer's life and had secretly started his campaign to capture the coveted position. Quiet conversations in dark rooms and promises exchanged between political players within the Central Committees in Beijing had resulted in his promotion and assignment to *Liaoning* as its senior commanding officer.

Finally, now as the commodore of the pride of the Chinese Navy, Jin Wang was where he wanted to be in this step of his career. From here, he could easily move up to admiral and command of one of China's three naval fleets. He was young enough to see himself in the fleet admiral's office, and from there, the defense ministry. He had ambition and family connections, and now this new assignment to protect China's expansion into the South China Sea would make future promotions come easily.

Jin Wang had breakfast in his personal three-room cabin. He had spent a considerable sum of the ship's funds to improve the living conditions of his quarters here on *Liaoning* and enjoyed the privacy the luxury space provided. Even on an aircraft carrier the size of *Liaoning*, space was still a premium. The higher the rank, the more individual space a person could have. He had also renovated his day cabin located just off the bridge. Jin Wang had decided a few creature comforts would help offset the smaller cabin's space.

Jin Wang glanced at the wall clock and decided it was time to make an appearance on the bridge. He rose from his desk and stopped to look at himself in the full-length mirror attached to the inside of his cabin door. At five feet ten inches and 155 pounds and dressed in a custom-tailored uniform, he was the perfect picture of a naval officer. He had considered offering himself to the Sub-Ministry for Naval Personnel as a candidate for the cover of their recruitment brochure. He smiled at the reflection in the mirror but decided that he would be pushing the envelope too far. Too bad, it was a great idea.

He left his cabin and made his way toward the bridge. Every sailor he met offered the proper salute and stepped aside to allow him easy passage. He reached the bridge, and all naval personnel not assigned to a task requiring their constant attention snapped their bodies to attention. Jin Wang ordered them to resume their duties and then began his survey of the bridge.

The bridge on the Chinese carrier was smaller in comparison to an American Nimitz class carrier but well organized to allow each sailor to work efficiently without interfering with the one in the next position. Round and evenly spaced, the windows in front of the helmsman allowed a good forward view of the sea as well as off to port and starboard. The helmsman stood at the steerage wheel and received his orders from the officer of the deck. There were voice tubes to his side for communications below deck as he was not to take his hands off the control wheel. Against the wall, where a person entered the bridge, were a number of telephones to connect with any department on the ship. Other equipment in the bridge was a table against the port side with a map of their current area.

Jin Wang walked over to the window with the best view of the naval group. In addition to *Liaoning*, he had three destroyers and the fuel tanker under his command. Almost three thousand sailors looked to him for guidance as they went about their duties. Off the ship's port and starboard side was a destroyer. Behind the *Liaoning* and the ship's large wake rode the tanker, and further back, the third destroyer protected their aft.

Jin Wang was happy with his command. He was happier still that he did not have to waste ten years of his life during the refurbishment of the massive carrier. The Soviet navy originally started construction on the ship as an Admiral Kuznetsov class aircraft carrier named the *Riga* in 1988. By 1992, the ship was structurally complete but without the electronic package. As the old Soviet Union dissolved, ownership transferred to Ukraine, and the ship lay untouched and stripped of her equipment. By early 1998, the ship was without engines and rudder, and most of her operating system had been put up for auction.

The government sold the hulk of the carrier under the pretext it would become a floating casino in Macau. Other former naval warships had found a last-stop home for the same purpose. However, officials in Macau voted against the proposed floating casino, and the stripped-out vessel began a long voyage to China. It required sixteen months for the passage because of a lengthy negotiations process with various governments who had to grant permission and allow passage through their territorial waters. Finally, on March 3, 2002, the hulk arrived at Dalian Shipyards in northeastern China. It was not until 2005 that the vessel was moved into a dry dock and her transformation began.

Dockworkers erected a large scaffolding around the vessel, and the hull was sandblasted. It received a new coat of red primer to prevent any further development of rust, and then a new gray paint coating was applied. Further work included installation of electronic systems, offensive and defensive weapons systems, and internal living quarters for the crew of nearly two thousand sailors.

In August 2010, the first of eight sea trials begin with varying durations of four to fourteen days. During this time, land-based facilities were designed to replicate the space of the aircraft carrier landing desk, and Chinese pilots began to practice landing on the mock carrier deck. Not until November 2012 did actual touch-and-go landing attempts begin on the *Liaoning*, and then another series of retrofits occurred based on the reports from the sea trial.

On December 22, 2012, the Chinese Navy reported it would take four to five years for the *Liaoning* to reach full potential, and the ship was used for ceremonial events and sailed to many foreign ports to show the world how China had entered the blue-water navy.

In late 2014, earlier than announced, the *Liaoning* received certification as fully capable of taking her position as a warship within the Chinese Navy. All sea trials were completed, and the ship was ready for active service.

The aircraft carrier was just short of one thousand feet in length and had a displacement of 74,368 tons and a draft of thirty-four feet. Propulsion was by eight boilers providing power to four shafts with fixed pitch propellers. Two 50,000 HP turbines, nine 2,000 HP turbo-generators, and six 2000 HP diesel generators created internal power.

All the propulsion power could move the ship at thirty-two knots and a range of 3,850 nautical miles. The crew could maintain the ship for forty-five days without any major need for resupply.

The carrier was outfitted with Type 1030 CIWS (close-in weapon system), FL-3000N (eighteen cell missile system), and ASW 12 tube rocket launchers. It has a complement of thirty folding-wing Shenyang J-15 Flying Shark aircraft and twenty-four Changhe Z-8 multifunction helicopters.

The navigation officer looked to Jin Wang. "Commodore, we are approaching the position for our turn to port."

Without turning from the view outside the bridge window, Jin Wang spoke to the officer. "Make the turn as scheduled, Lieutenant. Maintain current speed to conserve fuel."

Jin Wang heard a quiet throat clearing behind him and turned to the offensive noise. His air flight commanding officer was waiting to speak with the commodore. Captain Ji Liu was responsible for all air equipment onboard the *Liaoning.* Jin Wang had mixed feelings about the air commander. He felt the officer probably resented his being the commanding officer of the carrier battle fleet. He had been thinking of asking for a replacement upon their return to Zhanjiang after this mission.

"Yes, Captain, what can I do for you this morning?"

Ji Liu stayed at near attention as he addressed the commanding officer. "Commodore, we have perfect flying weather. I would request we use the opportunity to practice air cover operations over the carrier group. I would also like to allow our helicopter pilots to earn more time in ASW operations."

Jin Wang thought for several moments. "Yes. Your plan seems appropriate. Just make sure all aircraft are ready for inspection before Admiral Fang Li arrives either today or tomorrow morning. I would not want him to see us unprepared for his inspection."

Ji Liu saluted his commanding officer and offered a "Thank you, sir."

Jin Wang turned to the officer of the desk. "Prepare to go to flight speed when Captain Liu has his fighters ready for launch."

"Yes, Commodore."

Jin Wang looked back out the bridge window. From the senior side of the carrier, he could see the destroyer to front and the destroyer off his starboard. The starboard destroyer was out about five hundred meters and back about five hundred meters. He walked out onto the open deck from the bridge to look aft and saw the tanker riding back about five hundred meters in his wake. He reentered the bridge and crossed over to the port side open deck. The other destroyer was sailing back about a thousand meters. *Much too far away,* he thought. He called to the officer of the deck, "Order the port destroyer to increase speed until he is in proper position."

Again, he received only the briefest of responses, "Yes, Commodore."

A few minutes later, he heard the loudspeakers on the bridge emit a crackling noise followed by the voice from his air flight officer. The anticipated request came for a change in the carrier's speed to flight speed followed by the request to turn the vessel into the wind to allow flight operations to begin. The officer of the desk passed the order to the engineering officer below deck, and soon, Jin Wang could feel a stronger vibration through the soles of his shoes as *Liaoning* increased speed to turn and begin flight operations. From the outside bridge wing, he saw the first Changhe Z-8 helicopters arrive on the flight deck from below and the crewmembers begin to fold out the propellers to make the craft ready for takeoff.

He felt the warm air from the South China Sea move across his face and cause his uniform to rustle in the breeze. Yes, this was where he wanted to be until it was the right time for his next upward promotion.

Chapter 39

Bandar Seri Begawan
Wednesday, March 18, 2015
10:00 a.m. (CST)

The opening ceremony for the twenty-fifth ASEAN annual summit started with lots of ceremonial music and flag waving. The meeting room for the leaders and representatives was in the largest conference room available within the Empire Hotel. Already seated in their assigned locations, the lower-rank attendees waited for the official entrance ceremony for the presidents, sultans, prime ministers, or whoever were the senior representatives from the member nations. There was a large round table covered with a luxurious cloth and three chairs for the leader of each member nation and his senior associates. Extra chairs, placed in a second row behind the three leaders, were for addition support staff.

At 10:00, the loudspeakers began to play, and they all rose from their chairs. The national anthem of Brunei played, and the sultan of Brunei walked into the conference room followed by a flag carrier with his country's banner. He continued until he reached his designated seat but remained standing at the table. The flag carrier continued and placed the flag in a floor stand against the wall behind the country's representative. Today, the Sultan had elected to wear a traditional business suit in place of his ceremonial robes from the evening before.

The leaders would enter the conference room in alphabetical order. With the anthem for Brunei completed, the prime minister of Cambodia was next to enter. Its flag was a blue-colored band at the top and bottom with a red and slightly larger center band. Imposed within the red band was a picture of Angkor Wat, the largest Hindu temple in the country.

Next was Indonesia. The southeast nation stretched from the Indian Ocean to the Pacific Ocean and was the third most populous democracy with over 250,000,000 people, the world's largest archipelagic state and home to the world's largest Muslim population. The flag bearer carried their proud banner with its two horizontal bands of red and white.

The Laos national anthem signaled their prime minister to enter. The man represented almost seven million people in the Communist country. Their flag was three bands—a top and bottom red band and a center and double-width blue band. Impressed in the center blue band was a white circle that symbolized the full moon against the Mekong River.

Malaysia was the fifth country to enter. Their head of government was the prime minister. Its 329,847 square kilometers represented the sixty-seventh country in size with slightly fewer than twenty million citizens. The flag was fourteen equal horizontal stripes of red (on top) and white (bottom), with a blue rectangle in the upper hoist-side corner bearing a yellow crescent and a yellow fourteen-pointed star.

Myanmar, or Burma, paraded into the conference room next. Its 676,578 square kilometers supported 54,585,000 people under a civilian parliamentary government formed in March of 2011. The flag was three equal bands of yellow, green, and red from top to bottom. A large five-pointed white star, imposed on the center of the flag, extended into portions of the top and bottom band completed the detail.

The Philippine president Bayani Limbaco walked in next with his flag bearer a few steps behind. One hundred and four million Filipinos lived in this republic of 300,000 square kilometers. Their flag was two equal horizontal bands of red (top) and blue (bottom). A white equilateral triangle, based on the hoist side, displayed a yellow sun with eight primary rays; each corner of the triangle contained a small five-pointed star.

Singapore was the only city-state in ASEAN. The 697 square kilometer was home to 5.4 million inhabitants. It can brag about being the fourth leading financial center in the world and had one of the five busiest ports. The prime minister walked in front of his standard-bearer. The two equal horizontal bands of red (top) and white (bottom) made up the base of the flag. Near the hoist side of the red band was a vertical white crescent (with the closed side toward the hoist end of the flag), partially enclosing five white five-pointed stars arranged in a circle. The country had a parliamentary republic government.

Thailand made the ninth country to enter. The prime minister headed a constitutional monarchy and had sixty-seven million people living within the 513,120 square-kilometer country. The flag was five horizontal bands placed, top to bottom, red, white, blue (double width), white, and red.

Vietnam came last. President Tran Van Huong entered to represent his Communist country with 91,519,000 people living in 331,210 square kilometers. The standard-bearer carried the red-based flag with its five-point yellow star imposed in the center.

Throughout this thirty-minute procession, Randy Fisher had been standing with the junior representatives from the Philippines. Philippine President Bayani Limbaco, Ambassador Isko Bello, and Philippine Chief of Naval Operations Vice Admiral Crisanto Olan took the three chairs at the table for the senior representatives. The admiral was dressed in his daily working uniform but still cut quite a figure with his large six feet in height and 245-pound frame. Despite nearing the mandatory retirement age of sixty-two, he still possessed a full head of solid black hair.

Brunei was the host country, and the Sultan acted as the ASEAN summit president. As the final national anthem neared its conclusion, he started a round of applause, and all the attendees joined with him. After a reasonable time, he pulled the table-mounted microphone closer to his side of the table.

"Good morning to all my friends. Welcome to the twenty-fifth annual summit for ASEAN. This great organization, established in 1967, promotes our goals to improve economic growth, social progress, and culture development among its members. Additionally, it strives to promote peace and stability by offering member nations a platform to discuss differences openly and face-to-face.

"We have our differences, but we also have a way to work through them to maintain the peace. War is never cheap in material expense, and the cost in blood should be more than any country can afford. I hope we can always meet at these annual ASEAN summits as friends and realize we together are all part of Southeast Asia."

When the sultan concluded his opening remarks, the assembled group broke out into applause.

The secretary-general now assumed control of the meeting. ASEAN consisted of four departments, and he asked each department chairperson to provide a twenty-minute brief of their activities since the last regional summit meeting.

The first department chair rose from where he was sitting and walked to the microphone next to the secretary-general. For the next sixty minutes, Randy listened to the Economic Community Department, Sociocultural Community Department, and the Community for Corporate Affairs Department. He thought it amazing and lucky for himself that the working language for ASEAN was English.

At exactly noon, the secretary-general called for the ninety-minute lunch break, and the group filed out to another large room where the hotel staff had prepared a luncheon for the ASEAN attendees.

Ambassador Bello caught up with Randy as he left the conference room. He took hold of Randy's right arm and leaned in close to the senator. In a quiet voice, he said, "Fairly calm proceedings so far, but I'm afraid after lunch when the Political and Security Community Department makes its report, things will start to heat up. They meet quarterly, and after each meeting, the defense ministers or senior military advisors return home with more distressing news about China. I feel today several hot spots are going to boil over, and the calm demeanor of the morning will be forgotten."

Randy had to agree. "I don't think Admiral Fang Li won over any new friends at the social event last night. In fact, he probably made it worse."

Bello laughed with his next remarks. "I was told by several of your table guests how you were the only one able to make the admiral sit back and rethink his remarks about the Midway naval battle."

Randy shook his head only slightly. "I'm sure he would have thought of something to put me in my place if one of his junior officers had not pulled him from the dinner."

He looked around the group milling about before heading into the dining room. "Speaking of the admiral, where has he been keeping himself this morning?"

Bello waved his hand in a dismissive motion. "Oh, no doubt he would not want to participate in the ceremonial opening session. He knew the Security Department would not be making its report until after lunch. I think you can count on his appearance at the beginning of the next session."

Chapter 40

Sand Cay Island
Wednesday, March 18, 2015
Noon (CST)

Sub-Lieutenant Huynh Tan Phat of the motor torpedo boat *Ly Nam De* was sitting in his minimally furnished office inside the Quonset hut provided by the Vietnamese Naval Supply Depot for his men on Sand Cay Island. He was reading for the third time the decoded message his signal operator had delivered a short time ago. He could not believe the order from the Vietnam Naval Command Headquarters.

Each day since their first simulated attacked against the Chinese drill ships and escort warships, he had been ordered to run in closer and closer before making his breakaway. Each day, the Chinese warships had been slow to respond with gunfire, and he had faithfully reported this in his messages to Hai Phong.

However, the new orders went beyond a simulated attack. The paper in his hands instructed him to complete the attack and destroy the drill ship if the Chinese fired on his approach. He had seen the look on the face of his signalman when the messenger delivered the decoded message. It was a mixture of excitement and fear. No doubt by now, most of his crew was aware of the different instructions this order contained.

He looked once more at the authorization at the bottom of the order. Vice Admiral Dc Thuc Ho, the commissar of the Vietnam Navy, had issued the orders. He could only conclude the orders had come down from the People's Central Government in Hanoi. This was a major shift in their tactics. No longer would they be playing with the Chinese Navy.

The attack was to take place no later than 3:00 p.m. He looked at his wristwatch. He had two hours to prepare the ship. Tan Phat read the message one last time. The past wording had always said "simulated attack," but the new set of orders made the change very clear—"attack."

His petty officer walked into the room and waited for the captain of the *Ly Nam De* to look up from the message in his hand. Tan Phat finally raised his eyes to the face of his friend. "We are ordered to complete the attack if the Chinese open fire on our approach. Have all men report to the ship and prepare all weapons. Make sure every man has his flak jacket and helmet. Also make sure we have a full supply of medical gear on board."

The petty officer smiled back to his commander. "The ship has been ready since we started running these crazy stunts. The men are ready to push the Chinese back to their mainland."

"Fine," said Tan Phat with slightly less enthusiasm than his second in command. "We will shove off in two hours."

The petty officer saluted, turned from Tan Phat, and left the room. Tan Phat sat at his desk and thought for a full minute. He reviewed the previous simulated attacks through his mind. What should he do differently this time? Slowly, a plan started to form, and he reached for a blank sheet of paper. Maybe he could complete this mission and bring his men home alive.

Chapter 41

Taiping Island
Wednesday, March 18, 2015
2:10 p.m. (CST)

Sub Lieutenant Huynh Tan Phat was at the command wheel of the *Ly Nam De* and powered the motor torpedo boat away from the dock at Sand Cay Island. He set the course and headed northeast and well west of the drill ship and her escort warships. Each previous run had been directly east toward the floating platform, but today's approach would bring his vessel from behind their destination. Ever since the first run, the frigate and the destroyer had moved their ships between the oil-drilling platform and the normal approach of the Vietnamese vessel from Sand Cay Island.

Tan Phat was going to try to save his men and boat if possible while complying with his orders. The order said to attack if he drew fire from the Chinese Navy. To his way of thinking, there was no doubt if there would be an exchange of gunfire, so he planned to take the first shot today. He was hoping that his superior speed and maneuverability would give him an advantage over the slower ships with their heavier firepower. He could not hope to come out ahead in a prolonged standoff and exchange of gunfire with the Chinese warships.

His patrol vessel had two 57-millimeter machine guns mounted on swivel platforms aft and two 27-millimeter guns mounted forward on swivel platforms. The four twenty-one-inch torpedo tubes were loaded, but he carried no extra torpedoes so he would have only one chance against the Chinese ships. His orders called for him to take out the drill ship as the primary target.

The destruction of the drill ship would probably be an easy task, but Tan Phat did not intend to attack an unarmed drilling platform anchored above the well casing. If he could defeat the warships in a surprise attack, he would offer to allow the men on the drill ship to stop operations and leave the area.

For nearly an hour, he steered the ship northeast, and when his chart and navigation equipment indicated his ship had reach an area north of the drill ship, he turned the motor torpedo boat southeast. Another thirty minutes at this speed would put him east of the platform and slightly north of Taiping Island.

Always before, he had had the sun to his back, but this approach would have the afternoon sun in his eyes. He knew the approach would give an advantage to the Chinese, but he was hoping their normal slack routine would allow him to get close enough before the Vietnamese warship came under fire by the Chinese.

Tan Phat looked around the small bridge area. His men appeared to be ready for the engagement. He had made a quick inspection of all the ship's weapons and spaces below deck before they had left the dock at Sand Cay. He knew the petty officer would have every weapon and man ready, but it gave him an opportunity to visit with the men and offer some words of encouragement. He made sure they did not see any signs of worry on his face or detect any in the sound of his voice.

The warship moved forward at thirty knots. All hands kept watch for any other vessels or planes. If a Chinese plane spotted their approach too soon, the two warships near the drill platform would be ready for them. Then their mission would be doomed along with the men under his command.

Finally, his equipment indicated another turn to starboard and toward the target. In a wide turn, Tan Phat brought the motor torpedo boat around and on course for a direct run at the drill ship. He had no way of knowing if the ships would be in the same position from their previous simulated attacks. If the ships had returned to the positions in their first engagement, then Tan Phat was steering his ship directly at the Chinese warships. They would be spotted and brought under fire long before he could bring his torpedo tubes to bear on the enemy's ships.

His plan was to get close before they were able to bring their missiles and rocket launchers into position. He would take out the frigate first because it could respond more quickly. The destroyer had a faster top speed than the frigate, but it would take longer to build speed and Tan Phat knew speed and maneuverability would be his biggest advantage once the battle started.

He had two men up in the upper super structure with high-powered binoculars watching for the first sight of the top of the drill ship. He had ordered the radar turned off to prevent the Chinese from picking up his ship's signature on the approach. He estimated they were five kilometers away from the drill ship when one of the men called down with the first report—no sight yet of their targets. They were still too far away with the sun's angle in their eyes to determine the location of the warships. A few minutes later, Tan Phat received his first piece of luck. The topside sailors called down to him again. The drill ship was in sight, and now being placed between the warships and the drill ship's position would help to cover their approach from the Chinese naval vessels.

The distance between his motor torpedo boat and the target area closed quickly, and the spotters relayed the final information to plot the attack. The drill ship was still positioned with its bow due north. The ship maintained a permanent anchored position once it lowered the drilling equipment and proceeded to commence operation. Two of the support vessels were south and about two hundred meters off the aft section of the drill ship. The third support vessel was out beyond the bow of the drill ship and—he hoped—far enough away once the action commenced.

The two warships were exactly where he had hoped they would be. The frigate was positioned about two hundred meters to the front of the bow of the drill ship and heading southwest at a forty-five-degree angle to the drill ship. The destroyer was port side and lying parallel to the drill ship.

To Tan Phat's trained mind, ever since their first run against the Chinese warships, they had been in too close proximity to the drill ship. The seas were calm, but it did not make sense to position the ships so close together. He did not know Chinese marines had transferred from the warships to the drill ship and support vessels, a situation that required the Chinese commanding officer to keep his warships closer than protocol recommended.

At two thousand meters, Tan Phat knew he had achieved the surprise his plan called for. He ordered full power from the three M503 B2 diesel engines and their 15,000 horsepower, and he could feel the ship increase speed to the maximum forty knots. The bow came higher out of the water as the speed increased. At one thousand meters, they could see Chinese sailors running about on the desk of the frigate. From Tan Phat's position, the bow of the frigate, still behind the drill ship, allowed about three-quarters of the frigate for his target. They were below the sight of the deck of the destroyer, and its forward gun was pointing away from him and useless against his ship. Their CIWS (close-in weapon system) had not yet been activated.

At five hundred meters, he gave the order to fire the two outside torpedoes against the frigate. Immediately, his torpedo men pressed the launch buttons on the fire control panels, and the two killing monsters leaped from their launchers. The torpedoes' fifty-plus knot speed would close the distance to the frigate long before it could maneuver to safety.

Tan Phat did not wait to see the impact from the torpedoes. He pulled the ship into a hard turn to starboard. He hoped the destroyer captain would assume the Vietnamese warship would continue its course of attack and come forward of the drill ship and frigate, positioning itself for an attack on the aft section of the destroyer.

Instead, Tan Phat planned to make a full circle to starboard, cut across his own wake, and go around the drill ship from its aft end. He would pass between the drill ships and the two support vessels anchored off the aft of the drill ship. This would make it almost impossible for the destroyer to fire any weapons against his ship for fear of hitting their own vessels.

His ship leaned hard to starboard, exposing a large portion of the underside of the ship's hull. He had almost completed the circle formation when his two torpedoes hit the frigate. Tan Phat kept his eyes forward, but he could still see the two big flashes of the explosions. The noise caught up with the ship and drowned out the cheering of his men.

The first torpedo hit the frigate near the propeller shaft and ripped into the aft end before it detonated. The second torpedo slammed into the port side just slightly forward from the aft end of the doomed ship. The explosions almost ripped the tail end of the frigate from the main body. Boilers, steam pipes, and finally the fuel tank erupted and added to the fireball rising from the ship. The torpedoes were enough to kill the ship, but the additional internal explosions would bring the end much sooner. Most of the sailors below deck died instantly in the massive explosions. The few in the forward compartments who survived the initial explosion either were knocked unconscious or were too dazed to survive the water flooding into the internal spaces.

As in the earlier attacks, the men on the destroyer, taken by surprise, reacted slowly to the threat. Some who witnessed the explosion on the frigate first though it was an internal accident, but others realized they were under attack. The warning klaxons sounded the alert, and the sailors raced to their battle positions. Those on the aft end of the destroyers were training their weapons to either the starboard side, where the Vietnamese warship had approached during the previous encounters or toward their dying sister ship, expecting the attacker to appear from the smoke and fire consuming the frigate.

On the Vietnamese motor torpedo boat, Tan Phat knew it was too soon to celebrate. They still had the destroyer to contend with before they could force the drill ship to leave the area. Tan Phat yelled at the men to be ready to open fire with the forward 27-millimeter machine guns on the destroyer's bridge and other topside weapons systems as soon as it came into view. If the destroyer had not moved from its earlier position, he would have an easy broadside attack and from a very close range.

The Vietnamese motor torpedo boat approached the aft end of the drill ship. Its deck and drilling tower loomed high above the Vietnamese warship. Tan Phat had to reduce speed to make the turn and keep from colliding with the support ships. As his ship completed the turn and the destroyer came into view, his starboard-side machine gunner opened fire, raking the bridge of the destroyer. As his ship completed the turn to line up its torpedo tubes toward the destroyer, his port side machine gun added its firepower and was cutting down any exposed Chinese sailors on the desk.

Tan Phat ordered the last two torpedoes fired. His men responded immediately to the order, and the deadly weapons leaped from the weapon tubes. The distance from the destroyer was a short three hundred meters, and the two torpedoes hit the destroyer almost simultaneously just below the bridge area. The double explosion raised the destroyer partially out of the water and broke its back. Spray from the explosion splashed down on top of the speeding Vietnamese warship.

Tan Phat could not determine if the forward gun on the destroyer was out of action. He continued the turn around the drill ship and again increased to maximum speed. He planned to shoot between the destroyer and the sinking frigate. The narrow path of water forced him to run alongside the huge drill ship for about half its length before he could pull his ship to port and run through the gap between the two sinking Chinese warships.

Some of his men were cheering loudly and pointing at the two doomed Chinese ships. The frigate was sinking rapidly by the aft section. It was almost completely underwater; only the forward deck and bow remained visible.

The destroyer was settling back into the water but listing to its port side. The explosions from both ships caused the water to erupt and heavy waves to hit the drill ship. The six anchor cables holding the drill ship in the perfect position over the wellhead and casing were straining the sea anchors, and the ship was pitching about. The support vessel anchored in front of the drill ship was pitching heavily and threatening to pull its sea anchor from the ocean floor.

Tan Phat pulled the ship to port and was about to enter the gap. The first sign of trouble was the starboard machine gunner's body shaking like a rag doll. He saw blood spurting from the gunner's mouth as the sailor collapsed to the deck. Tan Phat knew they were under attack but did not know from where. More bullets from automatic weapons hit the structure of the ship close to his body. He could hear their pings as the bullets struck the steel of his ship. He turned in time to see Chinese marines along the deck of the drill ship firing down onto his ship as the distance started to widen between the Vietnamese warship and the Chinese oil platform. As the distance increased between the two ships, the angle for the men firing from the drill platform improved, and more weapons came to bear on the Vietnamese ship.

Tan Phat did not need to order the machine guns on the aft end of his ship to open fire. The bullets from the two 57-millimeter guns tore across the railing of the drill ship killing the men exposed to the machine gun fire. Many Chinese marines and oil wildcatters, hit by the heavy weapons fire, collapsed onto the deck of their ship. There was little protection from the heavier weapons on the Vietnamese warship, and for the first time in the battle, Tan Phat and his men had the superior firepower.

He powered the ship at full speed into the gap between the two dying warships, knowing the heavy smoke from the doomed vessels would quickly obscure his own ship and provide the needed protection to escape. Once beyond the effective range of the rifle fire from the drill ship, he could turn the boat around, establish contact with the captain of the drill ship, and allow him the chance to sail the oil ships away from the area and back to the Chinese mainland.

He had steered the warship between and beyond both Chinese warships when he felt the heavy blows to his back. His body, thrown hard against the forward part of the open bridge, bounced back and away from the structure. More bullets entered his body, and he slumped to the desk, never to know the outcome of his attack plan.

The huge explosion from the drill ship was lost on the dead captain. The 57-millimeter rounds from his twin aft machine guns had ripped into pipes and pressure tanks on the drill ship, and the volatile gas and oil blew the drill tower nearly completely off the vessel and left most of the ship engulfed in flames and smoke.

Of the 160-crew members on the Chinese frigate, *Yang Wei*, seventeen survived and were later pulled from the warm waters of the South China Sea. The 280 men on the *Yu Yuen* fared slightly better, as their fuel tanks did not explode before the warship slipped below the surface of the water. Their loss of life was eighty-one officers and men, including the captain.

On the Vietnamese motor torpedo boat, *Ly Nam De*, only the captain, Sub Lieutenant Tan Phat, and the starboard gunner sacrificed their lives for the oil and gas below the surface of the South China Sea.

Chapter 42

The vice chairman of CNOOC, Huang Zhao, was making his second trip to the drill ship at Taiping Island. He had a mutiny on his hands. Every day, the Vietnamese were running closer to his drill ship and the Chinese Navy was firing its weapons, sometimes over the drill ship itself. His men working on the ships wanted off, and the reports from his onboard supervisors were grim. Nobody could work under these unsafe conditions, and Huang Zhao had to agree with his men.

He was flying out to inspect the local situation and assess the problem to see if it was as dire as reported and then go to the Ministry of Land and Resources to make a formal complaint. If Minister Chang Chen did not immediately order the men released from their contracts and allow the support vessels to leave the area, then Huang Zhao would go to the Central Committee and find someone who would listen to him.

This whole project had to stop. He had been receiving distressing reports from other drilling locations, but Taiping Island appeared to be the worst. The efforts of the drilling operations had failed to produce any tangible results because of the daily interruptions by the Vietnamese navy, and CNOOC was bleeding red ink on these new drilling operations.

Lian Wu, the CNOOC chairman, was already trying to prevent the damaging financial information from leaking to the stock exchanges in New York, Hong Kong, and Toronto where CNOOC stock traded daily on the public market. Any information about the problems in their South China Sea operations would affect their stock value and reduce their ability to borrow additional funds.

Huang Zhao was riding in a Changhe Z-8 helicopter. The triple-engine multifunction rotary wing craft used by the military for transportation or ASW (antisubmarine warfare) was nearly empty. It could haul twenty-seven armed men and travel seven hundred kilometers with a maximum four-hour endurance.

The helicopter had left Zhanjiang with Huang Zhao aboard along with the pilot, copilot, and loadmaster. The Chinese Navy had stripped down this model of any luxury appointments for use, and all weapons had been removed to further reduce weight and improve travel distance. The loadmaster had provided Huang Zhao with a flight suit, helmet, and gloves to ward off the cold at the 1100-meter ceiling. The helmet allowed communication between the crewmembers. For the first half of the flight, he had listened to their conversation, but it was just normal talk about family, women, or if they would get back in time for some sporting event being broadcasted on the armed-forces network. Huang quickly became bored, tuned the conversation out, and opened his laptop computer to try to get some work done. Even with the helmet on, he still had to contend with the reduced noise of the engines.

An hour later, Huang Zhao checked his watch and determined the amount of flying time. They should be nearing the drill ship. They would land on the helicopter deck on the aft deck as before, and the pilots would refuel the helicopter while he met with the disgruntled crewmembers. The copter had no problem with fuel capacity for the flight from Zhanjiang but would need addition fuel for the return trip.

Huang Zhao was ready to power down the laptop and stow it away when he heard the pilots suddenly talking in an excited tone. He had not been paying attention to their conversation and with the background noise of the engines nor been looking out the bay windows.

The loadmaster, in his own seat, turned to Huang Zhao and motioned him to step forward. Rising from his web seat, Huang Zhao grabbed for the wall supports and made his way forward. He reached the end of travel distance for the cord on his mike and pulled the plug from its receptacle, losing all sound from the built-in helmet speakers. The loadmaster had opened the cockpit door and motioned Huang Zhao into the flight deck. Together, they crammed their bodies as far forward as they could, and Huang Zhao looked out the forward armored glass shield between the pilots toward their destination.

To his untrained eyes, the scene at first looked normal, but he noticed smoke from the smaller warship. It seemed to be sinking by the aft section. What was happening? He then noticed a smaller vessel moving at an alarming rate of speed and close to the drill ship. What was going on down there?

As the Changhe Z-8 copter drew nearer, he realized they had arrived during an attack by the Vietnamese navy. Hearing about the previous attacks from his men was different from seeing the real thing.

"Get to the drill ship!" he yelled over the noise of the engines. He was not sure if the pilots could hear him without the internal communication system, but he did not take his eyes off the surface of the water to look for a communication port to reattach the helmet cord.

The helicopter pilot responded to the order and pulled the collective hard to the side. The helicopter tilted to port and away from the ships to circle around and approach the helicopter flight deck from the south. Huang Zhao tightly gripped both hands to the pilot's seat back to keep his footing on the flight deck with the sudden shift in the direction of the helicopter's flight.

The sudden rapid change in the flight deck's angle blocked the view of the action on the sea surface from Huang Zhao's vision until the pilot completed his turn and made his approach to the landing deck. The destroyer was to their left, and they had just reacquired sight of it when they saw two large explosions amidships on the destroyer and the warship blew apart.

The pilot maintained his focus and prepared to set down on the helicopter landing deck. When they were only a few feet from touchdown, a fireball erupted from the deck of the drill ship. A second later, a huge explosion rocked the drill ship and a shock wave picked up the helicopter and knocked it over the side of the flight deck. The pilot lost any chance to regain control of the helicopter, and it fell forty meters to the surface of the South China Sea.

Chapter 43

Bander Seri Begawan
Wednesday, March 18, 2015
4:00 p.m. (CST)

The afternoon session for the ASEAN summit was anything but dull as the Political-Security Department commenced its twenty-minute presentation. The department chairman had barely finished talking when questions about the recent increase in Chinese naval and CNOOC drilling operations started coming from the leaders of Vietnam, Brunei, and Malaysia or their military advisors. Philippine President Bayani Limbaco remained quiet, but Randy Fisher could judge from his position behind the senior Philippine delegates that his body was tense. This discussion among the members of ASEAN was the highlight of this meeting. The outcome might determine if the South China Sea would see continued peaceful relations or war.

Throughout the initial presentation, Admiral Fang Li had remained silent, and from his facial expression, he seemed indifferent to the accusations being leveled at China. He was sitting in a section reserved for the ASEAN Plus Three group—China, Japan, and South Korea. Even here, his three staff members kept him apart from the South Koreans and Japanese delegates.

The talk had grown louder and the meeting was getting out of control when the secretary-general rapped his gavel to get the attention of the group and restore order among the delegates. The assembly became a bit less noisy, and he rapped the gavel again.

Finally, he had everyone's attention, and he looked toward Admiral Fang Li. "Admiral, as it seems all the member nations of

ASEAN are deeply concerned with your country's expansion into the South China Sea with new offshore drill equipment and expanded naval presence, perhaps you would like to address the delegates and discuss their concerns."

Fang Li remained motionless for almost thirty seconds. He appeared to be reading the contents of a paper in his hand. His indifference to their complaints was upsetting the delegates, and some were starting to mutter among themselves when he handed the paper to an aide and rose from his chair. He slowly walked around the huge round table and delegates until he reached the podium with the microphone. He placed both hands to the side and looked at the assembled delegates before starting to speak.

With a half-smile, he cleared his throat. "My friends, I am here today at the request of my superiors to inform you my country has moved more oil drilling equipment into the Chinese territorial waters of the South China Sea, and we plan to increase our operations over the next two years. Our current and future offshore drilling operations will remain in our territorial waters. China has made it very clear in many past announcements the location of our territorial limits, and we will used whatever force is necessary to protect those territorial limits. To that end, we have assigned two Chinese Navy warships to each location, and the *Liaoning*, our newest addition to the Chinese Navy, is now on station. With its complement of jet fighters, two of which you saw yesterday, we now can provide air protection for the entire portion of our territorial waters. As you are all aware, we have ample claims based on history for the entire South China Sea, and we intend to protect our territorial waters in whatever manner we deem necessary."

He paused shortly for effect but then continued with his statement, "We hope to continue our peaceful relationship with the member nations of ASEAN, but we are prepared to defend ourselves against any aggression against our production fields and our ships."

The president of Vietnam stood up from his chair. In heavily accented English, he addressed the admiral. "You can't be serious in your intentions to claim the entire South China Sea and all of its vast oil and gas resources for China. Too many of the ASEAN members require portions of those natural resources for our economies. If you continue to insist on claiming all of the South China Sea, you risk military conflict with my country and others from this group. Your claim of territorial waters out to almost five hundred kilometers from your shores is without sufficient proof or historical precedent and will not stand up in any court."

For almost thirty minutes, each president, prime minister, or senior delegate stood at his chair and repeated the same charge against the Chinese admiral. The words might not have matched exactly, but the meaning was clear. China was risking war with the ten member nations of ASEAN.

Philippine President Bayani Limbaco rose again after the last ASEAN member had made his unplanned statement to Admiral Fang Li. "We all know of the huge military advantage China possesses over the combined forces of these ten countries. However, let me remind you of two very important things. First, most of our members, including the Philippines, have defense treaties with larger counties and we would consider the expansion of China into our waters as an invasion of the Philippines. Second, by refusing our countries access to the oil and gas resources of the South China Sea, you are hurting our economies and therefore our people beyond what we can allow. We have enjoyed relative peace for many years, but if we have a war, the world will know that China is the aggressor nation."

During the time President Bayani was talking, the Philippine CNO Vice Admiral Crisanto Olan received a call on his cell phone. He was inclined to ignore it until he read the identity of the caller, and he pressed the accept button. Randy Fisher watched the Philippine CNO from his vantage point and saw the admiral tense up. Something was happening.

The admiral rose from his chair and walked to the outside wall in the conference room to hear the caller's voice over the noise of the delegates. A few minutes later, he returned to his chair and leaned behind the Philippine president to tap the shoulder of Isko Bello. When Bello looked toward the admiral, the naval officer indicated he needed to speak with both men. They huddled together for a full minute, and then President Bayani rapped his knuckles on the table to get everyone's attention.

It required several attempts, but finally, the room was quiet. "Gentlemen, we have just received some distressing information. I will let my naval chief of staff, Admiral Olan, brief you with what we currently know."

Olan rose from his chair to address the group. He did not waste time walking around to the microphone but spoke loudly from his position. "I have just received a call from my naval headquarters in Manila. They have received an SOS call from the Chinese drill ship and other support vessels operating near Taiping Island. Apparently, there has been an exchange of gunfire between the Chinese and Vietnamese warships. There has been a huge loss of life, and the drill ship has exploded. The Philippine Navy has a destroyer on its way to Taiping in response to the SOS. It should arrive in several hours. We also have a strategic Sealift vessel preparing to leave the dock within the hour. That is all we currently know of the situation. I am preparing to leave immediately to join up with our destroyer and supervise the rescue operations."

The room erupted in uncontrolled conversations and questions shouted at Admiral Fang Li. The Vietnamese president was yelling and pointing at Fang Li, accusing him of starting a war with Vietnam. Fang Li was ignoring the Vietnamese president and conferring with his aides. Others in the room were trying to reach their own military headquarters to learn of any more information.

Philippine President Bayani and Ambassador Bello with the Filipino CNO walked away from the table to stand near where Admiral Olan had been talking before on his telephone. Randy joined the three men.

Olan was explaining that his headquarters had arranged for a local helicopter to fly him out to rendezvous with the destroyer approaching Taiping Island. Once at the scene, he would gather the latest information and transmit a report back to the president.

Randy listened to the exchange between the men. He decided there was a greater need for him with Admiral Olan than here at Bander Seri Begawan. "Admiral, I'm going with you."

Admiral Olan looked at the US senator. His facial expression changed as he considered the statement. "Absolutely no way. That's no place for a politician."

He started to talk to his president when Randy intervened. "Mr. President, you invited me here on a fact-finding mission to see how the Chinese government was encroaching on your territorial waters. I believe I have learned all that is possible from within this conference room. The focus of my mission has now changed to what is happening right now in the South China Sea. I'm going out there with or without your assistance."

Admiral Olan was raising his hands in protest, but President Bayani indicated he wanted silence from his admiral. He looked at Randy. "You realize this situation could get a lot worse. If the Chinese have destroyed the local Vietnamese fleet, this could be all-out war. With the many mutual support agreements among the ASEAN members and your own country, this conflict could escalate quickly. It could become very dangerous out there, and we might not be able to pull you out to safety."

Randy had no hesitation in his voice. "I understand the risk, Mr. President. But right now, that is where I need to be."

Bayani looked at Ambassador Bello, who silently nodded his agreement. He looked back to his CNO and gave the instruction. "Take Senator Fisher with you."

Olan was shaking his head, indicating that he disapproved but would follow orders. He looked over to Randy. "All right, Senator, you're along for the ride. But when we get there, you do as I say."

Randy smiled at the admiral. "Admiral Olan, I will take every word you say with all the wisdom it contains, but I will not be subject to your orders."

Olan threw his hands up in frustration and forgot his diplomatic manners. "You damn North Americanos are still a stubborn lot."

Chapter 44

Bander Seri Begawan
Wednesday, March 18, 2015
4:45 p.m. (CST)

Randy Fisher was ready to board the rented helicopter, but the pilot had requested a ten-minute delay. With only one small overnight bag, he and Admiral Olan had grabbed a taxi from the Empire Hotel for the trip to the airport. Their taxi stopped long enough at the Brunei International Airport entrance gate for private chartered flights for them to wave their diplomatic passports and then drove directly to the waiting helicopter.

Randy used the time to remove his Blackberry and pull up Marion Bellwood's cell phone number. He knew local time in Washington was thirteen hours behind Brunei, but Marion needed to know about the latest developments. To his surprise, Marion answered on the second ring.

"Marion, I'm sorry to wake you, but there's been a military incident over here in the South China Sea. Apparently, the Chinese and Vietnamese navies have attacked each other—"

Randy was about to explain further, but Marion interrupted him. "We know about the drill ship. The bloom from the explosion was large enough to set off our missile launch early warning system. I'm on my way now to the White House to brief the president's National Security Team. Probably the president will sit in on a later meeting once we have more details. We know several warships were in the vicinity, but we don't know what caused the explosion."

Randy was amazed at the clarity of Marion's voice over the cell phone. "There was an exchange of gunfire between the Chinese and Vietnamese ships. We do not know if the gunfire set off the explosion on the drill ship, but it is a good bet. I will let you know when I get there and see what really happened. I'm getting ready to fly out there in just a few minutes."

Marion's voice boomed over the tiny cell phone speaker into Randy's ear. "Wait a minute, MP. You told me you were not going over there to spy, but now you're flying into what might be a war zone? You better think that idea over once again."

Randy had to yell back over the engine of the helicopter. He could see the pilot waving for him to board with the admiral. "We have ten countries over here ready to go to war with China over the oil and gas under those waters. I may be the only person here with an unbiased opinion. Besides, there are people hurting out there. I'll call you from the drill site once I get there."

Randy pressed the end button to close the call and hurried toward the helicopter. He climbed quickly inside the passenger compartment and strapped himself into the cushioned chair.

Admiral Olan leaned over to yell over the noise of the engine. "We had to wait until Admiral Fang Li's flight took off. Apparently, he was in one of the fighters. If he's on his way to rendezvous with the Chinese aircraft carrier, you might be wishing you'd stayed here."

Chapter 45

South China Sea
Wednesday, March 18, 2015
5:15 p.m. (CST)

The *Liaoning* was still steaming in the same rectangular box at a fifteen-knot average speed as ordered by Commodore Jin Wang. The fighter jets had been practicing flight operations and simulated dogfights for most of the day, and the helicopters were due to land shortly from the ASW exercise. Flight Operations Officer, Captain Ji Liu, had worked his pilots hard to ensure they could handle any hostile action planned against the carrier and sister ships or any enemy ships within their effective range.

He had been standing on the open bridge wing for most of the day watching his planes and helicopters going through the routines he had created. He was ready to order the final helicopters back aboard when the ship's communications received the SOS call from the drill ship's support vessels operating near Taiping Island.

Commodore Jin Wang was in his day cabin meeting with several of his personal staff officers when he received the information and quickly returned to the bridge area. The communications officer handed him the printed distress call. He slowly read the information and considered his options. "Do we have an ETA on Admiral Fang Li yet?"

The officer of the deck answered, "His jet is over the area of the disturbance now and should be leaving the area for the carrier any moment. His ETA from the scene is fifteen minutes. The second fighter acting as escort is ten minutes out."

Jin Wang looked at the bridge clock. "Turn into the wind and increase speed to flank to recover both aircraft." He walked on the starboard open bridge deck. "Have the destroyer on our starboard side leave immediately for the drill ship and begin rescue operations. The other two destroyers are to maintain their position around the carrier for protective screening."

The ship was starting its turn into the wind when the bridge speakers came alive. "Commodore, to the combat command center."

Jin Wang looked at the speakers and then started to move out of the bridge. "Captain Liu, please follow me."

The two men left the carrier bridge and stepped into the outer hallway. They walked a short distance and then turned sharply to access a steep and narrow ten-step flight of stairs leading to the deck below. Sailors starting to enter the lower portion of the stairway quickly moved out of the commodore's path. At the bottom of the stairway, they made another 180-degree turn and entered what on a US naval ship would be the Combat Information Center, or CIC.

Here, the noise of the carrier, silenced by the thick sound insulation, was very quiet. The room, darkened to allow the operators to read their electrical instruments more easily, was the hub for all military flight operations and the ship's defensive operations. The CCC officer in charge was looking at a sonar scope over the shoulder of the operator. He glanced away from the scope to see the commodore entering the electronics room.

"Commodore, one of the ASW Changhe helicopters picked up something just before the exercise was to end. It is nothing we have heard before. The contact is about three thousand meters off our port side. We've been listening to the sonar report from the repeater."

The ship's onboard sonar tech was monitoring the signal from the ASW helicopter and having the information repeated over the overhead speakers in CCC. The sound was indeed strange.

Everybody focused their hearing on the sound emitting from the sonar speakers and watched the digital display on the monitors. The sonar's computers were trying to identify the source of the sound but so far were returning negative information.

Captain Liu was the first to speak. "Didn't Naval Intelligence inform us the Vietnamese navy had received new Lada-class submarines several months ago? They're supposed to be a lot quieter than the old Kilo subs."

Commodore Jin Wang made another quick decision that was very out of character for him. "Sound General Quarters. Tell navigation to commence a zigzag pattern immediately. Order the helicopter to attack the enemy target. We can't let what happen at Taiping Island happen to the *Liaoning.*"

Captain Liu spoke up quickly. "Commodore, we have an inbound jet approaching now. It should touch down within minutes. It's got to be low on fuel."

Jin Wang looked at his flight officer. "We can't lose an aircraft carrier for one jet fighter. You have two minutes to get the fighter down or else the pilot can eject or ditch in the ocean."

Ji Liu raced from CCC and ran up the stairs to the bridge to check on the status of his jet. The ship's klaxons were sounding the alarm for general quarters before he entered the bridge. As he hurried to the open bridge deck, he could see the fighter on its final approach.

The officer of the deck was telling the navigation officer to prepare to assume a zigzag pattern as soon as the fighter landed on the ship.

The *Liaoning* was going to war.

Chapter 46

Vietnamese submarine captain Can De Ho was listening to the passive sonar equipment with an extra pair of headphones. A few minutes ago, his sonar operator had reported one of the helicopter's dipping sonar might have picked up their sister submarine, the *Ha Noi*, under the command of Captain Cam Le. The helicopter had changed its search pattern with the dipping sonar and seemed to be focusing in the area where they believe the sister sub might be currently positioned.

Since the carrier had first launched the ASW helicopters, De Ho had ordered a decrease in speed for the *Da Nang* to the minimal forward movement required to maintain navigation and allowed the distance to the carrier to increase. The *Ha Noi* had been too close to the carrier and was currently trapped inside the helicopter's operation area. They hadn't seen his signature on the sonar screen so De Ho hoped Cam Le had stopped and allowed his ship to slowly sink deeper in the water's depths and maybe to find a thermal layer to shield his ship from the dipping sonar's search from the helicopters. Once the helicopters moved to another area, Cam Le would be able to move his ship out of the area and to safety.

De Ho handed the headphones back to the sonar operator and moved over to the chart table. The XO, Lieutenant Le Van Hoach, had been updating the positions on the chart map for both submarines and the where they guessed the helicopter's sonars were being deployed.

The pattern was expanding toward them, and De Ho ordered the ship's course altered to starboard ten degrees to move them further away from the dipping sonars and the carrier.

He looked at the map again. "If the helicopters are working closer to us, then Cam Le should be able to move further away from the carrier."

"Let us hope he doesn't use this as an opportunity to move closer," the XO said. "He's more aggressive with the Lada-class submarine than other captains I've seen with the old Kilo class."

De Ho was looking at the charts when the sonar operator called back to the captain. "Sir, Chinese sonar has picked up *Ha Noi*, and they are moving to block her in."

De Ho moved back over to the sonar station and looked at the screen over the shoulder of the operator. He reached again for the headphones and listen to the passive search patterns of the ship's sonars.

He could hear the helicopter's active sonars pinging against the hull of the Lada submarine. The helicopters had the sister submarine boxed in. De Ho removed the headphones and handed them to the operator. "Keep the reports coming," he ordered. "Let me know of any change."

He moved back to the charts and the XO. "What is the water depth in this area?"

"Plenty. We've got four thousand meters below the keel."

The *Da Nang* was five thousand meters from the *Liaoning* and almost parallel to the carrier. De Ho issued new orders for a change in their position and speed. "Increase speed to maximum. Bring the sub up to periscope depth."

The orders were quickly relayed, and De Ho could feel the engineers increasing power. The deck angle moved to bring the ship closer to the water's surface.

"Periscope depth, Captain," the diving officer called out a few minutes later.

De Ho moved to the stainless-steel tube and activated the scope. Silently, the stainless-steel tube slid up from its well, and he let it break the surface. He lowered the handles, swung the tube, aimed the viewing lenses toward the carrier, and adjusted the focus. The carrier was in his sights. He moved the scope to the north and angled the viewer up to try to see the helicopters. There were two moving about a thousand meters behind the carrier. He moved the scope back to the carrier in time to see two more helicopters leaving the carrier deck.

De Ho had no doubt they were moving in on the *Ha Noi*. He hit the switch to lower the periscope and called out orders, "Sonar operator, switch to active sonar on the carrier. Hit them with full power. Let us try to pull them off the *Ha Noi*. Radio, make contact with Hai Phong and let them know our location and inform headquarters the carrier appears to be attacking the *Ha Noi*."

He walked over to the chart table and picked up the microphone from its retaining clip. He called to the forward torpedo room. "Load tubes one and three with torpedoes. Load tubes two and four with anti-ship missiles. Do not open torpedo doors at this time."

He walked over to the sailor sitting at the navigation wheel. "Turn forty-five degrees to port to line up on the carrier."

He could hear the active sonar lashing out from his submarine. He hoped the threat from his sub would pull the helicopters away from his sister ship. He had no way to attack the helicopters. Cam Le would have to use his skills to evade the enemy from the sky and save the *Ha Noi*.

On board the carrier, the active sonar signal from *Da Nang* slammed into the carrier and forced the three sonar operators to rip their headphones off to prevent damage to their eardrums. The senior operator called up to the bridge. Commodore Jin Wang heard the warning over the loudspeakers. "Bridge, new contact to starboard about five thousand yards. We estimate another submarine moving toward us at about twenty knots."

Commodore Wang immediately called out, "Hard to port! Turn fifteen degrees and go to emergency flank speed."

He looked over to his own XO. "What is the status on the possible submarine to our aft?"

The XO straightened up from over the chart table where he was tracking information on the suspected submarine to their rear and now the new report of a certain contact to their starboard. "Our helicopters are moving in on the submarine to our rear. They're attempting to box it in."

"Does it appear to be an attack against us?" the commodore asked.

"No, sir."

Wang walked over to the starboard side of the *Liaoning* to look toward the area of the latest threat. "Alter the helicopters over to the new contact. That's the real threat."

The XO walked up to the commodore, his body tense with the knowledge his commanding officer's decision was a mistake. "Sir, the new contact is trying to pull us away from the first contact. It's just a ruse. We need to allow our helicopters to move in on the first contact."

Wang looked at the XO. "No. Do as I order. Shift the helicopters now."

The XO continued to look at the commodore for a moment and then walked over to Captain Ji Liu. "Captain, shift your helicopters over to the new contact."

Captain Ji Liu hesitated too long. Commodore Wang moved over to the two officers. He put his body directly in front of Captain Liu. "Captain, issue the order now to move those helicopters, or I will relieve you of your command."

Ji Liu looked at the commodore and then the XO. "Yes, Commodore, but I request to launch two more helicopters to go after the first contact."

Wang nodded his head. "Approved, but get those helicopters already airborne over to the positive contact."

Chapter 47

On board the Vietnamese Lada submarine *Ha Noi*, Captain Cam Lee heard his own sonar operator whisper the welcomed information that the helicopters were moving away from their location. His own sonar equipment captured the loud active sonar pinging from the *Da Nang*, and he knew Captain De Ho was trying to draw the Chinese away from them.

"The carrier has turned from their course and increased speed," the sonar operator quietly announced.

Cam Le knew his sub could not keep up with the carrier's superior speed. "Are the helicopters on top of the *Da Nang*?"

"They're closing, sir. The other sub has stopped using its active sonar and turned again from the carrier. They're trying to lose the helicopters."

Cam Le was not a friend of Captain Cam De Ho, but the senior commander had put his boat and crew at risk to pull the *Ha Noi* from almost certain destruction. He needed to help the men on the *Da Nang* and perhaps make the carrier captain wish he had left the new *Ha Noi* in peace.

Cam Le walked over to the chart table on his sub and lifted the microphone from the clip. The Lada submarine had two torpedo rooms—forward with four tubes and aft with only two more. "Forward Torpedo Room . . . load all tubes with standard torpedoes.

Aft Torpedo Room . . . load both tubes with ship-to-ship missiles. Signal when ready to fire."

He moved over to the navigation and depth-control operators. "Bring the sub back on course with the carrier."

He looked over at the sonar operator. "Provide an update on the carrier and our sister sub."

"Carrier is pulling away at thirty-two knots, and they are increasing the distance to almost fifteen hundred meters. The *Da Nang* is about five thousand meters west of our position. The Chinese have four helicopters using their dipping sonars to triangulate on them. Our sonar indicates our sister ship is boxed in on all sides.

On the *Da Nang*, Captain Cam De Ho had pulled the helicopters off the *Ha Noi*, but now his ship was in trouble. They had four ASW helicopters working as a team to close the area around his sub. "Fifteen degrees down bubble. Take us down to three hundred meters."

He felt the submarine's angle change and grabbed hold of the chart table to keep from falling. He looked over to the gyrocompass. "Turn to port twenty degrees. They might not think we would be so stupid as to turn towards the carrier."

The navigation control for the Lada was very similar to a control yoke on a child's video game. The operator moved the yoke to the left and forced the sub to port and the new heading.

De Ho was still standing by his XO at the chart table, looking at the plot with all the ships' positions displayed to the best of their knowledge. His strategy was to order another course change in about ten minutes when his sonar operator called out with new information, "Captain, I think the *Ha Noi* has opened torpedo tubes."

Chapter 48

South China Sea
Wednesday, March 18, 2015
6:10 (CST)

Captain Cam Le picked up the microphone to ask the aft torpedo room when the missiles would be ready. The forward torpedo room had reported ready almost ten minutes ago. He knew the missile launch procedure would take longer, but they should have been ready by now. He pressed the mike button, but the overhead speaker came to life before he could open his mouth. "Aft torpedo room to bridge."

"Bridge. Go ahead."

"Missiles ready for firing."

Cam Le hung up the microphone and turned toward the navigation operator. "Be prepared to turn away from the carrier after we fire the weapons." He looked back to his XO and then over to the fire control officer.

"Open all tube doors."

The fire control officer called down to both torpedo rooms and passed the captain's order to the men in the torpedo rooms.

Less than ten seconds later, he looked over to Cap Le. "All torpedo doors open, Captain."

"Fire all torpedoes."

The officer had been holding his hand over the first fire control button. He immediately pressed hard on the firing button, and the red light above the fire control button changed to green to indicate the torpedo had left the tube. He repeated the process on the second button and again on to the third and the fourth. All the red lights were now glowing green.

"All torpedoes away, Captain."

Cap Le looked around the room. Most of the sailors were looking at him. Would he give the order to fire the deadly missiles? He waited for almost two full minutes knowing his torpedoes should have covered the distance to the carrier. He looked at his weapons officer still at the firing controls. "Time until the torpedoes hit their target?"

"Only a few more seconds, Captain."

Cap Le hesitated for only a moment. "Fire both missiles."

Chapter 49

The senior sonar operator onboard the *Liaoning* had seen the four miniature returns on his screen. He immediately felt sweat breaking out on his forehead and his heart rate jumped. He activated his head mike to issue the warning no sailor ever wants to hear. "Sonar . . . torpedoes in the water. We have four inbound tracks coming from 180 degrees at forty-eight knots. Estimated impact is ninety seconds."

Commodore Wang heard the message over the speakers on the bridge. The torpedoes were coming from the area he had pulled the helicopters from only minutes before. "Turn hard to starboard. Tell engineering we need every bit of speed to save the ship."

Flight control now came over the speaker. "We have an inbound aircraft on final approach. Admiral Li is on board."

Wang was nearing panic. "Order the aircraft off. Tell them we are under attack."

He moved quickly to the other side of the bridge to view the sonar repeater screen. He could see the torpedo tracks on the screen approaching the carrier. However, they were not the only signature showing on the cluttered screen. One of his destroyers was moving at maximum speed to cut across the carrier's wake and intercept the torpedoes.

The *Zheng He*, a type 052C destroyer, had moved in closer to the carrier, and its captain had reeled the fast-attack destroyer to starboard to try to prevent the torpedoes from hitting the carrier. His engines were putting out a maximum of 57,000 horsepower and had the ship propelling at thirty-one knots through the water. One hit by the inbound torpedoes could easily destroy the ship. Multiple hits would be certain doom.

The destroyer captain moved from inside the bridge to the outside bridge wing and looked off with his binoculars toward the direction of the incoming torpedoes. He could see the slight wake from the shallow moving underwater bullets. He estimated he would intercept several of the lethal monsters.

"Prepare to abandon ship," he ordered his executive officer.

The incoming torpedoes raced through the water, homing onto the magnetic field of the huge carrier. The destroyer cut across the carrier's wake but not in time to stop the first two torpedoes. They crossed in front of the destroyer's bow and continued their path toward the carrier. The third and fourth torpedoes slammed into the destroyer. Their detonation within the smaller ship was devastating. The bow of the warship rose high from the water with the destructive power of the two torpedoes. A break in the keel allowed the bow to sear away from the ship. The forward momentum of the ship forced seawater inside the vessel, and its own still spinning propellers forced the bow down even deeper into the water. The ship was doomed and would be soon heading for the bottom of the South China Sea. The captain had survived the explosion, and as he picked himself up from the deck of the bridge wing, he saw the sun flash off the two missiles as they broke the surface of the water nearly fifteen hundred meters south of his dying destroyer.

Chapter 50

The third torpedo from the *Ha Noi* continued unabated and struck the right spinning propeller of the *Liaoning*. The explosion snapped off the propeller and shaft as it entered the hull of the massive carrier. The explosion sent a shock wave up the remaining portion of the heavy spinning shaft into the reduction gearbox. The internal damage would require major repair by a dry dock repair crew.

The fourth torpedo entered the hole caused by the third torpedo and detonated inside the carrier causing massive damage to two of the other three shafts. Every sailor on the ship felt the drop in speed immediately. The normal slight vibration caused by the ship's spinning propellers was gone.

On board the carrier, Commodore Wang felt sick to his stomach. His brain was trying to cope with all that was happening around his ship. His precious carrier had sustained damaged. Men under his command were dead. He finally regained some ability to think and asked for a damage assessment. His words were barely out of his mouth when his radar operator called out with another warning over the speakers, "Missiles have broken the water surface and are heading our way."

The ship's antimissile weapons system, already tuned up by the GQ alarm, started to react to the incoming threat, but the missiles were moving fast, and there was no time for the three CIWS to be effective. The missiles' guidance systems had located their target, and nothing would stop their impact.

The Shenyang J-15 jet fighter was on final approach when the pilot received the wave-off from the carrier flight deck. The ship was already veering off from their flight path, and the pilot wanted to pull off for another approach.

The pilot declared a miss-approach and that he would pull away from his flight path and make another approach. However, he was interrupted by Admiral Fang Li seated in the second seat reserved normally for a weapons officer. "No!" the admiral shouted. "The ship is under attack, and I need to get on board."

The pilot brought his head up and looked into the small mirror allowing him to see the occupant of the second seat. "Sir, the carrier is changing direction and no longer moving into the wind. We must pull off and make another approach when they have resumed their course into the wind. Any attempt to land now would be suicidal."

Fang Li was shaking his head. He had already seen the destruction at the site of the oil-drill ship from their flyover and knew he had already lost two warships. "No. Land this plane. We are at war with Vietnam, and I need to get onto the carrier. Now land this plane on the carrier, or you'll never fly again."

The pilot reluctantly maneuvered the jet to realign with the tilting flight deck of the carrier and notified the carrier flight control they were still making their final approach. With tremendous skill, he brought the jet on-line with the carrier. He reduced the speed of the jet as low as possible without putting the plane into a stall. The plane was finally over the deck, and although he was farther along than he wanted, he forced the jet down onto the flight deck.

The landing gear hit hard once, bounced, and then came down hard again. The pilot released his braking parachute to bleed off additional speed. He felt the lowered tail hook catch an arresting cable, and the jet fighter came to an abrupt halt in its forward momentum. He was taking his first full breath since the aborted first landing attempt when he caught the flash of something moving incredibly fast across the deck in front of his fighter. The entire deck exploded in flames, and fire quickly consumed the fighter jet, killing the pilot and his high-ranking passenger. Neither man would ever fly again.

Chapter 51

South China Sea
Wednesday, March 18, 2015
6:30 p.m. (CST)

The four Changhe Z-8 helicopters, each equipped with ASW sonar and a single torpedo, had been on station tracking the second and positive submarine contact. They were finding it difficult to get a strong enough contact for them to launch their own torpedoes. The sonar / weapons technicians would get a possible contact but lose it before they could lock on for a launch. The Lada-class submarine's new and superior anti-sonar coating was proving itself effective against the Chinese technology.

All four pilots and their weapons technicians completely focused their efforts on the hunt for the submarine. None of them witnessed the impact of the other submarine's torpedoes against one of the two remaining destroyers acting as a screen for the carrier. They could not miss the explosion, and for several long seconds, all eight crewmembers' eyes locked on the destruction to their east. Helicopters hovered, and information from the underwater sonar equipment continued to stream into the receiving equipment, but the crewmembers ignored everything as they watched the destroyer's momentum drive the doomed ship deeper into the sea.

They were still watching the destroyer descend into the sea when the last two torpedoes stuck the carrier and their home. No sailor can feel worse than when he or she sees a vessel for whose safety he or she is responsible damaged by an enemy. The four helicopters continued to hover. Their sonar gear was returning possible contacts, but the techs were fixated on determining how grave the damage to their carrier was.

The *Liaoning* flight commanding officer, Captain Ji Liu, rushed to the bridge wing and looked toward the aft end of the carrier, trying to see the damage. Smoke was rising from the rear of the carrier, and he could feel speed bleeding off. The carrier's propulsion system had sustained damage, and he could see the destroyer was sinking. He turned back toward the bridge and yelled for three of the four helicopters to break off their pursuit of the second submarine and change course toward the destroyer to assist in the rescue of any sailors from the sea. The fourth helicopter was to try to find the submarine. His deck crew was working quickly to send additional helicopters toward the first contact. Two more ASW copters were almost ready to take off.

He turned to look at the destroyer again in time to see the water's disruption as the two missiles broke through the surface. They were moving so quickly that he would not have been able to track them had he not already been looking directly at them. They covered the distance from the spot where they broke the surface to the carrier in what seemed the blink of an eye. Although he heard the flight deck announce an incoming jet fighter landing on the carrier's deck, he continued to watch as the missiles impacted the carrier's island below where he was standing. Luckily, Ji Liu died before he could feel the fire from the explosion.

The four helicopter crews were shocked for the second time in less than mere minutes as they witnessed the missile's impact on their carrier. Was their home damaged beyond repair?

The flight leader recovered quickly and ordered the other three rotary wing aircrafts to take a quick reading from their latest sonar contact and launch their torpedoes. They needed to head back to begin rescue operations for sailors from the sinking destroyer. They would drop a lot of weight when they launched the torpedoes, and maybe they could get lucky with a hit on the second submarine.

Within fifteen seconds, the three ASW helicopters released their torpedoes and then banked their aircrafts hard toward the sinking destroyer. The fourth helicopter with the flight leader continued to hover over the South China Sea, and the weapons technician tracked the three torpedoes dropped into the water and renewed their search for the second target.

The torpedoes put on a burst of speed and angled down through the depths looking for the elusive submarine. After about thirty seconds, they reduced speed to conserve fuel and entered a passive listening mode. Each went into its own search pattern and followed the internal computer's direction programming to cover different parts of the ocean depths.

Deep below the water's surface, the Vietnamese submarine *Da Nang* was attempting to escape from the area. The crewmembers on the bridge had heard over their own sonar equipment the launch of the torpedoes followed minutes later by the missiles' launch. They had heard the four torpedoes detonate, but there was no information yet on the damage they had caused because of all the confusion and noise around the carrier. Had *Ha Noi* sunk the Chinese carrier?

Captain Cam De Ho ordered another shift in direction for the *Da Nang*, this time moving away from the surface ships. He was hoping the destruction on the water's surface would cause enough confusion to allow his escape. Still, he had no idea why Cam Le on the *Ha Noi* had fired on the surface ships. The sonar indicated the *Ha Noi* should have been able to sneak away. He had no doubts this incident would be the start of a war between China and his country. He had no illusion if the war continued unabated as to who would win. Vietnam had a proud and highly trained navy and army, but they would be no match for the superior numbers in men and equipment the Chinese could bring against them.

"Three new contacts, Captain," the sonar operator called out. "Torpedoes were launched from the helicopters, and they're sinking fast."

"Any direction to their search?" De Ho asked.

"No, Captain. They appear to be going into a passive sonar search mode."

De Ho ordered all motors to creeping speed. "Please keep reports coming, sonar."

"Yes, Captain. Torpedoes are still searching in passive mode. They do not appear to have any lock on us at this time. I believe they are operating in their fuel-conservation mode."

De Ho was standing by the chart table. "Sonar . . . what course would take us away from the torpedoes?"

The sub was moving northwest at 330 degrees. "Captain, a course of 240 would be the best direction to move away from the three torpedoes."

De Ho looked at the map and ran his fingers along the surface of the glass over the paper below. "Helm, make the turn to 240 slowly," he ordered.

The helmsman used all of his experience to make the turn, hoping not to cause any knuckle in the water from their own single propeller the circling torpedoes might hear. They were moving at only three knots and the turn took several minutes to complete. When the gyro finally hit 240, he straightened the rudder out and stopped the turn. "We are on the new course, Captain."

Above the water's surface, the fourth helicopter had moved west. It was the logical conclusion agreed upon by the pilot and weapons operator. They were relying on the submarine moving away from the three circling torpedoes, and the pilot wanted to be in place to catch the sub moving out of the area.

The smoke still engulfing the massive carrier would make it difficult to determine if he could still make a landing. They had not received any communication since the order to have three of the helicopters move to rescue sailors from the sinking destroyer. With one destroyer having left the scene for the site of the earlier conflict and in response to the SOS signal, only one destroyer remained with a helicopter landing deck, and there were four helicopters still in flight.

The helicopter pilot was looking at the craft's fuel gauge. He had already turned off the warning tone for low-fuel condition; the helicopter's systems would signal when they reached only twenty minutes of flying time.

He looked over to his weapons tech. "Anything?"

The weapon's operator held up his left hand with a raised index finger asking for another moment. He finally answered. "Move about five hundred meters further south of our position. I think I might have a weak signal."

The pilot powered the aircraft for a few minutes to the new position. The weapons tech lowered the dipping sonar again and waited for the signal to stabilize from the insertion into the water. The pilot was looking at the fuel gauge and reviewing their emergency-landing procedures for a landing at sea. They had an emergency inflatable raft and plenty of food and water to last until the destroyer or tanker ship could pick them up.

His radio came alive with an inquiry from the carrier requesting his fuel status. The voice filled him with relief. The carrier was still capable of communicating with its fleet of helicopters. He had a big smile on his face when he looked at the weapons tech. The operator's attention seemed completely focused on his equipment.

"Positive contact 250 meters further west. I am preparing to launch our weapon in twenty seconds. Hold our position."

The pilot maintained their position as he stole another look at the fuel gauge. He was certain even if they left the area this moment for the carrier, they would not make it back before their fuel ran out.

"Weapon away!" the weapons tech called out. The pilot waited another two seconds and then turned the helicopter east toward the carrier. He thumbed his radio to contact the carrier.

"Helicopter One is on its way back to mother nest. We probably will not have enough fuel. We are preparing for emergency landing in the water."

He looked over to the weapons tech. "Get in back and break out the emergency raft. We're going to need it."

Chapter 52

South China Sea
Wednesday, March 18, 2015
6:45 p.m. (CST)

The sonar operator onboard the *Da Nang* heard the splash of the torpedo immediately as soon as it broke the surface of the water. "Torpedo in the water. It is circling and trying to pick us up."

Captain Cam De Ho picked up the mike from the clip holder. "Torpedo rooms . . . prepare to launch countermeasures. What about the other three torpedoes?"

Sonar now gave Cam De Ho the worst news yet. "Captain, the fourth torpedo has locked on us and is increasing speed. It is about seven hundred meters away and closing the distance. The other three are far off now to the east and pose no danger."

De Ho called out to his helmsman. "Turn 30 degrees to north and increase speed to maximum. Sonar, keep giving me the ranges as the torpedo approaches."

Sonar came back immediately. "Torpedo is moving at forty-nine knots and range is down to six hundred meters."

De Ho spoke into the mike. "Launch two countermeasure devices."

Two countermeasures popped out the small side ports of the submarine. They immediately activated to imitate the sounds of the submarine. De Ho hoped they would distract the torpedo away from the submarine.

The sonar operator was listening closely to his equipment. The submarine's speed was near maximum, but the faster torpedo was closing the distance.

Cam De Ho called down to the torpedo room again. "Prepare to fire another two countermeasures."

The torpedo room's answer over the overhead speakers came immediately. "Ready, Captain."

"Sonar, Captain . . . torpedo is closing. Impact is fifteen seconds."

"Launched second group of countermeasures. Helm. Turn thirty degrees to port and maximum rise on the forward planes. Blow all ballast tanks. Let's make the biggest knuckle we can."

The *Da Nang* tilted hard to port, and the submarine's hull groaned from the stress of the hard turn and decrease in depth at maximum speed. The diving officer quickly changed several levers and blew out all the water in the diving tanks. The now buoyant submarine raced to the surface. Sailors throughout the vessel not strapped to seats at their work positions struggled to keep their footing as the submarine made the radical change in direction and depth.

De Ho had done everything he knew to evade the torpedo. The rapid change in the submarine's depth, speed, and direction would create a large disturbance or knuckle in the water. Would it be enough to distract the torpedo? Would the countermeasures work? Only a God he did not believe in would determine if they lived or died.

Chapter 53

The Situation Room in the basement of the White House was full. With the president of the United States was Vice President Jimmy Diamond, the secretary of defense, the national security advisor, director of homeland security, the director of the CIA, and his DDO, Marion Bellwood. The chairman of the joint chiefs of staff, accompanied by the chief of naval operations sat at the table, and their deputies assumed chairs along the outer wall with other assistants waiting to provide any information their respective superior required.

The president settled into his chair, and a navy steward placed a cup of black coffee in front of him. "All right, what's going on in Southeast Asia?"

The members in the room turned toward the CIA director Julius Stone, who spoke first. "There has been a military incident in the South China Sea between the naval forces of China and Vietnam. My DDO has the details as we know them."

Marion Bellwood leaned forward to the table and opened the folder in front of him. "Several hours ago, our satellites picked up an explosion in the South China Sea. It was large enough to trigger our alarms for a possible ballistic missile launch, and our military went into an emergency response mode until we made a positive determination.

"It has been confirmed that an oil-drilling ship exploded off Taiping Island in the South China Sea. The Chinese National Offshore

Oil Drilling Company, CNOOC for short, operated the oil platform or ship. However, this was not an oil-drilling accident. The explosion resulted from an armed conflict between naval forces from Vietnam and China that took place at the oil-drilling site. We don't yet have information on the makeup of the vessels, but I expect to have the information shortly."

Secretary of Homeland Security James Coleman asked the next question. "Did we have any previous knowledge the situation in that part of the world was nearing a boiling point?"

Bellwood looked at National Security Advisor Terry Smith to see if he was going to take the question, but the NSA was looking down at the table. Bellwood plunged ahead. "Yes. There has been a history of armed skirmishes between China and Vietnam going back many years. In recent weeks, we have watched a buildup by the Chinese Navy as they expanded their oil-drilling operations in that part of the world. For those of you not familiar with the South China Sea, a lot of countries claim ownership of many of the island groups with China laying claim on the entire South China Sea."

"What other countries?" the president asked.

"All of the countries having a coastline with the South China Sea are involved. Brunei, Cambodia, Indonesia, Laos, Malaysia, Myanmar, Philippines, Singapore, Thailand, and Vietnam all lay claim to the island groups and the oil and gas below the surface."

"Why am I only now hearing about this?" Harold Miller asked.

Finally, Smith spoke up. "It's been a relativity quiet spot and not worth your time, Mr. President. We've been focused on Afghanistan and reducing our forces there."

"Well, it's on my radar now." The president looked hard at his national security advisor as if Smith were personally responsible.

The president looked back at Bellwood. "What was the makeup of the ships before the incident?"

Bellwood turned several pages back in the folder lying in front of him on the table. "The Chinese had one drilling ship and three other support ships for the drill ship. In addition, they had a destroyer and frigate on-site for protection. Our latest satellite pictures show the three support ships and a badly damaged drill ship from the explosion. I suspect our next satellite coverage will show the drill ship to be sinking or completely gone."

Vice President Diamond leaned forward to ask a question. "Are you suggesting, Mr. Bellwood, both of the Chinese warships have been sunk?"

Bellwood nodded. "Yes, Mr. Vice President. As I said, we should have more information shortly."

Diamond followed up with another question. "What were the losses inflicted on the Vietnamese navy?"

Marion was about to answer when his Blackberry lying on the table went off. He glanced at the caller and looked at the president. "I need to take this, sir."

President Miller nodded his head and raised his right index finger to signal his approval.

Marion picked up the phone, hit the receive button, and listened for almost a minute while the others in the room waited in silence. "All right, shoot the information to my Blackberry and call me with any updates."

He ended the call and looked back to the group. "There has now been a second and perhaps worse incident. A Philippine patrol boat has been monitoring for several days the Chinese aircraft carrier, the *Liaoning*, and her three escort destroyers. The Chinese carrier group came under attack shortly after the first attack near Taiping Island. The damage from the attack left one destroyer sunk and the carrier badly damaged. It is too soon to know if the carrier will remain afloat or sink. Number of dead is unknown, but we must assume it will be high. The Philippine patrol did not report any other vessels in the area, but their sonar registered what they thought were torpedoes and their radar recorded two missile launches. The anti-ship missiles were out of the water and on target almost before their radar could pick them up. We have to assume this was a fight between the carrier group and a submarine. However, we do not know if it was Vietnamese or another country. It's most definitely getting hot in the South China Sea."

US Navy CNO Admiral Jeffrey Gardner looked down the table toward the president. "Sir, the United States has defense treaties with many of the countries in that part of the area. The Philippines, Singapore, and even Vietnam and most of the member nations to ASEAN are treaty members. We need to begin to move assets into the area before it gets more out of hand."

The president sat back in his chair and looked at the flat-screen monitor on the wall to his right as he contemplated his actions. The display on the screen changed with the latest information as he spoke. "What assets do we have in the immediate area?"

The CNO did not need to look at any papers to answer the question. "We're thin in the Southeast Asia area, Mr. President. We have the *George Washington* battle group at dock in Yokosuka, Japan. They returned to dockside about forty-eight hours ago from a two-week exercise cruise with South Korea and Japan. We need to get her crew back on board and ready for sea. We can have her ready for sailing in forty-eight hours. It would be about fifty-eight hours steaming time to reach the South China Sea and where the *Liaoning* was hit."

The CNO could see the reaction to this information from some of the other members sitting at the table. "We have other assets in the Middle East near Iran, Iraq, and Libya, but it would take longer for them to travel to the South China Sea than the *GW*."

The president was shaking his head. "Eleven carrier groups in our navy and the best we can do are four and a half days before we can have any major naval assets on station to keep this from exploding into a worse situation?"

Secretary of Defense Mathew Myers spoke for the first time. "The government of India has military treaties with many of the counties affected by this. They have been complaining for some time about China trying to restrict naval passage through those contested areas. With this sudden explosion of naval warfare, we can assume they will send their two carrier fleets into the area to make sure the seas are passable by commercial shipping."

Assistant Secretary of State Cynthia Miezis was nodding her head in agreement. "I can concur with the secretary of defense, Mr. President. We have had several discussions with the Indian government about this. They are looking to expand their own presence in South East Asia. This is the excuse they are looking for to move their fleet into those waters."

The president threw his pen onto the table. "So to sum this up, we have the world's largest naval fleet but no assets we can bring into action in less than four and a half days. It appears we can only sit back and let the Indian navy move into this part of the world. I am not happy about this, people. Someone give me some other options."

Nobody spoke up for several moments. The president looked at the assistant secretary of state. "When will Secretary of State McGowan be ready to leave Afghanistan?"

Miezis looked at her watch. Secretary of State William McGowan had been negotiating with the Afghan government on the US troop withdraw. The current exit plan called for only a small force of about five thousand troops to be in country by the end of the year. They would be there for training and support, including a rapid-response force to help with any flare-ups of the Taliban forces.

"He's due to leave there in forty-eight hours and then fly back to Washington to meet with you, sir."

The president was still not happy. He looked at Marion Bellwood. "Mr. Bellwood, you mentioned your asset would have more information shortly. Whom do you have over there, and when will they be back to you with their next report?"

Marion Bellwood had hoped that question would not come up at this meeting, but his luck had run out. He was aware of the president's feelings toward Senator Randy Fisher. He was about to disclose who his source of information was when his cell phone rang again. He stole a quick look to identify the caller. It was his asset from the South China Sea.

Chapter 54

Taiping Island
Wednesday, March 18, 2015
6:45 p.m. (CST)

US Senator Randy Fisher and Philippine Naval Chief of Staff Admiral Crisanto Olan landed by private helicopter on the BRP *Gregorio del Pilar*. The ship was a former US Coast Guard Hamilton-class high-endurance destroyer sold in July 2011 to the Philippine Navy. A second USCGC, the *Dallas*, was sold and renamed BPR *Ramon Alcaraz* in May 2012, and Olan informed Randy the cutter was preparing to leave dock should the need arise.

The sight of the drill ship told a lot of the story of what happened. The ship was still afloat but listing heavily to port, and smoke continued to escape from holes on the starboard side. There was still plenty of daylight in this part of the world to see flotsam on the water surface mixed with the oil from the ship. Small patches of fire burned on the surface, and the service ships, along with the Philippine destroyer, were keeping a safe distance from the drill ship. The positioning anchors used to hold the ship over the wellhead had pulled free. Only the sea anchor kept the drill ship from becoming a menace to navigation. There was no sight of the Chinese warships except for their floating debris mixed with the floating material blown off the CNOOC drill ship by the explosion.

The need for the second Philippine destroyer came quickly to Admiral Olan when they stepped out of their helicopter onto the raised landing pad on the BRP *Gregorio del Pilar*. The destroyer's executive officer, Lieutenant Commander Rodel Quiambao, was waiting with new information for the admiral. Olan read the teletype and passed the two-page message to Randy.

From: Philippine Navy Headquarters—Manila—Commanding Officer—Communications

To: Admiral Crisanto Olan, CNO Philippine Navy

Security Classification—**Top Secret**

Subject 1: At approximately 18:30 hours Chinese Naval forces operating west of Scarborough Reef came under attack by unknown forces. Chinese forces consisted of one (1) aircraft carrier, the *Liaoning*, and three (3) Type 052C destroyers . . . identity unknown, and one (1) fuel tanker . . . identity unknown. One (1) Type 052C destroyer, hit by two (2) torpedoes and sunk with unknown loss of life. Aircraft carrier, hit by two (2) torpedoes and two (2) anti-ship missiles and sustained severe damage. Aircraft carrier is at dead stop and adrift in current of South China Sea. No menace to navigation at this time. BPR *Ramon Alcaraz* is ready for duty and awaiting instructions to leave port at Naval Base Cavite to assist in rescue operations.

Subject 2: Philippine Naval Attaché in Bombay, India, reports two (2) aircraft carriers and support vessels leaving India Eastern Naval command at Visakhapatnam within the hour. Estimated steaming time is 69 hours to your location. Carriers are INS *Vikrant* and INS *Vikramaditya*. Two (2) guided missile destroyers and two (2) Type 15A destroyers attached for support-identity unknown.

Subject 3: Philippine Naval Attaché in Beijing indicates additional naval assets preparing for sea from Chinese East Sea Fleet command at Ningbo, Zhejiang Province. Fleet disposition is unknown at this time. There are no additional assets from Chinese Southern Command available at this time.

Subject 4: Vietnamese President Tran Van Huong, Ambassador

An Nguyen, and CNO Admiral Binh Huy Pham have left ASEAN summit and returned to Hai Phong. No known information on possible Vietnamese Naval deployment but situation would assume to be likely.

End Message

Randy read the message a second time to fix the information firmly in his mind. He handed the sheets back to Admiral Olan. "Where is Ningbo in China?"

Olan took the message sheets, folded them into quarter size, and stuffed them in his shirt pocket. "It's along the eastern coast about halfway between Taiwan and southern Japan. The Chinese fleet there is nearly the same size as their Southern Command except for the carrier. Their only carrier is now dead in the water, and the Chinese Navy is looking for blood."

He turned toward the XO and introduced him to Randy. Without further formalities, Olan ordered the XO to take them to the bridge and the captain of the BRP *Gregorio del Pilar.*

Randy was looking at the remnants of the drill ship off in the distance. There were still small pockets of fire fed by surface oil. He could smell the smoke drifting across the water from the burning oil. From what he could see of the wreckage, it was amazing the ship was still afloat. The drill tower, partly collapsed from the explosion, was leaning heavily over the port side of the ship; its weight was pulling the ship over. How the ship had not capsized was a mystery to Randy.

Randy followed the two naval officers down the steep steps of the landing pad to the destroyer deck and up another set of steps to the bridge. This was his first time on board a warship at sea, and he had to work hard to keep his feet steady on the deck as the ship swayed with the waves from the sea.

They reached the bridge, and several sailors popped to attention at the sight of their chief of naval operations. Olan returned salutes to the men and called out for everyone to return to duty. He quickly introduced Randy to the commanding officer of the BRP *Gregorio del Pilar.* "Senator, this is Lieutenant Efren Lanta. Captain, our special guest is US Senator Randy Fisher from South Carolina."

Randy quickly offered his hand. "Thank you for allowing me to come aboard, Captain."

Lanta was medium height for a Philippine native and possessed the typical jet-black hair. His smile was relaxed and formed winkles at his eyes. "Welcome aboard, Senator. I received a signal you were coming with Admiral Olan. Would you like a cup of coffee to start things off right?"

Randy smiled back at the younger man. "I would enjoy a cup of coffee, but only if everyone else aboard has been taken care of. I don't want to take anybody away from helping the men you pulled from the ocean."

Lanta quickly turned to a young sailor standing off to the side of the bridge and held up four fingers to indicate the number of black coffees to bring. He turned back to the admiral and Randy. "We arrived in time to pick up about twenty from the drill ship. Most are workers from the ship, but a few were Chinese marines assigned to the destroyer that went down. The servicemen have been completely mute so far, but the wildcatters have been very talkative. It seems they wanted to leave the drill ship soon after it arrived at the production field so the Chinese captain in charge of the naval units ordered marines from his ship on board to maintain order."

The mess boy arrived with the coffee, and Randy took a quick sip to test the heat and taste. It was a perfect cup of coffee. He had met plenty of men and women from all the branches of the service. Everybody claimed the food and beverage in the navy was the best.

Admiral Olan pointed at the drill ship. "There doesn't seem to be a lot of oil on the surface. Did the explosion allow oil to blow from the well?"

Lanta was shaking his head as he answered. "We don't think the well casing blew. It seems the well's blowout preventer must have worked. At least we do not have an oil spill problem to deal with. The last thing we need is another Deep Water Horizon incident on top of the mess we already have to work with."

Lanta was referring to the deep-water drill platform that exploded in April of 2010 in the Gulf of Mexico that dumped over 4.9 million barrels of crude oil into the water, which then drifted onto the Louisiana coastline.

Randy set his empty coffee cup down on the bridge table where the group had gathered. "Captain, I'd like to visit with some of the survivors you picked up. I'd like to hear what the talkative ones are saying."

The commanding officer looked at his admiral. Upon receiving a nod of approval, he turned to his XO. "Take Senator Fisher down to meet the men we rescued."

As Randy was leaving the bridge, he heard Admiral Olan ordering the second Philippine destroyer to set sail for the Chinese carrier to offer any possible assistance.

Randy followed Quiambao out of the bridge and down two flights of stairs to the level below the main deck. They walked past sailors who were carrying large and heavy plastic bags. Quiamnao informed Randy the bags contained the survivors' clothes, which were soaked with oil and water.

The two men entered the crew's dining facility containing several long benches bolted to the deck. The room was only half filled with the twenty men pulled from the sea by the crew of the BRP *Gregorio del Pilar*. Randy looked around at the men for a few moments, taking in the sight. They must have received showers and clothing supplied by the Philippine Navy. Most were drinking coffee or tea, and the table was partly filled with dishes from the meal supplied by the galley.

A Philippine officer walked up to Randy and the XO. Quiambao introduced the ship's medical officer to the senator who explained that most of the rescued men were in decent shape—a few cuts and abrasions with only two broken arms. They were alive and very lucky.

Randy looked around the room as the doctor continued describing the injuries. The men were rough-looking with shaggy, uncut hair and dark features from working long hours in the sun. Many had heavy beards, indicating they had not used a razor for many weeks. Some he could tell were not Chinese but from different ethnics backgrounds. He did not have firsthand experience with oil wildcatters, but figured they probably came from a similar mold no matter what their country of origin.

As he looked at the men quietly drinking coffee and eating sandwiches, his gaze shifted from one to another. Something suddenly made him return to one of the men. This one did not seem to fit in with the general aspects of the group.

Randy looked carefully at the man sitting apart from the other men pulled from the sea. It took only a few seconds for Randy to determine this man was not a member of the drill ship or a Chinese marine. That he was Chinese was unquestionable, but he obviously did not work on the drill ship.

He was dressed like the other survivors in hand-me-down clothes. However, the similarities ended there. His hair, now combed in a fashionable style, had obviously recently been trimmed by a skilled barber. He was clean-shaven, unlike the other men from the drill ship. Probably the biggest telltale clue was the man's shoes. Most of the wildcatters were still wearing the heavy leather steel-toed work boots they had on their feet when they went over the side of the drill ship and into the water. This man was wearing high-quality leather wingtips. They were still wet from the oil and water and badly scuffed but certainly different from the other survivors. Only someone earning a lot of money could afford these very expensive shoes. The last fact setting him apart from the other survivors was the man's position in the dining room. He was sitting away from the other men, as if he did not belong with the others.

Randy decided to walk over to see what information he could get from the stranger. He stopped by the coffee service table. Selecting an empty mug, he filled it with coffee. On a whim, he grabbed a second cup and filled it as well. Picking up both cups, he walked over to the stranger, placed one of the cups in front of the Chinese national, and then sat down on the seat at the table across from him.

Randy did not speak any Chinese or any other foreign language. Despite taking French in high school, he had barely gotten through the class with a passing grade. He just could not learn any other language other than English. It had been as frustrating for him as it was for his instructors. He had probably received a passing grade simple as a courtesy by his teacher because of his hard work.

He decided to just open up and see where things went. "Is there anything we can get for you? Or is there someone you would like us to try to contact for you?"

The man gave a small smile toward the US senator. "No, thank you. You've been very generous to all of the men." The man's English was almost without an accent.

Randy felt stupid to have not considered their guest could speak English. He reached across the table to offer his hand. "Hello. I am Randy Fisher. I'm a guest here of the Philippine Navy."

The Chinese man took the offered hand. "I am Huang Zhao. I'm vice chairman of CNOOC, and this was my drill ship. I am responsible for this catastrophe."

Chapter 55

Taiping Island
Wednesday, March 18, 2015
7:15 p.m. (CST)

It took a few minutes for Randy to convince Huang Zhao to leave the dining room and follow him out into the hallway. Lieutenant Commander Quiambao followed quickly to see what was going on.

Randy waited until the ship's executive office had caught up with them. "Lieutenant Commander, this is Mr. Huang Zhao, Vice Chairman of the Chinese National Offshore Oil Corporation, and he has valuable information we need to hear, information we might be able to use to help us stop what could be the biggest naval gun battle since World War II. We need a place where we can talk quietly with the admiral and your captain."

Quiambao made a decision in just a few seconds. He walked down the hallway and picked up a telephone on a wall hanger. Randy correctly guessed he was calling the captain. Quiambao came back and asked them to follow him one level up to the captain's personal cabin.

A few minutes later, Randy had Huang Zhao were sitting at a small table for four in Captain Lanta's cabin with Admiral Olan. After a quick round of introductions, Randy decided honesty would get this session off to a good start.

"Huang Zhao, I want to fill you in on what's been happening since the explosion, but before I can do that, we need to know what happened here. Can you brief us?"

Huang Zhao looked around the room. He was not sure if he could trust these people. His gaze settled back onto the man who first talked with him. He looked slightly familiar, as if he might have seen his face in the news. Looking straight into Randy's eyes, he asked him if he was an important American.

Randy had to smile. "I am a United States senator representing the people from my home state of South Carolina. That does not make me an important person but just a concerned citizen of the world. We need to find a way to prevent this incident from blowing up into a full-scale war between the ASEAN members and China."

It was Huang Zhao's turn to smile for the first time. "I received my bachelor of science degree in geology from the University of Houston. I know what a US senator is, and I now know who you are. You prevented a nuclear explosion several years ago in your home state."

He paused again, and it seemed he had come to a decision. "I think you are a man of peace, and I will trust you." Huang Zhao paused as he organized his thoughts. After taking a deep breath, he started to explain how this mess had started.

"Several months ago, the chairman of the Ministry for Land and Resources came to our offices for the annual report. Afterward, he demanded we start twelve new production fields this year and another twenty-four in the next two years. He really gave us no choice in the matter. Increase production quickly or face what would be an unpleasant future. These instructions forced us to put safety aside and to hire men we would normally not approve. We purchased old equipment and needed to bring it into use quickly.

"I am proud to say that despite those problems, we were doing all right until the Vietnamese ships started making their attack runs at the drill ship. They would run their ship in close, and our warships would fire at them. Sometimes, my country's ships were on the wrong side of the drill ship, and they would fire over the top of the drill ship. It was insane with the volatile oil and gas we were pumping to the surface. I was not here for any of the earlier naval incidents, but my men wanted no part of this mess. They were asking to be relieved of their contracts. It became so bad the captain of the destroyer placed the marines on board the drill ship to control the oil men."

Randy was watching Huang Zhao's eyes. He felt the Chinese

executive was telling the truth. "What about the attack today? Did you see it happen?"

Huang Zhao was sadly shaking his head. "We only witnessed the last part. I was coming out here today to hear about the latest demands from my people to be relieved from their contracts. As we approached by helicopter, the attack was already underway. We thought the frigate received a hit by a torpedo from the Vietnamese ship, and then it made a 360-degree turn to run behind the drill ship to avoid fire from the destroyer. I think now the captain of the destroyer thought the torpedo boat would burst into sight from the smoke of the damaged frigate, but instead the torpedo boat came from the aft end of the drill ship and took the destroyer by surprise."

Admiral Olan had a surprised look on his face. "You're saying one Vietnamese torpedo ship sank two Chinese warships?"

Huang Zhao silently nodded his head. "My people reported there were three or four previous attacks by the Vietnamese. I say attacks, but they never fired a single shot until today. It seemed they were testing how close they could approach the warships before they would draw a response."

Lanta spoke for the first time. "This is a common tactic in these waters, and the Iranians have used the same tactic against the Americans in the Middle East. This gave the Vietnamese navy important strategic information to develop a plan of attack for today's operation."

Randy asked the next question. "Why the big push for more oil and gas? Was your country facing an immediate shortage?"

Huang Zhao shook his head no. "No. In fact, we had a good year. Most of our production fields were up from last year, and we exceeded the requirements set by the ministry for last year. It made no sense to my company's chairman and me for the ministry to press us for these higher production figures. I know every country needs more energy or cheaper energy, but we were not facing any type of national shortage that I was aware of."

The men were quiet for almost a minute as they digested this information. Randy broke the silence. "Huang Zhao . . . I am going to break security to convince you how we really need your help. Right now, your navy is making ready their Eastern Fleet. The Indian Navy has already ordered two aircraft carriers and their support vessels into this area. We suspect the Vietnamese navy is preparing to come out, and I have to assume the US Navy will be coming here as well. That is a huge increase of warships without considering what other counties here in Southeast Asia will do. Some will honor their treaty commitments and add more warships to the mix."

Olan now broke into the conversation. "I don't care how well-coordinated these navies may claim to be, but with the large number of warships in the South China Seas, what we've seen so far will only be the beginning. There will be more armed engagements and more dead sailors."

There were murmurs of agreement from the men sitting at the table. Randy looked at Huang Zhao. "We need to reduce the tension between Vietnam and your country immediately. You already have what appear to be twenty-plus warships in this area now with more on the way. Who is the senior naval officer you were dealing with?"

"That was Admiral Fang Li and his senior operation officer Admiral Yang. Both of them were gung ho for this whole misadventure. We'll get no help from them."

"Then we'll have to go over their heads. Is there anyone else you know we could reach out to and try to stop any more buildup by the Chinese Navy?"

Huang Zhao was quiet for almost a minute and then slapped the tabletop. "Why did I not think of this sooner? Dong Zhang. Yes. Dong Zhang. I could contact him, and he is very powerful. He's a member of the Politburo Standing Committee."

Randy looked around the table and back to Huang Zhao. "Please forgive my ignorance of the Chinese Government political structure, but how high is this man and can you simply reach out to him?"

Huang Zhao motioned with his head he understood Randy's lack of knowledge. "We have a general secretary, who is the most powerful person in China. He may not hold any official office, but he would be the general secretary of the Communist Party of China, the president of the People's Republic of China, and the chairman of the Central Military Commission. Under the general secretary is the premier of the People's Republic of China. Then we have four vice premiers, and Dong Zhang is the first vice premier."

"So he's similar to a cabinet member in my government?" Randy asked.

"Yes. Not like your secretary of state or defense but more like a slightly lesser cabinet officer."

Admiral Olan was looking at Randy with a slight grin on his face. "You've had dealings with slightly lesser cabinet members before, Senator. I seem to remember you tangled with your secretary of energy some time ago."

The look the admiral received from Senator Randy Fisher made him wish he had kept the comment to himself.

Randy chose not to reply to Olan. Instead, he looked back to Huang Zhao. "Can you get us an audience with the first vice premier?"

Huang Zhao was nodding his head in an affirmative manner. "I believe so. We are the same age and shared several classes together during our early university years until I left to attend the University of Houston. We have not seen each other since, but he will remember me. For certain, I can assure you."

Randy looked at Lieutenant Lanta. "What are your plans for the survivors you have on board?"

"We are supposed to transport the survivors over to one of the support vessels as soon as that is possible. We delayed starting the process until the admiral was able to get here so he could have a chance to question them."

He looked quickly at Huang Zhao. "Sorry, but we needed to know what really happened here."

Huang Zhao motioned with his hand. "Do not concern yourself. You treated us very well, and nobody forced any of the survivors to talk. I appreciate everything you've done for my men from the drill ship."

Randy spoke up next. "Well, we can't have you going back on a slow boat to China." He stopped speaking for a moment. "Sorry, no pun intended with my remark."

The three men had to laugh at Randy, and he broke up in a slight fit of laughter himself. "Well," Randy said. "It's amazing we can laugh in the midst of all the disaster that has occurred today."

Huang Zhao raised a hand slightly from the table. "I think I can solve the transportation problem. I arrived on a helicopter. If I can contact my company, I can arrange for another helicopter to fly out to pick me up."

Randy looked back to the Chinese man. "What happened to the helicopter you traveled on out to the drill site?"

Huang Zhao's face took on a dark look. "I ordered the pilot to land on the drill ship. We had just about touched down on the drill ship when the explosion occurred. The force of the explosion blew the helicopter off the landing pad and into the sea. I was the only one able to get out before it went under. The pilot, copilot, and loadmaster all drowned."

Chapter 56

Washington DC
Wednesday, March 18, 2015
6:15 a.m. (EST)

Marion Bellwood knew from the face of his ringing Blackberry that Randy Fisher was calling. He let the phone ring once more but hit the green receive button before anyone in the Situation Room could wonder why he was hesitating so long. "This is Bellwood."

He heard his friend's voice loud and clear over the satellite connection. "Marion, I wanted to update you on what's going on out here. Are you someplace where you can talk?"

Marion knew he could not have a whispered conversation in the Situation Room with the president of the United States sitting two chairs to his left. "Hold on just a moment, Senator."

He placed his hand over the speaker of the phone and addressed the group. "This is my best source of information at this moment. It's Senator Fisher, who is on-site at the first naval incident."

President Harold Miller nearly came out of his chair. "What the hell is he doing over there? You mean to tell me all of your human intelligence is coming from that son of a bitch? If he is the best you can do, then you had better start looking for a new job when you leave this room. My God, we're relying on a damn upstart from South Carolina."

Randy Fisher was up on the flight deck near the strapped-down helicopter and away from the rest of the crew and passengers of the BRP *Gregorio del Pilar*. He could hear the conversation from the room where Bellwood was located. Despite Marion Bellwood's hand over the speaker of his Blackberry, Randy knew he was listening to an outburst from the president of the United States. He pulled the phone away from his ear and looked at its face. For several seconds, he considered throwing the damn device into the South China Sea. His common sense and words of caution against making rash decisions spoken by his mother years ago caused him to rethink his action.

He brought the phone back to his ear and tried to get Marion's attention. He called out his friend's name several times but to no avail until finally on the sixth or seventh attempt, he could hear Marion's voice back in his ear. "Hold on, Senator. We are attempting to work something out over here."

"No!" Randy shouted into the phone. "You put me on speaker right now so every other son of a bitch in the room can hear what I've got to say."

Bellwood kept the grin off his face. He only said, "Okay," and Marion hit the speaker button on the Blackberry.

"I'll bet the next round of beers I'm not the only son of a bitch in on this conversation right now." Randy's voice came in loud and clear to every person in the Situation Room. There was a mixture of snorts and coughs, and several cleared their throats to cover up their surprise that someone had referred to the people in the Situation Room by a questionable name.

The president was speechless with anger. Others in the room did not know what to say or to appear to accept the junior senator from South Carolina as equal to themselves.

Vice President Jimmy Diamond broke the silence with a light tone in his voice. "Randy, this is Jimmy Diamond. Several people have called me a son of a bitch to my face several times in my life but never from halfway around the world. I hope you're in a safe place right now and can help us with this terrible situation."

Diamond was looking at the president as he continued, "We've been going around the room trying to figure out what to do. It seems we can't get our own navy down there for almost five days, and things are a little too hot where you're at right now to let it string out that long. What can you tell us?"

Randy was smiling now as he visualized the vice president and the rest of the members of the national security team sitting in the same room this very moment with Harold Miller.

"You're correct, Jimmy," he said. He had purposely used the vice president's first name to inform the other people in the room how close he was to the second most powerful man in the world. "I'm at the site of the drill ship with Admiral Olan of the Philippine Navy. I do not know for sure what you already know so I will just give you a recap of today's events. We had a little skirmish between the Chinese and Vietnamese navies, and the Chinese lost two warships and an estimated two hundred sailors. The drill ship is threatening to sink, and most of the wildcat workers were killed when the drill ship exploded. Off to my east, we had a second naval battle, and the Chinese lost another destroyer and their only aircraft carrier is also threatening to slip beneath the ocean.

"I believe you're up to speed on the situation here where I'm located. I can also report the Chinese are preparing to launch their Eastern Fleet and the Indian Navy has already put to sea with both of their carriers for this region. The Vietnamese navy's intentions are unknown, but they have already made a big bang with today's events. In much less than your five days, I expect the South China Sea to fill with naval warships. We could see a surface action, like we haven't experienced since World War II, going on here unless we can figure out how to stop it."

Randy paused for a moment to let things calm down a little. He figured he had pricked the president's thin skin enough for the moment. Still not hearing anything over the phone, he plunged ahead. "I have something else to tell you. One of the survivors pulled from the water by the Philippine Navy here is the vice chairman of CNOOC. He explained to me who ordered this massive buildup by his company. We have discussed a plan to get the Chinese Navy to pull back, and we hope to allow other countries over here to reconsider their actions and maybe resolve this in a more peaceful manner. We plan to leave by helicopter tomorrow morning and fly to China. He has a strong contact with the Chinese First Vice Premier Dong Zhang. We are going to try to meet with him tomorrow and get this thing under control."

The assistant secretary of state for the Southeast Asia area was sitting up in her chair next to the president vigorously shaking her head at the president. Cynthia Miezis quickly took a sheet of paper from her business portfolio, wrote a short note, and turned the sheet around so the president could read her message.

Miller read the message and agreed they needed a seasoned diplomat over there to handle this situation. The president had decided he had been silent long enough. He was about to tell Fisher to stay on board the Philippine destroyer and they would get someone else over there to handle the negotiations. As he crumpled up the sheet of paper, the navy communication officer walked into the room and over to the president. He handed him a pink message slip stating the president of the Philippines was on the telephone wanting to speak with the president.

Miller looked at the paper and then at the Blackberry lying on the table. "Hold on, Senator. We'll get back to you." He rose from the table, catching the others by surprise, and they struggled to get to their feet as he left the Situation Room.

The president walked to the waiting elevator and entered along with two Secret Service agents. A short ride up and he was on the first floor making his way to the Oval Office. As he walked into his office, a secretary spoke into the telephone she was holding. "One moment, please, President Limbaco. The president just walked into the Oval Office."

Miller took the telephone from his staffer and held it for a moment as he collected his thoughts. "President Limbaco, it's a pleasure to talk with you, but I wish the circumstances were under better conditions. My staff has just brought me up to speed about the terrible naval battles between China and Vietnam. I was just in a meeting with my national security team when you called."

Limbaco's voice came through the long-distance lines clearly, and his accent was easy for the president to understand. "Thank you, President Miller, for taking my call. We are very concerned with the escalating situation in our part of the world. I am sure your national security team has provided you with a clear picture of the situation here. This latest outbreak of war between China and Vietnam will only lead to their continued buildup of naval warships in the South China Sea and further destabilize the situation. My military advisors have already informed me the Chinese Navy is making plans to send additional assets into the South China Sea and India has already ordered their carrier fleet into the same area to protect the open waters we all enjoy and need to conduct our trade with the rest of the world. I can only assume the United States is also planning to send naval warships into this area."

Miller was standing by his desk looking out the windows as the Rose Garden started to become visible in the morning sunlight. This time of the year, there was not a lot of color provided by the plants. "I can assure you, President Limbaco, the United States is making preparations to assist our friends in the region to keep the sea lanes open. As we speak, our aircraft carrier group based in Japan is preparing to set sail to provide assistance."

"Mr. President, my advisors have informed me your carrier fleet, the *George Washington*, could not be here for almost four or even five days. Before it arrives, the Chinese and Indian navies will have already reached the South China Sea. We can also assume Vietnam will increase its military presence in the same ocean waters. With an overwhelming number of naval warships trying to protect territorial waters too many countries already claim, the situation could become untenable. I'm afraid with such a huge amount of naval firepower in one small ocean, the odds of another armed naval conflict are very high."

Miller now sat down at his desk and ran his fingers through his hair. He had to agree with Philippine President Limbaco. Too many warships in the same ocean were bound to result in more incidents. These damn military people just needed to use their guns, planes, and ships to justify their positions and ever-growing budget requests.

"Please be assured the United States wants to preserve the peace in your region. The last thing we want to see is an escalation of the fighting between all the naval forces currently or that will be in your area. Our aim is to bring in our carrier battle group and keep the various naval warships apart and unable to wage war."

This was followed by several seconds of silence from the Philippine president. Miller thought maybe he had lost the connection, but finally, President Limbaco's voice came back over the line. "President Miller, do you know your Senator Randy Fisher is with my Admiral Olan at this very moment? He was at the ASEAN summit at the request of both the Vietnamese governments and mine to observe the situation. Admiral Olan has just reported to me that Senator Fisher has developed a contact within the Chinese oil industry and can get an audience with a senior vice premier in the Chinese government."

President Harold Miller's fingers tightened into a fist at the mention of Randy Fisher's name. "That bastard, that bastard, that bastard," he repeated to himself but finally got control before he spoke back to the Philippine president. "Yes, President Limbaco, Senator Fisher was talking with the members of my national security team in the Situation Room just before your call arrived. We were discussing that very diplomatic option when I left the room to take your call."

"Good. Very good," the Philippine president said. "We have found your Senator Fisher to be very capable. My Ambassador Bello also tells me the Vietnamese government holds the same level of respect for Senator Fisher. I suggest we allow him to proceed with his diplomatic mission to China. He might be able to get the Chinese and Vietnamese governments to lower their military posture even before your navy and the Indian Navy arrives in the area. We must use every possible opportunity to quickly resolve the situation."

Miller was having trouble controlling his temper but kept it in check. "Of course, Mr. President. I will instruct Senator Fisher to proceed along those very lines. Thank you for calling, but I need to return to my meeting. I will make sure you are kept informed of all developments, and I trust you will do the same."

"Yes. Thank you, President Miller. I knew my government could rely on your sound judgment. Thank you and good-bye."

The telephone line was dead when the president of the United States slammed the phone handset down into the base cradle.

Chapter 57

Washington DC
Wednesday, March 18, 2015
6:45 a.m. (EST)

Randy Fisher had been on hold with the White House Situation Room for almost twenty minutes when he heard Marion Bellwood's voice again in his ear. "Senator, the president has some instructions for you."

There was a slight delay again, but finally, Randy heard Harold Miller's voice on the phone. "Senator, I've been in consultation with President Limbaco, and we want you to proceed with your trip to China tomorrow. We want you to get the Chinese to reduce their navy's presence in the South China Sea. When our own fleet arrives, their presence should further reduce the tension in the area."

Randy's voice came over the Blackberry lying on the tabletop for everybody to hear. "Mr. President, I respectfully ask that you keep our fleet at its home port. If I am to ask the Chinese and Vietnamese to curtail the number of ships they have in the South China Sea, I have to be able to say we are not moving our fleet in to take control instead. Without your assurance, I doubt my mission would be successful. Further, we need to pressure the Indian government to pull back their fleet for the time being to avoid inflaming the situation. There is still time to stop this from getting worse, but not if our and the Indian fleet sail into these waters when we are trying to get the Chinese and Vietnamese to pull back. I would suggest you use your influence with the Indian prime minister to get them to recall their fleet."

Jimmy Diamond was rubbing his hand over his mouth to keep

anyone in the room from seeing the smile on his face. Marion Bellwood was mouthing to himself a warning hoping Randy would not push the president too far. Others in the room were making slight coughing noises.

President Miller displayed a tremendous amount of control. "Yes. We will see what we do to that effect, Senator. I trust you will reach out to the Vietnamese government as well as to the Chinese to see if you can control them."

Randy could hear the irony in the president's voice over the phone. "Yes, sir. They are my next call."

Chapter 58

Beijing, China
Friday, March 20, 2015
10:00 a.m. (CST)

China Southern Air was the fastest commercial air transportation company from Hanoi, Vietnam, to Beijing, China. Senator Randy Fisher was sitting in the first-class section of an Airbus A380, having left the Vietnamese capital city at 5:30 in the morning for the slightly over four-hour flight to the capital of China.

It had been twenty-four hours since the Vietnamese helicopter had lifted off the BRP *Gregorio del Pilar* and flown him to Ho Chi Minh City in Vietnam. He had waited on board the Philippine destroyer to see Huang Zhao and as many of the oil wildcatters as possible board another helicopter provided by CNOOC, which flew them to the nearest Chinese mainland airstrip on Sanya, China, in Hainan Province. Sanya was one of China's southernmost locations and a popular tourist attraction. Huang Zhao would retrace his previous steps, fly back to Beijing, and contact his friend, Vice Premier Dong Zhang. Randy was planning to arrive in Beijing the next day if Huang Zhao could help expedite the travel arrangements. Meanwhile, Randy had to go to Vietnam and meet with President Tran Van Huong and Ambassador An Nguyen to try to slow down Vietnam's own military buildup.

From Ho Chi Minh City, he flew on a Vietnamese military transport plane to Hanoi. For over an hour the previous evening, while still on board the destroyer, Randy had talked over his Blackberry with both the Vietnamese president and their ambassador to the

United States in an attempt to reduce their military's response. He asked they not move any more vessels into the South China Sea until he had a chance to go to Beijing and meet again with Huang Zhao.

He recalled the moment he felt had achieved his goal. "Mr. President, just like the Philippine government, you asked me to come to the ASEAN summit to learn about your problems with China. Okay, I have done as you asked. What did you expect me to do with the information? I have heard what is going on between your country and the other members of ASEAN and China. I have seen firsthand some of the destruction and heard about more in the last fifteen hours. Now let me try to help you. Maybe I can reach some sort of agreement that will reduce the tension within the area. As it stands, your naval forces have inflicted far more damage on the Chinese than they have to your country's military, at least from what I now know of the situation. Please let me come to your country and let's meet together."

There had been a long pause with no words spoken between him and the Vietnamese president. Randy could faintly hear a conversation in the background but was not able to understand the language. Finally, President Tran Van Huong came back on the line and told him a Vietnamese helicopter from the mainland would be arriving early in the morning to bring him to Vietnam and then a transport plane would fly him to Hanoi. They would meet as soon as he arrived in the Vietnamese capital city.

Almost as soon as he had ended his call with the Vietnamese president, his Blackberry rang again. He had no problem understanding Marion Bellwood's message. "MP, you're in shit up to your neck. I thought the president was going to send the FBI after your butt to arrest you for meddling in foreign affairs, but I think he expects you to fail or even make things worse over there. If that happens, he will flay you in front of the press. You need to watch your back when it comes to *His Majesty*."

Randy thought for a while before replying to Marion. "From what I understand, the Chinese Ministry of Land and Resources forced all this increased activity in this area. We have not heard anything publically from the Chinese Central Government of their plans to expand their presence out here. I think maybe we have a minister trying to make a name for himself and he picked an ambitious naval admiral to help force his idea onto CNOOC."

Marion's voice came back with skepticism and caution. "Listen, Randy, you're risking your political career on a guess from a conversation with just one man. What else do you have to support your decision?"

"Admiral Fang Li. I saw his performance at the Philippine Embassy during the Christmas season a few months ago and then again just yesterday before we received the information on the battle out here. He was just too damn cocky. He acts like he's working on his own agenda."

Marion came back quickly. "That's not a lot to go on. I hope you know what you're doing."

"Me too," Randy replied. "Speaking of our Admiral Li, he left the ASEAN meeting before us in one of their carrier fighter jets. I think he probably made a flyover here and then headed for the carrier. Will the carrier be out of action long enough to allow our carrier to get into the South China Sea if we need it?"

"The last overhead picture we have showed their big ship dead in the water and a lot of damage to the flight deck. If any sailor or pilot was near the island when those missiles hit, then I doubt they'll be making war on anybody for a long time."

Randy was hoping Admiral Li and his carrier would be out of the picture for at least seventy-two hours.

"Listen, MP, I've got something for you even the president doesn't know about yet. I know you were uncomfortable when I could listen in on your Blackberry conversations, but you might be glad with what I've got to tell you."

When Marion heard nothing from Randy, he went on with his information. "The background conversation between President Tran Van Huong that you could barely hear was with Admiral Binh Huy Pham. He was informing the president that Vice Admiral Dc Thuc Ho ordered the Vietnamese torpedo boat to attack the drill ship. The Chinese have been firing at the Vietnamese torpedo boat on its last three or four runs, but the Vietnamese never retuned the fire. The vice admiral exceeded his authority, and the Central Committee relieved him of his command. The report about the attack said the torpedo boat captain refused to attack the unarmed drill ship. They only retuned the fire from the Chinese marines who were stationed on the drill ship."

"Well, the torpedo boat captain was very effective in his attack. Two Chinese warships sank, and his ship escaped."

Marion came back again. "He might have been effective, but he paid for his victory with his life. He was hit by the marine rifle fire just before the drill ship went up in the explosion."

Randy digested the latest information before speaking again. "That must be why President Tran Van Huong suddenly changed his attitude and allowed me to come to Vietnam. His country might not have started this mess, but they're not completely blameless."

"You're correct," Marion replied. "Plus, it appears they're way ahead in the score count. Three sunk Chinese warships and one badly damaged so far. That's a lot of notches on someone's belt."

"That's only one side," Randy said back to his friend. "We might not know the loss on the Vietnamese side."

The next morning had been a real juggling act, as the rented Philippine helicopter had to lift off from the destroyer and hover in a fuel-conserving pattern to first allow the CNOOC helicopter to land and pick up Huang Zhao and then the Vietnamese helicopter to land so Randy could board.

From Ho Chi Minh City, he traveled to Hanoi, and government-provided transportation drove him to the Presidential Palace for his meeting with Tran Van Huong. When he entered the office of the Vietnamese president, he also found Ambassador An Nguyen and Admiral Binh Huy Pham together in the president's office. The president was sitting behind a large wooden antique desk, and the ambassador and admiral Binh Huy Pham were sitting in straight-back chairs to the left of the president's desk. There was an empty chair to the right of the president's desk for Randy.

Randy decided to surprise the Vietnamese. Without the appropriate greetings to the Vietnamese leaders and without taking the offered chair, he looked at Admiral Binh Huy Pham. "How many submarines did you have tracking the Chinese aircraft carrier? Please do not deny that your submarine attacked the carrier. No other country would have a reason for the attack, and I'm not sure you can convince me your navy had any good reason to kill a bunch of Chinese sailors."

The three Vietnamese sat speechless as they stared at the young

American. No one had ever talked to them in this manner before. Randy decided to press his advantage. "You asked me to come over here to see how China was trying to expand their influence, and before I could form a clear picture of the situation, you launched an attack on their warships. How do you explain your war-like actions to the world?"

President Tran Van Huong found his voice. "I find it very upsetting when an invited guest would enter into our country and the Presidential Palace and talk to the sovereign head of our country in such a tone of voice. Perhaps it was a mistake to allow you to come?"

Randy kept a straight face. "If you don't like my tone of voice wait until the Chinese find theirs. You sank three warships and badly damaged their navy's flagship. We do not know the number of dead sailors, but it is probably many times more than your country has lost. Together, it is enough to turn the blue waters of the South China Sea red with blood, and it is enough to bankrupt your country if China demands compensation for their material loss. Even before we get to that question, how are you are going to handle the additional naval forces they're going to send your way or the army probably being made ready to invade your country?"

His goal was to shock them and force them into a frame of mind to compromise with whatever agreement he could hope to negotiate with the Chinese when he met them tomorrow.

Admiral Binh Huy Pham had lowered his head. Randy could not see the old man's face, but he sensed it would show shame. For a moment, he felt sympathy for the admiral. He knew Binh Huy Pham had not ordered the attack, but he could not ease up on the three Vietnamese.

Binh Huy Pham squared his shoulders and looked back up at the senator. He did not look toward his president to obtain permission to speak. "The order to attack the warships at Taiping Island came from Vice Admiral De Thuc Ho, and he did so on his own accord. The torpedo boat was to observe only and test their reaction to practice runs against the Chinese fleet and report back to their headquarters."

"Practice runs designed to draw fire from the Chinese vessels," Randy said. "How many practice runs do you require to test their reactions?" He saw the look on the old man's face and hoped he had not gone too far. In a more respectful tone, he continued, "And the attack on the carrier? Was that once again one officer going too far?"

Binh Huy Pham looked down at his hands as he intertwined his fingers. "Dc Thuc Ho claims he gave no order to attack the carrier. We cannot confirm his answer yet. The submarine responsible for the attack on the carrier has missed several scheduled times for reporting in. The other submarine reported hearing underwater explosions, and we suspect we have lost a submarine with all hands."

Randy looked back toward the old sailor. "I hope it's a case of communication equipment failure. What is the number of sailors on board your submarine?"

"Thirty-eight officers and crew," the old admiral replied.

Randy had continued to stand during this entire exchange. Ambassador An Nguyen used his right hand to indicate the empty chair. "Please, Senator Fisher, sit down and tell us more about your conversation with the Chinese gentleman from CNOOC."

Randy accepted the offer and sat down in the chair. "His name is Huang Zhao, and he is the vice chairman for CNOOC. He has been responsible for all the drilling operations for his company and forced into this whole affair by the senior minister from the Ministry of Land and Resources. He was totally against this huge buildup but was powerless to stop it. He is now hoping to get to the first vice premier and explain the situation. I am hoping that when I arrive in Beijing tomorrow, he will be at the airport to meet me. If not, I may be taking the first flight out of Beijing and back to the United States where my president will use the opportunity to bury my political future. As you know, he and I are not on the best of terms."

Vietnam President Tran Van Huong had been silent for some time. He had allowed his temper to show before, but now, it was under control. "How can we resolve this without further war and bloodshed?"

Randy smiled at the older man. "I've an idea I want to discuss with you, and tomorrow I need An Nguyen to come with me to Beijing."

The Airbus A380 jet now pulled to a stop at gate 21, terminal 2 of the Beijing Capital International Airport. It was the only gate large enough to handle the A380. Randy looked outside his window at the modern airport. It was the second busiest airport in the world next to Hartsfield-Jackson Atlanta Airport in Georgia. With three terminals, the airport handled over seventy-five million passengers and 1.75 million tons of freight each year. It was a symbol of the new China.

Randy looked across the aisle toward Ambassador An Nguyen to see how he was faring with their arrival in Beijing. The elder statesman unfastened his seatbelt, looked up toward Randy, and rewarded the younger man with a small smile.

Randy reached inside his suit coat and tried to work the stiffness out of his shirt collar against his neck. He had only grabbed a few personal items when he left the Empire Hotel in Bander Seri Begawan. On the destroyer, a Philippine steward had insisted on cleaning and pressing his suit coat, pants, and shirt for the ride to Hanoi. Just before he retired in the hotel in Hanoi, a hotel valet had taken all his outer garments and he found them cleaned and pressed again, but this time with too much starch.

Randy removed his Blackberry and powered up the device. He had been sending and receiving emails from Marion Bellwood with updates on the various naval ships heading toward the South China Sea. At this time, the Indian Navy was still en route. The president had ordered the *George Washington* battle group to leave their home base in Japan but to hold up about halfway to Manila. Randy was thankful the Chinese Eastern Fleet was still in port except for one destroyer escorting a small fleet of rescue tugs that were heading for the Chinese aircraft carrier. It was another break for everybody. The carrier apparently would not sink but instead be towed back to the Chinese mainland.

A new email from Marion informed Randy that US Ambassador to China Jay Buckingham would be meeting him at the capital airport with instructions from the president to offer any assistance to the peacekeeping process. It was a welcomed surprise to Randy, as he had received no other communications from the White House.

Randy and An Nguyen were among the hundreds of passengers exiting the giant Airbus at Gate 21. They were the only two passengers met immediately inside the terminal building. Randy was delighted to see Huang Zhao waiting at the passenger boarding area with several other Chinese officials and one tall American he suspected was Ambassador Buckingham.

Huang Zhao had a small smile on his face as he stepped up to Randy and gripped his hands. Before Randy could make any introductions, Huang Zhao spoke his first words. "There's been a new development."

Chapter 59

Randy looked toward the tall American. "You must be Jay Buckingham. I don't think we've met before."

The six-foot-two-inch tall diplomat from Delaware stepped in to shake Randy's proffered hand. "Welcome to Beijing, Senator. I have wanted to meet you ever since your name came across my desk in a message from the vice president."

Randy took a closer look at the ambassador. "You've heard from Jimmy Diamond?"

Buckingham flashed a bigger smile as he leaned down to speak more quietly into Randy's ear. "Yes . . . he and I are two old sons of a bitch from way back. He asked that I might make myself available while you are in China. Maybe smooth the way just a little more."

Randy smiled back. He finally was not flying solo on this mission anymore if Jimmy Diamond had requested that Jay Buckingham work with him. "I'm glad to meet you, Ambassador. You must be high on the VP's list of friends and very low on the president's to be here with me."

Buckingham let a quiet laugh escape between his lips. "I'm not one of the president's old Wall Street buddies, if that's what you mean."

Randy turned to introduce Ambassador An Nguyen to Buckingham and Huang Zhao. He could pick up the immediate tension between the Chinese oilman and the Vietnamese politician.

He decided to let things go unsaid for the time being until he heard the latest developments from Huang Zhao.

Looking toward the Vice Chairman of CNOOC, he was going to inquire about the new developments but instead asked if there was someplace better to talk than in the middle of the airport concourse.

Buckingham came to his rescue. "I've got several embassy vehicles outside prepared to transport the four of us into the city. Why don't we collect any luggage you have and let Mr. Huang Zhao's people take it to the hotel? We can all travel in my car." Randy immediately agreed with the ambassador's suggestion and indicated his one overnight bag as his only piece of luggage.

Twenty minutes later, they were through the VIP customs inspections and piling into the middle black Suburban. Two more embassy Suburban vehicles made up their caravan with the one for Randy and his entourage placed in the middle for security.

Once they were outside the airport grounds, the entourage entered the Jichang Expressway for the thirty-two-kilometer ride into the city. Randy reached inside his suit coat inner pocket. He pretended to remove an ink pen but actually turned on the anti-scrambler device built within his Blackberry. It was the first time he had used the phone's secret feature but decided now might be an opportune moment to employ it. He had no idea of what Huang Zhao was going to reveal and no idea if the ambassador's car was free of listening bugs.

Randy was sitting in a bucket seat behind the driver and beside Jay Buckingham in the opposite seat. He had forced Huang Zhao and An Nguyen into the third row bench seat so they were sitting side by side. It was time he forced an alliance between these two men.

He turned in his seat to bring his legs into the small space between the two-bucket seats he and Buckingham were using. This allowed him to look at both Asian men. "Gentleman, if we are going to avoid a war between your two countries today, we need to start with both of you. You both know neither of your countries is blameless in this whole mess, but you better decide right now to work with each other to help resolve the problems."

Huang Zhao looked at Randy and Buckingham and then out the side window. After a few moments, he turned inward toward An Nguyen and offered his right hand to the Vietnamese man. "Please excuse my terrible manners. It has been a trying seventy-two hours for me. I lost many men on the drill ship. Some of them were friends for many years."

An Nguyen reached out with his right hand and then brought over his left to enclose Huang Zhao's hand. "Too many from both sides have needlessly died for oil. Let us resolve to make today's mission a success."

Randy had a smile on his face. If they could bring détente into this car, then maybe they could do the same for the two countries. "Good. Now Huang Zhao . . . what is this latest development you want to tell us?"

Huang Zhao could not keep the smile from his face. He felt relieved he was with the senator again. A strange bond had formed between them during the few hours they were together on the Philippine destroyer. "I had no problem getting back to my office and meeting with my boss, Lian Wu. We have not received any communication from the Ministry of Land and Resources. We consider that good news but still a little unsettling. I was able to talk briefly over the telephone with a personal assistant to Dong Zhang. I requested a meeting with my friend and was told by his assistant to wait for a return call. I finally got a call early this morning ordering me to bring you to Zhongnanhai this morning. We are going there now."

Randy looked at Ambassador Buckingham for clarification. He nodded as he started to talk. "That's good. Zhongnanhai is where the Chinese Central Government has all their main offices. The general secretary lives and works there, along with many of the senior government leaders." He looked back at Randy. "It means your visit is being taken very seriously."

Randy was a little confused. He looked back toward Huang Zhao. "Then what is your concern if we are going to Zhongnanhai?"

"I received the call at four thirty this morning. They either were working very early or had been there all night. In addition, this morning, all radio and television information about the general secretary stopped. The party is acting as if he never existed. Very unusual."

Buckingham needed to talk. "Huang Zhao is correct. Every morning, the news broadcast starts with high praise for the general secretary and the Central Government. For their state-owned news agency to go dark about the Central Government is unsettling at the least. I had to send a warning to Washington just before I left to pick you up."

Randy was quiet for several moments. He was looking out the side window behind Jay Buckingham as the caravan drove past the mixture of modern buildings built within the last dozen years and the much older buildings with the typical Chinese architectural design. He refocused back on the group. "What have you heard about the naval battle on the news?" He was looking between Jay and Huang Zhao.

Both men spoke one word together, "Nothing."

Buckingham spoke again. "You can't really assume too much from the lack of information about the battle, Randy. From all accounts I've read, the Chinese took quite a beating out there, and the Central Government won't allow the information to reach the media." He looked at Zhang Zhao for confirmation.

Huang Zhao was nodding his head. "Unfortunately, Ambassador Buckingham is correct. Our government will prevent any bad news from reaching the people."

Randy was rubbing his hand across his face. It had been almost five hours since he had shaved in the early morning hours. He could feel new growth of beard on his face. He looked again at Huang Zhao. "How well do you really know this Dong Zhang?"

Huang Zhao was smiling again but a little sheepishly. "As I told you before, we shared a number of classes together during our first two years at university. However, we also share the very same date of birth. When we both reached our eighteenth birthday, we went out together to celebrate. It was a night neither of us will forget."

He could tell his fellow passengers wanted more details. "I had too much to eat and drink. I started with *Pinyin*, which is a type of beer. After drinking too much of the beer, I was goaded into trying several types of *Huangiu*, which is a wine made from rice or wheat. Dong Zhang had been drinking heavily. He was not much better than I was by the time the restaurant owner wanted to kick us out of his establishment. I am afraid I mixed too many different types of alcohol and food. I was trying to get up from the table, but suddenly, I tripped and fell toward Dong Zhang's chair. I threw up all my food and beverage into his lap."

The American Embassy security guard riding in the passenger seat in front of Ambassador Jay Buckingham let out a muffled snort. He tried very hard to get control of himself, but Buckingham and Randy both started to laugh and then nobody could hold back, including Huang Zhao. It was a welcomed relief from the tension everybody was feeling.

Randy was shaking his head and laughing at Huang Zhao. "This is the guy we are all betting on will help stop a war. Is it too late to turn around and return to the airport?"

The caravan crossed over the fifth road ring that circled the city. There were only five road rings, but they numbered from two through six. They helped to keep the twenty-plus million people who lived in Beijing moving smoothly throughout the huge city.

Finally, their three-car caravan reached the Xizhimen Bus Station. After waiting for the light to change, they turned south onto Zhaoyangmen Street and traveled a number of blocks. Randy could see out of his car window the Workers' Stadium complex used for some of the 2008 Olympic Games.

At Changan Street, they turned right and continued for several more blocks. Their caravan passed the northern edge of Tiananmen Square, site of the 1989 protests held against the oppressive government of China. Randy had only been fifteen years old as he watched the news coverage from the Forbidden City. He would never forget the video footage of the young Chinese student standing alone in front of an army tank brought in to support the three hundred thousand members of the military to restore order in the capital city. Was the current Chinese Central Government any less harsh than the government from twenty-six years ago?

On his right was the Working People's Cultural Palace, and then they turned again to their right onto Nan Changile Street. The famous Zhongshan Park was now on their right, and their final destination, the Zhongnanhai Government Complex was on their left. From the street, it resembled the typical ancient Chinese architecture seen in the city. Xinhuamen or the "Gates of New China" was the name given to the entrance. Any person outside the high walls could see nothing else about the location of the heart of the Chinese Central Government.

Chapter 60

Chinese security personnel stopped the caravan at the entrance gate. Chinese army soldiers stepped up to the center vehicle and opened the doors. Ambassador Jay Buckingham looked over his shoulder at the men in the third bench seat. "We need to get out here. They will not allow our cars or the security guards to enter Zhongnanhai."

Randy stepped out the opened door and turned around to pull the seat forward to ease the exit for the older Vietnamese ambassador. When he turned back around, he had his first unobstructed view of the seat of the Chinese government. In front of him was a wide, two-story building with eight double wood columns painted red along the front of both stories of the building. Both the first and second floors facing the street had a veranda that in other circumstances might encourage someone to sit comfortably and watch the world go by. Randy doubted anyone had relaxed on that veranda anytime recently.

He looked from the building to the tall flagpole a few feet from the front bumper of their lead car. The red flag with a large star near the upper hoist end and four smaller stars arranged as a crescent around it was flying briskly in the mild breeze. The temperature in Beijing was normally about the same as in his home city of Columbia, South Carolina, with an average high and low temperature of 49 and 30 degrees Fahrenheit for the end of March. Today was in the upper fifties, and a mild, warm breeze added to their comfort, but it was still cool. Maybe the nervousness he was feeling made the mild temperature feel colder.

From the main entrance to Zhongnanhai, a well-dressed Chinese official, who looked to be in his mid-twenties, walked out to greet them. He ignored Huang Zhao and An Nguyen as he bowed slightly before addressing Randy and Ambassador Buckingham. "Good morning, Senator. Good morning, Ambassador. I am Kia Zhou, special assistant to the general secretary. Please follow me. I will show you a little of Zhongnanhai before you meet with the general secretary. He is very busy this morning but will make time for your visit."

Randy gave a slight bow back to the general secretary's assistant. "Thank you, Kia Zhou. Please let me introduce Vietnamese Ambassador An Nguyen and a fellow countryman of China, Mr. Huang Zhao."

Kia Zhou seemed not to know what to do next but suddenly bowed to them. "Yes . . . of course. Please now follow me."

The group of four followed the young man through the doorway and into the main entrance. The interior of the two-story building was an open area extending to the ceiling. Inside, one large water fountain placed in the middle of the room dominated the opening with several smaller fountains placed throughout the sizable room. Many different species of large leafy plants, placed to create several pathways to or near the fountains, helped to create a relaxing atmosphere. Near the south end, a large stature of Mao Zedong, flanked by two identical paintings of the late Communist leader, dominated the area. The effect was to give the room a look of peace and tranquility.

While the four visitors walked along with Kia Zhou, there were numerous uniformed and plainclothes security guards moving with the group but keeping a respectful distance.

Once through the first building, they were able to see more of the garden-palace complex. Zhongnanhai was the equivalent of the White House and US Capitol building in one—an immense and beautiful mixture of palatial buildings, constructed in the traditional Chinese architectural style, set among the grounds and lakes within the walls of the complex. As Randy walked away from the entrance building, he could not see any modern buildings except an egg-shaped titanium-and-steel dome off in the distance. Jay Buckingham located the object of Randy's attention. "That's the National Centre for the Performing Arts. I'm surprised they allowed it to be built so tall and to be seen inside here."

Randy continued to turn in a full circle to take in the view of the beautiful gardens and buildings. "There's a very solemn atmosphere here. I keep waiting to see a line of priests or monks walking to a temple for their midday prayers."

For over an hour, their guide took them on a private tour of the beautiful grounds built around the two manufactured lakes, the "Central Sea" and the "Southern Sea." They would pause at each temple, pavilion, or shrine to examine the architecture. All the buildings and landscaping blended together in harmony. It was very restful, and had Randy not witnessed the destruction of war less than forty-eight hours ago, he would have wanted to play the part of a tourist and enjoy the visit.

As 1:00 p.m. approached, Kia Zhou escorted them to a larger building set in the center between the two lakes. Buckingham whispered into Randy's ear. "This is the home and office of General Secretary Lei Feng. In China, he has more power than any other person does. He is the general secretary of the Communist Party of China. In addition, he is the president of the People's Republic of China and the chairman of the Central Military Commission."

As they walked up to the front of the gray brick building, the front door opened and six very large plainclothes men walked out to form an aisle for a seventh man to walk through. The man was about Randy's size, which was large for a Chinese, and he appeared to be slightly older. He was dressed in a well-made dark pinstripe suit. Randy guessed his age at about forty-five. He came to a stop at the end of the human aisle and near the end of the covered porch to the building's entrance. Randy thought this must be another "special assistant" to the general secretary but was surprised when Huang Zhao suddenly moved forward, calling the name of the man.

"Dong Zhang . . . it's good to see you at last." Huang Zhao was about to reach Dong Zhang, but two of the large men, obviously security agents, suddenly stepped in front of him to block his path.

Kia Zhou, the general secretary's special assistant, and their guide, yelled out a warning, "Stop. Do not address the general secretary until you have been properly recognized."

Chapter 61

Beijing, China
Friday, March 20, 2015
1:00 p.m. (CST)

China's new general secretary waved the security men back to their earlier positions and approached Huang Zhao with a smile and an outstretched hand. "Huang Zhao, it has been much too long since we have seen each other. Please introduce me to my first official guests."

Huang Zhao was speechless for several seconds but quickly recovered as he accepted the hand of his old college friend. With Dong Zhang at his side, he walked back to the group and approached Randy first. "This is United States Senator Randy Fisher from the state of South Carolina, US Ambassador James Buckingham, and the honorable ambassador from Vietnam An Nguyen. We have come here to meet with you on important matters concerning the recent events in the South China Sea."

Dong Zhang walked up to Randy Fisher and offered his hand in a warm greeting. "I have been especially interested to meet you, Senator Fisher, ever since I was informed Huang Zhao was bringing you to Zhongnanhai. We have discussed your history from several years ago at great length within my country. I wanted to look into the eyes of a man who has faced death and survived." His English was slightly accented but easily understood.

Randy offered an equally firm grip to the new leader of China. He thought he was doing a masterful job of keeping the surprise out of his voice at the sudden change in leadership in China. "Thank you, Mr. General Secretary. I am afraid the American news media has overly dramatized my reputation. You are looking at a man who had a very lucky day."

Dong Zhang continued his smile and handshake. "Good. Never discount luck. Let's hope we all have a lucky day today." He turned to Jay Buckingham. "Mr. Ambassador, welcome. We have met several times in the past."

Jay Buckingham offered his own hand in greeting. "Thank you, General Secretary. Let me congratulate you on your new position. I look forward to working with your government to improve the relations between my country and yours. Please never hesitate to call upon me for anything the United States can do."

Dong Zhang moved to Ambassador An Nguyen. He looked carefully into the eyes of the older statesman. He kept his voice calm and cordial as he spoke. "Ambassador, it's a pleasure to meet you. Our two old and very proud countries have tested each other over the past few days. Let's hope today we may chart a new course for peace and prosperity."

An Nguyen looked up into the eyes boring down into his own. Using all the diplomatic skills honed from years of experience, he replied in a calm voice. "Mr. General Secretary, I have no greater wish than that we may reach a peaceful understanding between our two governments. There has been far too much death and destruction, and we must find a solution today."

Dong Zhang stepped back and first looked at the group, and then he moved slightly to look at the grounds and buildings around them. "It is a beautiful day here at Zhongnanhai. I hope you were able to enjoy the small tour. I apologize for not being able to meet you directly, but there has been much to do already this day. Perhaps you will allow me to make up to you for my tardiness with a light lunch. I know you had to leave Hanoi early this morning for your flight to Beijing. My day started very early as well, and I am sure we are all hungry. Please, let us eat and we can learn more about each other."

With a slight wave of his hand to indicate the direction of their next steps, Dong Zhang moved to walk beside Randy Fisher as he led the group inside his new home. This particular building was not as large as the White House, which Randy had only visited once, but it served as just the private office and home to the general secretary.

Once inside the building, Randy discovered the interior to be a pleasing mixture of traditional and antique Chinese artwork and furniture, hardwood floors covered with oriental carpets, and walls painted in neutral colors. Natural light entered through tall glass windows starting above the wainscoting and continuing to within two feet of the twelve-foot ceiling. As they moved through several rooms, Dong Zhang would stop to describe a small ornament or painting and provide its history to his guest. Randy was not sure if the general secretary's personal possessions had already been moved into the residence in the very short time since Dong Zhang had become the new leader or if these were belongings from the former general secretary, Lei Feng, now just a name in Chinese history.

They came to a large room that Randy assumed was the office for the general secretary. It commanded a beautiful view of the grounds through the windows on the south side. They could see the "Southern Sea" lake off in a short distance within the gently rolling landscape. A large map of China was hanging on the north wall and bookcases lined the east wall divided by the door they had entered. A large antique wood desk commanded the west wall and two large sofas were setting with their backs near the bookcases. A large fireplace in the corner near the window contained a small blaze, providing some needed warmth to the room now that they were indoors and out of the bright sunshine.

In front of the fireplace was a table set for five diners. Dong Zhang led the group over to the table where several servants were waiting. He motioned for his guests to take the seats. As the group approached, each man found a place card to indicate his position to sit.

The seating arrangement in ancient Chinese times consisted of a four-tier social strata: first, the imperial court; second came local authorities; third, trade associations; and last, farmers and workers. The respective structure in modern dining etiquette had been simplified over the years to the master of the banquet with guests occupying a lower status.

The seat of honor, reserved for the master of the banquet or the guest with the highest status, is the one in the center facing east or facing the entrance to the room. Those of higher position sit closer to the master of the banquet.

If the dining table is round, as it was in today's lunch, the seat facing the entrance is the seat of honor. The seats on the left-hand side of the "honor seat" are second, fourth, and sixth in importance, while on the right are the third, fifth, and seventh, and so on.

Randy was the only one in the room not familiar with the seating arrangement but found his name tag at the seat facing the doorway they had just entered. To his left was a place card for Dong Zhang, and to his right was a place for Ambassador Jay Buckingham. On the other side of the round table were place cards for Ambassador An Nguyen and Huang Zhao.

Randy looked over the cloth-covered table with cut-crystal glasses and fine china plates and cups. The table was the perfect size for the five men who were going to dine together or play poker, and perhaps a high-stakes meeting would be the ultimate game played here today.

As the men took their assigned places, two servants quickly filled their glasses with water and then another white-coated servant entered with a silver serving tray filled with a clear decanter of a beverage and small crystal glasses. As the servant placed one of the glasses in front of each man, Randy noticed a very small diamond set in the stem. Randy was not a wine connoisseur, but he had read about these glasses before. They were Riedel wineglasses made from borosilicate. It was a material known for its resistance to thermal shock, which maintained the wine's properties to normal levels even with the glass in warm hands.

The servant filled the small wineglasses from the decanter and left the room. Dong Zhang picked up his glass, and his guests followed suit. He looked around the table with his glass raised. "To peace and common sense. Perhaps both will find a path to this table today."

The men reached out to clink their glasses together, and each took a small sip. As they set their glasses down, new servants approached with small bowls of a clear vegetable soup.

As he picked up his soupspoon, Dong Zhang looked over the table at Huang Zhao. He had a small smile on his face. "I seem to remember you had a problem with mixing different types of alcohol, so you will only be served water with the rest of our meal."

Huang Zhao was taking a sip from his water glass and starting to choke on the water in reaction to Dong Zhang's comment. Jay Buckingham reached over to slap him lightly several times on the back to help restore his breathing. There was a round of laughter from the table guests. Dong Zhang laughed the hardest. "I see your reputation has already become known to your associates. Well, it's too good of a story not to be told many times."

Following the soup, the main course was a baked fish with roasted potatoes. It appeared the new leader of China was concerned with eating a healthy diet. For the balance of the lunch, they talked of sports and family as any regular group of men would. The conversation revealed that Randy was the only man at the table without children or grandchildren.

Dong Zhang chided Randy for not being a father. "Children change every man's perception of life. Decisions become more important and require careful study. As the new leader of my country, I have to look at all my people as my children and make very careful decisions."

Randy laid his cloth napkin on the table next to his empty plate. "I can assure you my wife, Annie, and I plan on having children. However, like you, I look at my own state of South Carolina with the same careful thinking process. I don't have 1.3 billion people to worry about, but I take the same importance in my decision-making process as you, General Secretary."

The servant had begun to clear away the dishes, leaving only the water glasses on the table. "Good," said Dong Zhang. "If we keep that thought in the forefront of our minds, we will bring this meeting to a good conclusion."

He waited until the servants had left the room. As they were leaving, Kia Zhou entered, along with another man dressed in business attire. They went to the antique desk across the room, picked up two straight chairs, and brought them over to sit behind Dong Zhang. "My personal assistant and private secretary will keep a record of our talks. So now, let us begin to undo what has transpired over the last several months that resulted in a mini war in the South China Sea."

He looked at Huang Zhao. "You explained some of what happened several months ago to my assistant last evening. At the time, I was involved in discussions with the senior leadership within the Central Government and was not able to talk with you. Please, dear friend, tell us how this whole terrible affair was started."

Huang Zhao picked up his water glass but only moved it farther back on the table and away from himself to allow more space in front of his body. He knew he had a tendency to use his hands and arms when he spoke and got excited.

He carefully laid out the history of events starting with the CNOOC board meeting months ago when Minister Chang Chen announced the expanded oil import requirements for his company. He recounted the atmosphere at the meeting at the Southern Naval Command headquarters in Zhanjiang with Admirals Fang Li and Deshi Yang. He described the efforts by himself and CNOOC chairman, Lian Wu, to meet the production schedule and the dangerous shortcuts they were required to take. He came to the problems on the drill ships when the Vietnamese navy initiated the simulated attacks, which prompted the Chinese naval warships to recklessly fire their weapons over the drill ship, threatening to cause explosions of the volatile gases from the drilling operations. He concluded the report with his own personal story of arriving at the drill site during the actual sinking of the Chinese ships and the frightening experience when the explosion thrust his helicopter off the ship's landing pad and into the sea.

He could not finish his summary without voicing a criticism of the minister for Land and Resources. "All this happened because Minister Chang Chen forced my company to increase production beyond any reasonable time frame and safety procedures. We were meeting annual production needs and were stunned at their new requirements. So many men were killed over this terrible insistence to increase oil production."

The men around the table were silent for several moments as they contemplated what Huang Zhao had revealed. To Randy and Ambassador An Nguyen, it was a well-known story. To Jay Buckingham and the general secretary, it was the first time they had heard everything from Huang Zhao's perspective.

An Nguyen was the first to break the silence. "General Secretary, I am here on behalf of my government to offer our apology for the warlike actions by members of the Vietnamese navy. I want to assure you that my government leaders never issued any orders for our warships to open fire on your navy vessels. Orders by our military leaders were to test the response of your forces to a possible attack but never to attack your ships. I can further assure you the man responsible for issuing the attack order has been relieved of duty and is in custody awaiting his fate."

Dong Zhang was quiet as he considered what the two men had revealed. He was looking down at the table, but finally, he looked up and found his voice. "There is blame on both sides for this terrible event. Minister Chang Chen was an ambitious fool who conspired to achieve a seat on the Central Committee by bringing in high-level energy production for my country. He was able to convince General Secretary Lei Feng to approve the operation to expand the oil production in the South China Sea. Then he teamed up with a megalomaniac in the form of Admiral Fang Li, who used his position to enforce Minster Chang Chen's plan."

He looked around the table at his guests. "As you now know, the Central Committee decided General Secretary Lei Feng needed to step down due to poor health. He will live the rest of his life in quiet comfort and be remembered as a great leader."

He stopped again to consider his thoughts before continuing with his next statement. "Minister Chang Chen has been relieved of his power and position. He will face criminal charges for exceeding his authority within the ministry of Land and Resources. Fate has already decided Admiral Fang Li's punishment. He died, along with the pilot of his jet aircraft, on the *Liaoning* when the missiles struck the carrier along with the ship's commodore and the captain of flight operations. Admiral Deshi Yang has been relieved of his command and will be retired from the navy."

There was silence again from the group. Randy felt the general secretary was revealing a lot of information not normally made public. Perhaps he was taking a forward step in trying to normalize relations.

Randy wanted to speak about the sailors on both sides of the war. "Mr. General Secretary and Ambassador An Nguyen, please accept the condolences of my country for the terrible loss of life both your navies has experienced during this terrible event. It is my desire today that we discuss how to prevent this from happening again."

Dong Zhang was moving his head in a motion of agreement. "Yes . . . we must never want to decide how oil and natural gas is removed from beneath the oceans with the use of warships. My country has lost three vessels and many members of their crews.

Our navy's flagship will require billions of yen to make it seaworthy again."

He turned toward his assistant and nodded his head. The men at the table watched as Kia Zhou reached into his suit coat outer pocket, removed a computer flash drive, and handed it to the general secretary.

Dong Zhang looked at the small electronic storage device and then laid it on the tablecloth and with two fingers on his right hand, slowly pushed it across the table to An Nguyen. "This is a sonar recording from one of the surviving destroyers attached to the *Liaoning*. They picked up the signature of your submarine that attacked the carrier and pursued it with all possible weapons. It will provide the answer as to why you have not received any messages from the vessel."

An Nguyen slowly reached out for the memory stick and carefully picked up the small plastic-encased device. He looked at it for several moments as if to see within the electrical circuitry the souls of the men who died on the submarine. Looking back toward the general secretary, he spoke very softly. "Thank you, General Secretary. It will bring some peace for the families of the crew members to know for certain the fate of their loved ones."

General Secretary Dong Zhang took in a deep breath and slowly released it. "So, both of our countries have lost ships and sailors. Tell me, how do we resolve our dispute over the islands and natural resources of the South China Sea? We have more countries involved in this affair than just China and Vietnam."

Randy spoke up now. "Mr. General Secretary, I would like to offer a suggestion to help resolve this. Most of the member nations to ASEAN lay some sort of claim for parts or all of the Spratly Islands and most of the South China Sea. Would it be possible to form a business alliance between your country and the ASEAN members and jointly mine the South China Sea? This idea, based somewhat after the Organization of the Oil Petroleum Exporting Countries, or OPEC, would reduce tension, as all the countries would be working together. There would be a joint funding for the costs of exploration and mining. A proportional distribution of benefits based on the percentage of investment. Everybody shares on both the expenses and rewards. It could be administered by a new division of ASEAN with China becoming the newest voting member."

He paused to let this idea sink in for a few moments. "Ambassador An Nguyen is a member of the ASEAN delegation, and I feel certain he would be willing to lead the discussion within the ASEAN organization."

Jay Buckingham now added his voice to the idea. "Mr. General Secretary, I would also be willing to use my office as an ambassador to help in any way possible to make this idea become a reality."

An Nguyen spoke again. "Mr. General Secretary, indeed, I would be willing to sponsor China's entry into ASEAN. My president has already spoken to several other ASEAN members and all have replied with a very favorable response. It would mean an end to the tensions existing between the ASEAN members and China going back many years."

Randy again added his voice. "We find in the United States business partners are more likely to try to work out their differences rather than to spend money to injure each other. As a member of ASEAN, your country would have a full voice within the organization to help work out other issues that might arise."

Dong Zhang looked around the table and then to Randy Fisher. "This was your idea, Senator Fisher, or from your President Miller?"

Randy, a little embarrassed by the question, plunged ahead. "This was my thinking, sir. I am afraid I do not enjoy the total confidence of my president. Nevertheless, it is a Capitalist idea. We'd rather make money than war."

Chapter 62

The idea of China becoming a member of the ASEAN organization and the creation of SEAOC, the Southeast Asian Oil Company, took on a life of its own. Randy and the group required several breaks during the day, and telephone calls were made to organize a small conference call among the leaders of the ASEAN membership. Most of the leaders from the ten member nations were aware of the ongoing discussions held in China and hoped they would prevent further naval conflict.

By late afternoon, the members had agreed on a schedule for a new ASEAN summit and rough plans were made to welcome a new member into the ASEAN organization.

Randy and the other delegates were relieved when Dong Zhang gave the order for the Chinese Eastern Fleet to stand down and most of the Southern Fleet was ordered to return to their base at Zhanjiang. Only the ships required for the continued rescue operations were to remain at sea.

Emails and text messages were flying back and forth to Washington and the various leaders of ASEAN as they all were expressing their thanks for Randy's small part in preventing further naval conflict within the region. Marion Bellwood called again on his Blackberry to inform him President Miller had ordered the *George Washington* fleet to return to Japan along with its battle group of warships. The Indian Navy was also returning to its homeport except for one missile cruiser, which was continuing with what the Indian government called a "goodwill mission to the Philippines."

The world press was slow to notice the events in the South China Sea. This was partly due to the restrictive press allowed to exist in China and Vietnam and to the relatively low importance given to the ASEAN organization by the world news agencies. Most Americans had never heard of the Asian organization until news organizations in the Philippines broadcasted the assistance by the Philippine Navy in the rescue operations.

When the news broke in the United States, it was in the middle of the night, given the thirteen-hour time difference. The American press, caught unprepared when the information revealed three warships had been destroyed and the Chinese's only aircraft carrier badly damaged, quickly brought the American public up-to-date.

By 5:00 a.m. (EST) in the United States, White House Press Secretary Alison Warden had released a statement that the president, informed of the situation from the beginning, had issued all necessary orders to keep the conflict from expanding. The carrier *George Washington*, ordered by the White House into the area to help prevent further conflict, was later recalled when it was determined the situation was under control. To all the reporters' questions in the White House pressroom, Alison Warden downplayed the situation.

Somehow, information had leaked out that Senator Randy Fisher had been instrumental in negotiating a truce between the two antagonists, and his Blackberry was constantly vibrating. He was contemplating turning it off as he approached the room where the Chinese general secretary had ordered an elegant dinner to celebrate the new truce between his country and Vietnam.

Randy entered the room to see the General Secretary and Huang Zhao near the windows quietly talking. He caught sight of Dong Zhang motioning him to come over to join them. As he neared the two men, he could tell from Huang Zhao's face that something good must have happened.

Dong Zhang accepted Randy's handshake and placed his own left hand on Randy's right shoulder. "I wanted to introduce you to my new Minister of Land and Resources." He looked at Huang Zhao. "What did you call the job of working on an oil-drill ship?"

Huang Zhao had a sheepish grin on his face. "Wildcatting."

Dong Zhang gave a little laugh. "That's it. He has agreed to retire from wildcatting on the oil rigs to become my newest minister and head the Ministry of Land and Resources. I plan to keep him very busy."

Randy was all smiles as he reached over to shake Huang Zhao's hand. "Let me be one of the first to congratulate you on your new position. I'm sure you will serve your country in your new assignment admirably."

As the three men continued to talk, official Chinese photographers were recording the first meeting of the new secretary general with his foreign guests. These same photos would find their way to the world news agencies. It was rumored Warren Fletcher broke the information to President Miller that Senator Randy Fisher's picture with the new secretary general would be on the front page of many US newspapers the next day. The president's comments back to his chief of staff never found their way to the public.

Randy was about to continue with his praise for his new friend when his Blackberry vibrated once again. He was hesitant to answer the phone but changed his mind when he recognized Annie's cell number. For almost three days, because of the time difference, they had been communicating only by email. He looked at the General Secretary and Huang Zhao and requested they excuse him for a few minutes to accept a call from his wife.

He walked across the room as he hit the green accept button on the telephone. "Annie, it's great to finally hear your voice."

The soft voice of the person he wanted most to hear from had a slight edge to it. "I suppose you're up to your neck in that mess over there. It is starting to come out over here. You never told me navy warships were exchanging gunfire. You better be okay, or I will be very angry at you."

Randy laughed back into the mouthpiece of the phone. "I'm fine and everything is going to be okay over here. What is happening back there? It seems I've been gone forever from you."

There was silence over the phone for several moments. Randy was beginning to think he had lost his connection with Annie, but her voice came back over the phone. "You remember the idea we had to remodel the bathroom?"

Randy took several moments to switch his thinking from foreign affairs to domestic plumbing. "Yes. We were talking about gutting the bathroom and installing a combination whirlpool and air spa tub and wall system with a series of body sprays and a large rain-style showerhead."

He could hear a little cooing sound creeping into Annie's voice. "Well . . . I took advantage of you being out of town, and the renovation has been completed."

Randy was surprised and pleased by what he had just heard. Annie was an electrical engineer, but she had designed a new bathroom and actually had the work completed on her own. She never failed to surprise him.

"What about the old hot-water boiler. Will it be able to keep up with the extra demand for hot water in the shower?"

"I had the plumber install one of those new gas tankless hot-water heaters that never runs out of hot water." The cooing sound in Annie's voice had changed to more of a purring sound now.

He swallowed before he spoke. "So how do the new shower body sprays work now with all that endless hot water?"

He was not expecting the question coming back over the phone. "Why don't you come home and we can discover just how well it works together?"

Randy looked around the room to see if anybody was listening. He hesitated briefly but brought the phone back to his lips. "Hold on a moment."

He walked over the secretary general of the Chinese Communist Party, who was still talking to Huang Zhao. "Sorry for interrupting, but I need a ride to the airport."

Author's Notes

The ASEAN organization as described in the novel is real. The ten-nation membership covers a land area of 4.46 million square kilometers, which is 3 percent of the total land area of earth. The six hundred million combined population, if a single entity, would be the tenth largest economy in the world.

The contested waters of the South China Sea are also real as described in this novel. The Chinese Navy continues to pressure the ten ASEAN nations for control over the oil and gas beneath the waters in that part of the world.

This is a work of fiction. Names, characters, businesses, organizations, places, events, and incidents either are the product of the author's imagination or are used fictitiously. Any resemblance to actual persons, living or dead, events, or locales is entirely coincidental.

Acknowledgments

I want to thank Amanda McNulty, contributing author to newspaper articles in Sumter and Columbia, South Carolina. Amanda has earned numerous awards for her work, including the Distinguished Agent Award, 2009; the NACCA Media Award for newspaper column, 2007; and the National finalist NACCA media award for radio, 2007 and 2009.

I also need to thank my best friend, Chery Gilmore, for her inspiration, support, and patience. Many times, she would spend hours alone while I hammered out another chapter. She would take the loneliness in stride after she would ask if I was ever going to leave the office. My reply was that I could not stop now as I was "on a roll." Thank you forever.

Mike Gilmore

Michaelgilmore1.com

scauthor@yahoo.com

Levels of Power

The Chairman

Watch for the next Senator Randy Fisher Novel

Levels of Power

The Chairman

Due to a vacancy on the high court, President Harold Miller must appoint a new chief justice. As a member of the Senate Committee on the Judiciary, Senator Randy Fisher must take part in the confirmation process. A sudden illness of the committee chairperson compels the Senate leadership to appoint Randy as the temporary chairperson of the committee.

The president's nominee, by all standards, appears to be perfect for the coveted position and only a slight slip of the tongue during his courtesy meeting in Senator Fisher's office sets off warning bells in Randy's mind. Why had the nominee lied about his wife when there was no reason to lie?

Join Randy Fisher and his Senate staff as they launch their own investigation into the private life of the nominee and his wife. Is there a reason to prevent Randy from supporting the president's nominee?

The further they dig, the darker the information they uncover.